He'd gotten a promotion, wanted her to leave her job and move, and she was torn—until she saw the picture...

Francis turned to face her. "It's not the first time I've mentioned it. Do you even listen? I was hoping for Regional, but Rosemary kept hinting it was National, and I've been doing the what-ifs. I can't pass this up, obviously. But the girls—well, there's college applications and graduation and all that. They need to stay here."

"Who exactly is this Rosemary?"

"A VP, actually. Human Resources. She's been super helpful."

He wanted them to move. All those monologues about mortgages and interest rates had been leading up to this. Charlotte drew a deep breath. "This is a lot, Francis. It doesn't seem real. I need to think."

"It's real, all right. And I need to stop thinking. I'm going down to exercise I'm wound up tighter than a drum."

As was her habit for happy occasions, she decided to find a celebratory poem to recite for Francis. She normally consulted the anthology in the den, but Francis's laptop was still on the dresser, convenient for a quick search. She was no tech genius, but she knew how to use Google.

She passed her hand over the screen saver. A photograph appeared and she drew back in surprise. It was unlike Francis not to close out his e-mail.

In the background—the ocean and a cloudless blue sky. In the foreground—Francis standing behind a woman in a jeweled swimsuit that surely never touched water. The woman's hair was perfectly highlighted and her even tan contrasted with Francis's reddened skin. His head was resting on top of hers, and his arms were wrapped tightly around her in an X, covering her breasts. Her breasts. Touching them. Close. The way he was holding her. That was the worst.

Charlotte Murphy—trusting wife, loving mother, and dedicated teacher—comes to suspect that her wealthy, arrogant husband of eighteen years has been cheating on her and that the principal of the inner-city vocational high school where she teaches English has been changing answers on state-mandated standardized tests. Seeing their teacher's unhappiness, her students convince her to let them give her a movie star makeover. When they're done, Charlotte doesn't recognize herself and vows to change her life. Charlotte's new life is further complicated by the unwelcome attention of Theo Lagakis, the school's dean, who has a hidden agenda. Whom can she trust?

Charlotte's story is enhanced by the poetry she loves to teach, as well as with first-person commentary from her student and close observer, Valerie Martin. Valerie, a serious student, faces not being able to graduate from high school due to the allegedly forged scores.

KUDOS for *Ms. Murphy's Makeover*

"Authentic, humorous and tender, in her big-hearted debut, Jacqueline Goldstein's *Ms. Murphy's Makeover* will open your mind as it warms your heart." ~ Sally Koslow, author of *The Widow Waltz*

"A funny, yet poignant tale of betrayal, resilience, and second chances." ~ Marian Thurm, author of *Today Is Not Your Day* and *The Good Life*

"Charlotte, Ms. Murphy, would be at home on the pages of a Jane Austen novel, but where she belongs is here, on the pages of *Ms. Murphy's Makeover*, navigating between the landscapes of an inner-city classroom in the Bronx and on the verge of a collapsing marriage in the suburbs of Connecticut. I love this book. I must warn readers: It will haunt you in the way only a story as courageous as *Ms. Murphy's Makeover* can." ~ Patricia Dunn, author of *Rebels by Accident* and Director of The Writing Institute at Sarah Lawrence College.

"*Ms. Murphy's Makeover* will make you laugh and cry with its roller-coaster ride of ups and downs—gangs and scholars, truth and treachery, love and lust, death and rebirth. A must read for anyone who loves a good book." ~ Rebecca Marks, author of *On the Rocks*

"The true-to-life situations, the three dimensional characters, and the tension-filled romance make this the perfect book club pick. *Ms. Murphy's Makeover* deserves to be savored, but the action and romance make it hard to resist flying through the pages." ~ Eileen Palma, author of *Worth the Weight*

ACKNOWLEDGEMENTS

Thank you to The Writing Institute at Sarah Lawrence College; to my incredible Advanced Novel Writing instructors Patricia Dunn and Jimin Han; to my teachers Marian Thurm and Sally Koslow; to the "fantastic" writing group: Ahmed Asif, Marlena Baraf, Rebecca Marks, Nan Mutnick, Eileen Palma, Jessica Rao, Ines Rodrigues, with special thanks to Rebecca for guiding me to Black Opal Books.

Thank you to Lauri Wellington and the entire team at Black Opal Books; to Joan Schulman and the writers at the Chappaqua Library; to my early readers and dear friends, Janet Mayer and Iris Farber; to my wonderful daughters, Jessica Phillips and Elena Nielsen; and, of course, to my beloved husband, Zachary Goldstein.

I also want to acknowledge the many fine educators I have worked with, who give their all every day to the students they serve. Most of all, my thanks go out to the kids in the New York City Public Schools, whose courage, determination, and sheer goodness in the face of adversity made teaching them a joy.

Ms. Murphy's Makeover

Jacqueline Goldstein

A Black Opal Books Publication

GENRE: WOMEN'S FICTION/ROMANTIC SUSPENSE

This is a work of fiction. Names, places, characters and incidents are either the product of the author's imagination or are used fictitiously, and any resemblance to any actual persons, living or dead, businesses, organizations, events or locales is entirely coincidental. All trademarks, service marks, registered trademarks, and registered service marks are the property of their respective owners and are used herein for identification purposes only. The publisher does not have any control over or assume any responsibility for author or third-party websites or their contents.

DEDICATION

*To my dear and loving husband, Zachary Goldstein,
our terrific daughters,
Jessica Phillips and Elena Nielsen,
and in memory of my parents,
Susan and Leopold Grandsire*

CHAPTER 1

Charlotte

It seemed the farther she was from her Connecticut home, the more attractive she became. Charlotte Murphy speed-walked past a construction site near the parking lot, charting a winding path through broken glass, dog feces, and other souvenirs of a Bronx weekend. At thirty-eight, the mother of teenagers, she hoped to pass the workmen unnoticed. But wolf whistles soon began. It could not be what she was wearing, a modest gray twin set and matching skirt. Probably it was just the hair, as her husband claimed. Red hair and white skin were exotic in this neighborhood. As she hurried to the brick building where she worked, Charlotte looked straight ahead, ignoring the barrage of catcalls and comments.

She also chose not to see the smirking face of Ted Lagakis, the new dean of discipline, who lounged against the iron fence surrounding the school. As she approached, he also gave a wolf whistle, low and mocking. Tall, burly, and far from handsome, Lagakis looked more like a bouncer in some seedy club than a fellow teacher. At least he was not smoking, but Charlotte knew that would change when Bertha Trombetta arrived. Those two had a morning ritual of puffing away in full view of the students.

A few of those students stood slightly apart from the

dean, munching on chips and sipping fruit punch in neon colors rather than eating the free breakfast provided in the cafeteria. Charlotte managed to greet Lagakis and the kids with a crisp "Good Morning" when her foot chanced on something slippery and she skidded, just as she neared the dean.

He caught her easily. "Good Morning? *Now* it is."

Thick fingers, sprinkled with dark hairs, gripped her arms. The blue stone in his pinky ring winked at her. Heat radiated from his large body, in spite of the chilly September breeze.

Charlotte made her own body rigid, definitely off limits. Lagakis dropped his hands and pointed at Charlotte's feet. She followed his gaze and realized that a used condom was stuck to the sole of her shoe. Lagakis's smirk deepened as Charlotte tried to remove the condom without letting it touch her skin. She scraped her foot repeatedly against the concrete step at the doorway. Lagakis nearly doubled over, laughing. When the repulsive thing finally came off, Charlotte glared at him.

The dean raised his hands before his face, as though to ward off a blow. "Sorry, doll. I couldn't help it." His laughter followed her into the building.

Inside, the vestibule was dark and cool, its walls plastered with student-made posters welcoming visitors to The Bronx High School of Aesthetics. Charlotte paused and took several deep breaths, pretending to admire the newly decorated area. It had felt like a full day's work, just getting from her car to the school.

"Go right in, girly." George, the ancient security guard, waved Charlotte past the metal detectors and toward the marble staircase that led to the main office. There she moved her time card from Out to In and greeted the secretaries. She checked the cubby for her mail and then headed up a dimly lit staircase to her classroom—a sunny, high-ceilinged refuge with a thriving philodendron spilling tendrils over the window ledge.

As she paused to water the plant with standing water left over from Friday, she looked out the window and saw boys in gang colors throwing lit matches into the mailbox outside the school.

These were not her students. Her students were nice kids who wanted to be cosmetologists, or whose parents wanted them to be in a school where they'd be relatively safe. Teaching them enough English to pass the state exam was Charlotte's job. Dealing with security was not.

Where was Lagakis? Most likely, he'd gone inside to call for backup.

Automatically, she locked the door, secured her purse in a metal cabinet, and then removed a pile of journal notebooks from the wooden closet. She selected the one on top. Purple cover. Purple ink. It had to be Valerie's.

Charlotte knew that some kids needed a safe place to write about their lives. She promised she would keep their writing confidential and would not penalize them for poor spelling and grammar. Valerie had written *PLEASE DO NOT READ* on her latest entry. And so Charlotte set the purple notebook aside, and took up the next one on the pile.

She had barely opened it when she heard the familiar clicking sound of the principal, Natalie Albert, using her master key to open the locked door. The principal, tall and model thin, had the reputation of never wearing the same outfit twice.

Today a red power suit complemented her dark hair. Her chocolate brown eyes sparkled.

"I hate to say it, sweetie, but we just caught a break." Natalie was about to say something else when her eyes zoomed in on Charlotte's new ring. "Oh my. What's old Francis done now?"

Charlotte was stung, and more than a little annoyed. "A lot of hard work, that's what."

She knew better than to tell Natalie that her husband had lost his wedding ring. He thought maybe it slipped off when he was swimming. He'd been filled with remorse, replaced it immediately, and bought Charlotte a diamond celebration ring as well.

"Oh, Charlotte. Don't be so sensitive. Anyway, that's not what I want to talk about, my friend. Bertie Trombetta died last night. A heart attack. The witch is dead!"

It took a moment for Charlotte to process this information. In the distance, a church bell chimed. *Ask not for whom the bell tolls.*

Natalie bowed her head and folded her hands in pretend piety, their lacquered red nails pointing to the ceiling. "There is a God, after all."

Charlotte closed her eyes and swallowed hard. "Dead? Are you sure? She was here Friday, teaching across the hall."

The image of Bertha Trombetta, smoking, floated before Charlotte's eyes.

"Screaming her head off, probably. I bet she gave herself the heart attack. But I must say her timing was perfect."

This was cold, even for Natalie. But the principal was under a lot of pressure. Charlotte thought she understood. "Are you saying the visitors won't come?"

Natalie gave a short laugh. "Nothing can stop that." She placed her hands on Charlotte's desk and leaned in close. "Life goes on. That's actually why I'm here. Charlotte, I need you to go to Bertie's funeral."

Charlotte immediately shook her head no.

Natalie waved a hand, anticipating Charlotte's objection. "I know, I know. I should go myself. Normally, I would. But I can't this week. Not with the visitors from State Ed here. And someone has to represent the school."

Charlotte thought of an escape. "Does Lagakis know?"

Natalie nodded. "I just told him. He's in his office, on the phone with the family."

"Perfect. Send him. Or do we need him in the school?"

Natalie laughed a second time. "Be serious. But yes, he asked and I can't very well refuse. You'll have to go with him. I'm sorry."

Charlotte exploded. *"No!* And Bertie wouldn't want me there."

Natalie smiled, showing newly whitened teeth. "She won't know."

Technically, Charlotte could refuse. But Natalie was more than her boss. She was a friend, of sorts. Twenty years ago, they had attended the same college. Natalie recognized Charlotte at a job fair three years ago and offered her the position of teaching English at a vocational high school for cosmetology.

At the time, downsizing at Francis's firm had made the Murphys anxious, and Francis had been relieved when Charlotte was offered work. He'd kept his job, however, along with a big raise. Now he was after her to quit. And Charlotte didn't want to.

Natalie pressed her advantage. "You owe me, sweetie. I need this."

Charlotte made a last ditch effort. "Look." She pointed at her stack of journals. "I'm swamped."

"Sweetie, I know you don't read those things, anyway."

"I read every word. Unless they ask me not to. It's for critical thinking." Charlotte put air quotes around the last two words.

"Save the buzz words for the visitors. I need this, Charlotte. With you there, maybe Lagakis will behave himself."

"Good luck with that." Charlotte sighed. "But all right. Under protest. And you owe me."

"Excellent. Now. A *teensy* suggestion. At the funeral, glam up a little. Lose the librarian look for a day. Black dress. Heels. Hair down."

"The librarian look? Is it that bad?"

"Look, we are a school of beauty here. So. You have a black dress?"

"I do, but Francis says black makes me look— conspicuous." Her husband had used another word, but Natalie didn't need more ammunition.

"Oh, yes. Pope Francis. Was he speaking *ex cathedra?*"

Charlotte had to smile at the image of her husband in papal vestments.

"I'd be on the phone to my lawyer so fast."

Maybe that's why you're divorced. Aloud, Charlotte said, "What does it matter what I wear?"

One of Natalie's more annoying habits was whispering behind her hand. She did so now, although they were alone in an empty room. "You never know who will show up at these things. Bertie was always threatening to go to the media. There may be reporters. That woman had a big mouth."

"So? Wait. Is something wrong? Is that why State Ed is coming?"

Natalie looked Charlotte full in the eye. "Don't be ridiculous. It's a purely routine visit."

A bell signaled the start of class, and Charlotte could hear students in the hallway. "Showtime. I have a class coming in."

Natalie placed a hand on the doorknob, but turned back. "Bring a student with you tomorrow. Someone presentable. And keep your eye on Lagakis."

Students had already gathered outside, awaiting admittance. Bertha Trombetta's wide, homely face was before Charlotte's eyes, and lines from Walt Whitman's *Leaves of Grass* resounded in her ears.

For my enemy is dead, a man divine as myself is dead,
I look where he lies white-faced and
still in the coffin—I draw near,
Bend down and touch lightly with my lips
the white face in the coffin.

಄಄಄

Valerie's Journal
DO NOT READ!
Everybody knows the job. We take care of our

teachers. Even Suzette. She got pulled out of class to do a mural on a big sheet of shipping paper from Staples to cover up graffiti on the long wall and it looks crazy professional. I did an essay for the bulletin board, only the principal said I had to copy it over, being I did it in purple ink. At least I was only copying from myself. I mean other essays on the board were from a couple years ago. The principal saves them in this file and she just gives them to kids to copy on fresh paper and sign their name and this month's date. The cosmetology teacher did our hair, took pictures, and put them up like it was our work too. I have to do a presentation when the visitors come—wax the cosmetology teacher. Just her legs. She's been growing them out mad hairy, but I'm getting graded on it, and I think she's being observed too, which is like a test they give our teachers.

We rehearsed all the questions, in case the visitors ask us like how come we study for Regents Exams. The answer is so we can pass the tests and graduate, duh, but they make us practice and we don't mind since it wastes class time. Oh and there was that dorky substitute in the building today because Ms. Trombetta died last night, RIP, and people in her class who hadn't studied for the quiz were like, Yes! To me it made no difference, being I get Murphy for English now.

CHAPTER 2

Before the Funeral

Francis X. Murphy liked to joke that he never saw his house in daylight. He arrived at the office early and stayed late, often going in on weekends when he wasn't traveling.

But the morning of the funeral, he slept in. He descended the oak staircase in the blue brocade robe that set off his Irish coloring. Dark hair, rosy complexion, and Shannon blue eyes. It had been well after two when he'd slipped into their bed, actually twin beds with a joint headboard and a crack down the middle they used to call the Continental Divide.

Uneven planks creaked as he walked to the kitchen. Both Murphys had been mystified to find, when they'd started looking in Connecticut, that antique floors equaled enormous prices. They'd paid full measure to own a home that had been a school a hundred years ago, even though it was turned around on the property and the front didn't face the road.

But Charlotte loved the high ceilings and tall leaded windows that let in so much light. She'd grown up in a first floor apartment with a mother who was always switching off lamps.

As for Francis, he loved describing the property more

than actually living there. Two wooded acres and a pond. Practically a private park. On the Gold Coast.

In the breakfast nook, he inhaled long and deep as Charlotte poured his coffee from her mother's old pot. They both preferred that brew to what came from the beeping machine on the counter.

"Service with a smile. Why so late this time?" asked Charlotte.

He stretched long thin arms above his head, and the wide sleeves slid down. Thin wrists. Thin ankles. Long feet encased in leather slippers. A tall, elegant man of forty-one.

"Thank you. The coffee is perfect. And trust me. I had to stay till the meeting finished."

"I thought it was just a dinner thing."

"You don't understand business and I'm glad you don't have to." His eyes flicked over her dress. "Why are you wearing *that*?"

That was a black sheath. It had been too expensive to throw out and she hadn't gotten around to donating it.

She watched him struggle to be diplomatic. He took a sip and closed his eyes. "Ah. I miss your coffee when I'm on the road. But, um, poetry girl, I don't think you should wear black. You need to neutralize that hair with soft colors."

"It happens there's a funeral. A woman at school died."

She waited for another comment, but he patted his mouth with the cloth napkin, leaned back, and took another sip. Linen was something he insisted on for all his meals, even breakfast. When he did speak, his tone was mild, patient. "Even so. Black is wrong for you, poetry girl. It's too much of a contrast with hair like yours."

When did you become the fashion police? Charlotte bit back the words before they escaped. She knew Francis meant well.

"Who died? A friend of yours?" he asked.

"Not really."

"Then why wear that? Why are you even going? I bet Natalie's making you."

"Someone's in a good mood," she said.

"I was, until a minute ago. It just bothers me. Natalie says jump and you say how high."

A thump on the front porch meant the newspaper had arrived. Glad for a change of subject, Charlotte went out, removed its plastic cover, handed the first section to him, and took Arts for herself. He accepted the paper, but said, "You know, we should drop home delivery. Most people read on line now. I always do now, when I travel."

"Not for me," she said.

"When will you join the twenty-first century?"

"I'm still trying to get to the nineteenth." Charlotte's aversion to technology was a Murphy family joke.

They read in silence, hearing the settling sounds of the old house, along with the shower running and the hair dryer whirring, as the twins got ready upstairs. Sunlight streamed through the sheer curtains Charlotte preferred to heavy drapes, like a benediction on this rare time together. Outside, a family of deer feasted on apples that littered the ground. The arborist had said that tree was in trouble—he'd prune before the cold weather set in.

Footsteps thudded on the stairs, and the twins, Emily and Abigail, appeared. Although they were fraternal twins, no more alike than ordinary siblings, both had red hair like Charlotte's. Emily's was carefully blown dry. Abigail's was a mass of wet ringlets.

Abigail ran to her father and Francis ducked. "You're dripping on the newspaper, Abby. Why the wet hair?"

"No time. Mom kept me up writing the stupid college essay over and over."

"What's the big deal about an essay? You just sit down and do it," said Emily, who had written her essay without any help.

"When I was in high school, I had to do everything on my own. You both are lucky to have a mother who can help you. Although she wastes it on future hairdressers," Francis added.

Charlotte shot him a look, but he pretended not to notice.

"Whatever. So, where are the protein bars, Charlotte?" Emily was rummaging in the cabinet.

"I forgot," Charlotte answered. "But I made banana muffins."

"Those?" Emily's lips turned down in a pouting grimace. "Full of carbs and gluten."

Their father looked at Charlotte and rolled his eyes. In spite of his comment about her students, Charlotte was grateful for that eye roll.

Abby pulled on her sister's hand. "Come on, Em. We'll get some bars from the vending machine."

"Buy more, Charlotte. Don't forget. Write it down. Go to the store," Emily said.

"I don't like you to call me Charlotte. Call me Mom or Mother."

Emily muttered under her breath. "Then act like one."

"What's that? What did you say to your mother?"

Emily backed down immediately at Francis's stern tone. "Nothing. Don't forget. Rodeo Drive, Daddy. Have fun playing school, *Mother*."

"Abigail?" Charlotte held up the folder containing the essay they'd worked on past midnight.

"Oops! Thanks, Mom. You're the best."

Emily pointed at the muffins and pretended to gag, two fingers pointing at her throat. The back door slammed, the car the girls shared started, and they were gone. Francis continued reading. Charlotte tapped on his paper hard enough to make noise. "Thanks for backing me up before. But I wish you wouldn't run down my students."

"What's that? All I said was future hairdressers. That's what they are."

"You said *wastes* it on hairdressers. They are nice kids, and they deserve an education."

"I suppose, some of the better ones, anyway. But do they need someone like you? We don't need the money anymore. We never did."

"You thought we might."

"That was three years ago. Crisis averted."

"Till the next crisis."

"Charlotte, we're fine. They were firing people left and right, but I'm still there."

"And you're doing the work of all the people they fired."

"That's the price, poetry girl. Long hours equals high pay. And I'm a cinch for another raise soon. Why can't you get that? Don't you believe in me?"

"Of course, I do."

"Then it's time for you to quit. It doesn't look right, you going there."

"Maybe I like the job. Maybe I'm good at it."

"Anybody can do what you do. And you're neglecting your own kids. Where are your priorities?"

"Where are yours? Why are you never home?"

As soon as the words left her mouth, she regretted them. He was holding up the paper. He'd be good for another ten minutes now, explaining just how much he sacrificed for her and the girls. Charlotte looked longingly at her school things as Francis rattled on.

"Listen to this. The market is softening. Interest rates…"

"You're right, Francis." She nodded, having no idea what he said as she gathered her things and got ready to leave.

"Now you're being sensible. Rosemary's been saying—"

"Who is that?" Charlotte asked.

"Just a friend from work."

"You keep mentioning her. Rosemary for remembrance?"

Francis chuckled. "*Hamlet,* right? My God, it's rubbing off on me." He rattled the paper and turned away.

CHAPTER 3

Lagakis

Ladies and gentlemen, get to class. The bell rang." Lagakis stood in the crowded hallway, tapping his watch. He wore a dark suit today, funeral attire, which made his broad shoulders seem even wider. An ever expanding circle of Dominican girls greeted each other with kisses, like long-separated relatives. Two ninth grade boys played at fighting, wrestling around on the floor. Lagakis interposed his large body between them, knuckled both their heads, and sent them away laughing.

Several couples were kissing against the long wall. A girl whose legs were wrapped around a boy's waist said, "Hi, Mr. Lagakis."

"Get to class, China," Lagakis said and approached a trio of girls who formed a ring around a fourth, a tall girl named Suzette. She was talking at full volume, tossing her braided extensions, and waving long powerful arms.

"Ladies, the bell rang." Lagakis pointed a guiding hand, palm outward, in the direction he wanted them to go.

Suzette brushed it away like a pesky fly. "Don't you put your hands on me," she said.

Her fingers ended in lethal blue nails decorated with tiny flowers. But although Suzette sucked her teeth and raised a blue-tipped middle finger at the dean, she finally went to class, and so did all the others. Lagakis could do crowd control. Teaching was his second career, following twenty years of service with the New York City Police Department. Although he was new to teaching, Natalie had immediately made him the dean, giving him only one class to teach.

As per Natalie's instructions, Charlotte escorted her student Valerie to the principal's office. The girl was ushered past the waiting room to the inner office, probably to rehearse her condolence handshake and speech. Natalie left nothing to chance. Charlotte had to stand in the small outer office. Two gloomy assistant principals, summoned to meet the visitors who were expected that day, occupied the only chairs. After a few more minutes of hall patrol, Lagakis also entered the tiny waiting room, completely filling it.

"A shepherd, that's all I am. They should issue me a crook."

"A what?" said one of the assistant principals. "Did you say crook?"

"A shepherd's crook, boss. Like my papou had in Greece. Only the sheep he herded were white."

The other assistant principal, an African American, looked up at that.

"Just kidding," Lagakis said. "No offense."

In his dark suit, Lagakis looked quite the professional today, but he always managed to be so...inappropriate. He stared at Charlotte as though reading her thoughts. "Yes, I do own a suit. But clothes don't make the man. Isn't that what you're thinking?" He smiled, showing deep dimples. "That's Shakespeare, right?"

Wrong.

"Now *you* look gorgeous in that black," he continued. "Redheads generally do. Of course you always look gorgeous. Or is it okay for me to say that? I don't want to harass you and—" He nodded toward the principal's door. "—get in trouble with your buddy. But could you turn around? I want to check out your shoes. Make sure there's nothing stuck to them."

Charlotte knew better than to engage. When he wasn't acting smarmy, Lagakis needled her. Why did he always stand so close? He loomed over her now as they waited together. Perhaps he didn't realize how much space he took up in the small room. Fortunately, Valerie's handshake seemed to have passed muster, and the principal beckoned the teachers to enter the inner sanctum.

"You finally managed to clear the halls?" Natalie said to Lagakis. "I told you today everything has to look perfect."

His eyes darkened but he said nothing, and Charlotte took pity on him, despite his needling tone.

Natalie, you should be thanking him instead of carping, Charlotte thought. *Your precious halls are clear.*

In Natalie's office a wooden conference table reeked of furniture polish. To the right of the doorway, a smaller table was set up with coffee and a tray of miniature muffins for the visitors. The tray was still covered in plastic wrap. Photographs of long ago students giving finger waves in the beauty shop were arranged along the long wall. A bookcase held yearbooks dating back to the 1950s. On top of the bookcase was a statue of a girl bowling.

Valerie looked at it closely. "I never saw that before," she said. "I didn't know we used to have a bowling team."

"This school used to have a lot of things," the principal said. "Before the Regents became a graduation requirement. You understand about the Regents, Valerie?"

Valerie recited in a monotone. "Yes, ma'am. We study for Regents Exams so we can pass the tests and graduate. The Regents measure how well we meet New York State Standards."

Natalie pointed to charts displayed prominently on the office walls. "There are standards for every subject."

"Yes, ma'am."

Charlotte was afraid Natalie would start in about graduation requirements in a vocational high school, but Lagakis spoke first. "This one knows how the game is played. How come she never saw the bowling trophy? Guess she doesn't spend much time in this office. Unlike some of her friends."

Valerie is right here, thought Charlotte. *Speak to her, not about her.*

Lagakis was staring at the muffins.

"They're for the monitors," the principal said. "I mean, the visitors."

"You have to sweeten them up, huh?"

"I think you should get going," the principal said. "Who is driving?"

"I'll drive. If that's all right," said Lagakis. "I don't want to step on any toes."

"I'd be most appreciative if you'd drive," Charlotte said.

"And will you show your appreciation, my lady?" Lagakis pulled at an imaginary forelock, mocking her formal diction. When he saw her face, he said, "Sorry. You need to keep me in my place, don't you?"

Charlotte shook her head in frustration. Bad enough she would have to spend the afternoon facing Bertie's mortality and her own. How much worse to do so in Lagakis's company. *Natalie, you owe me big time*, she thought.

As they left, Lagakis lifted the plastic wrap and helped himself to a miniature muffin, nestled in a cradle of pleated paper. He swallowed it in one gulp and dropped the paper into what had been a spotless wastebasket. "That one's for Bertie," he said. "Since she isn't here to share with the monitors—I mean—the visitors."

☙❧☙

Valerie's Journal
DO NOT READ!

So they picked me. I didn't mind going. The principal of course had to check me out before I could leave with Murphy, but I know how to represent. I had on a black skirt and white blouse with long sleeves. No jewelry. My hair was tied back in a low pony tail. I just had gloss on my lips in peachy amber and some eye make-up.

Valerie cleans up pretty good, doesn't she? Lagakis said, and you could see Murphy wanted to die.

Lagakis has a pretty nice car, black with leather seats. Kind of like a gypsy cab. Too bad somebody keyed the doors. I bet Lagakis was pissed. I know who it was too. The car dings like crazy if you don't put on your seat belt, which was a good thing.

You'd think I'd be used to smoke from the girls' bathroom, but it was starting to get to me. I wanted to open the window but I figured the car would take over and alarms would go off. Plus Murphy would probably freak and make Lagakis put out his cigarette. Besides I didn't want to spoil Murphy's hair which looked good for a change. She must have blown it out instead of just letting it air dry. Her dress was a knockout. She's mad pretty and crazy nice and guess what? She does have a figure which you generally can't tell. I wish she would come up to the shop once in a while. I'd like to get my hands on that red hair. My hair would have been ok with the window open since I had it tied back and of course I had used product. But I stood quiet and it was interesting watching the two of them. I mean Murphy never took her eyes off him except once or twice when she turned around to talk to me. And he practically got us killed looking at her.

I wondered if they were ever together. If they ever did it in the olden days.

I'm sitting on the toilet writing this but the foster kids will probably bang on the door in a minute unless my grandmother keeps them off me. Murphy let me take it home as long as I bring it back tomorrow. So anyway. It's a funny thing, to think about teachers doing it. Murphy must have done it at least twice. She has two kids, she told us. But they're twins so maybe that's only once. They're going to college soon.

Trombetta. I swear never did it in her life. She probably never even fooled around. Maybe that's why she always came up to the shop for manicures. At least she got somebody to hold her hand. And Lagakis is just a dog. Ask anybody.

So we get to the funeral home and I spotted this van that says LAGAKIS in humongous letters. A guy gets out and carries this gorgeous wreath into the place. It was the biggest one I'd ever seen. Mr. Lagakis, I said, that van has the same name as you. Yes, that's one of ours, he said. So Murphy says you own a flower shop? And he says no, it's my uncle. We're Greeks. Flowers fur and food. Not to mention the other F-word. She looks nervous. He waits a beat and then laughs. Fine jewelry, he says. What were you thinking? She got all red. He shouldn't do that to my teacher. She's not like that. But he opened the car door for Murphy and helped her get out, like she was some delicate flower. He was going to help me too, I swear, but I jumped out before he had the chance. Anyway he says to me, Valerie. College isn't for everybody. I should have joined up with my cousin Gus. He never even finished high school and he's a millionaire. I was a fool. Went to college and became a shepherd.

Murphy says but Valerie is college material.

Hello, miss, there's no money for that. I heard just the books cost like a hundred dollars. Each.

So we walk in the room, sign our names, and guess what? There's hardly anybody there. And not a lot of flowers or anything but this really nice furniture all empty lined up on the sides. They had dressed Trombetta in a blue dress with sequins all over the jacket, like old women wear to weddings. She had pearls on. Pearls with sequins. They don't match. I wondered if they were real pearls, and if they would bury them with her. The hair was all right. But her foundation was caked and the lipstick could of used liner.

A great loss to the teaching profession, Murphy was saying to someone behind me. I'd never actually heard Murphy lie before, but I guess sometimes you have to. She loved her work. She loved her students, Lagakis says.

Sure she did. She loved failing them.

Lagakis just stared down at Trombetta lying there. I guess they were friends and all and she practically had him on speed dial she wrote so many dean refer- rals. I was actually feeling bad for him. But Trombet- ta's sister was busy with some other people so Lagakis already moved to the back. Eventually me and Murphy go back there too. Lagakis starts telling a couple of Trombetta's relatives how dumb us kids are, how we can't read. His voice was so loud. Trom- betta herself could probably hear him. He had every- one's attention—Trombetta's cousin and nephew or great nephew and another old lady.

I was kind of checking out the nephew, since he was like the only guy my age there and since I don't get to see that type too much in person. Nice build. Total J Crew blond straight hair falling in his eyes and a tie and I swear to God plaid sneakers. At his aunt's funeral.

I rather thought Aunt Bertha was exaggerating, says the genius nephew Trombetta was always brag- ging on. She used to say I could read better than her students when I was in kindergarten.

I figure Trombetta said that. Sounds like her. An- yway I'd give him about five minutes on my block. Ten tops. But his eyes were really blue, or maybe he had contacts.

Then Lagakis goes on about Trombetta. How she said some teachers passed the students if they could

*fog a mirror. He gave a kind of salute toward Trom-
betta in her coffin. She called it like she saw it, he
says. She wasn't afraid to tell the truth.*

*So Murphy gives him a look like, don't you see Va-
lerie is standing right there?*

*I wish Murphy would take it easy on herself. It's
cool. I get Lagakis. Murphy she's a nice lady and all
but she has no idea.*

*All of a sudden Murphy gets this look on her face
like she's figured something out at last. She kind of
puts an arm around me and whispers, on the low, he's
doing the best he can. She looks up at Lagakis and
then back at Trombetta. Most people do, she says.*

*I feel like Trombetta is right here alive again. I
swear I could hear her voice saying it. Sometimes,
your best is not good enough. But I don't say it to
Murphy. Meanwhile, old J. Crew has put something
in my hand. I ignore him and shove it in my pocket.*

*Lagakis finally notices me standing there. And at
that moment in time he actually looked embarrassed
that maybe I'd heard him.*

*I felt Murphy's hand on my back. Valerie, come
and meet Ms. Trombetta's sister.*

*So this was Trombetta's sister. The moment had
arrived. I stuck out my hand. I'd rehearsed this part
with the principal. I'm very sorry for your loss, I say.*

*Here is one of her former students, Valerie Martin,
Murphy said.*

*The woman looked a little bit like Trombetta, only
thinner. Her hair desperately needed conditioner. She
ignored my hand and kind of grabbed me in a big
hug. The buttons on her jacket pushed into my chest.*

*Valerie Martin. She talked about you all the time.
My sister loved you so much.*

*Weird. The even weirder thing was Murphy bent
down and gave Trombetta a kiss.*

CHAPTER 4

Remembering Trombetta

As Charlotte bent over the open casket, she half expected the body to rear up like Grendel's mother in protest. Bertie Trombetta had certainly done her share of rearing when she was alive. She had huge thick arms and hands like bear claws. She would hammer the table at faculty meetings. Sometimes she would bang her cane. "Standards!" Her voice was a bellow. "We can't keep passing these kids along. We've got to start failing them. It's not fair to the good kids."

"We've got to start teaching them," Charlotte would counter.

"They're unteachable."

"Then what do they pay *us* for?"

"They pay us to baby sit juvenile delinquents."

Each morning, Charlotte would see Trombetta standing outside the school with Lagakis, both smoking right in front of the kids, getting their last nicotine fix before beginning the day.

The last time Charlotte had seen Trombetta alive had been the previous week, at lunch. It had been unusually noisy and crowded in the staff cafeteria, and teachers were lined up like prison inmates, pushing trays along a silver railing. Charlotte usually brought a sandwich to eat at her desk, but today she had forgotten it at home, and so she stood at the end of a long line just to purchase a container of yogurt and some tea.

When she finally obtained her food, she looked around for a place to sit, but the only empty chair was at a small table where Bertie Trombetta ate alone. Charlotte contemplated carrying her lunch upstairs to the classroom, but her feet hurt. She had been standing for three full periods, and she needed to sit down and eat something right away. Against all judgment, she took the seat opposite Trombetta.

Bertie Trombetta had been one of the first ones on the line, and she was halfway through her meal. She shoveled the food in rapidly—first a bite of fried fish triangle, then some macaroni and cheese, then the canned corn. Her round arm was a machine, moving from plate to mouth, steady as a metronome. Her huge uplifted breasts created a shelf for bits of food that fell from her lips. A container of whole milk and a plastic cup of fruit cocktail waited their turn at the back of her tray.

"What time does the bell ring today?" she called out to the entire room. "I hate the way they keep changing the schedule."

No one paid any attention. Three brand new teachers, blonde recruits from Teach for America, were busy comforting a fourth, a Miss Knudsen from Minnesota who was crying into her coffee. "Anders! I should have stayed with Anders and sold bait."

The slaughter of the innocents, Charlotte thought. The crying girl had been assigned to Renaissance House, a dumping ground for incorrigible students. Charlotte promised herself that she would seek the poor thing out later and offer to help.

Seated next to the new teachers was Mr. Harney, a social studies teacher. Each day he wore a tiny Confederate flag pin on his lapel. No kid had ever asked him about it, he boasted. No curiosity, these kids. No wonder they couldn't pass American Studies. He turned the pages of his *New*

York Times and drank what he said was coffee from a tall silver thermos. By the end of the day he was singing gently to himself, obviously buzzed.

At another table, the special education teachers were shrieking with laughter. Apparently, a special needs student, Monroe, who refused to open a book in any of his classes, had distinguished himself that morning when the principal accidentally locked all her keys inside a special vault where important documents were kept. The principal was on the verge of hysteria until Monroe, sent to the office for a discipline interview, opened the vault with a credit card.

Lagakis stopped at Charlotte's table, holding a cup of coffee. "Ted, when the hell does this period end?" Trombetta asked. "Nobody put out a memo for the time schedule."

She was probably the only person in the school who used his first name.

The walkie-talkie on his hip crackled as he spoke. "What that woman doesn't know about running a school would fill a book. The bell rings at ten minutes after. It's assembly schedule today. Take your time."

Charlotte looked away from the yellow corn kernels on Bertie's gray sweater and concentrated on her own strawberry yogurt. Not her favorite, but much more appetizing than Trombetta's fried fish stuffed with melted American cheese.

Trombetta picked up the book Charlotte had brought down to read. "*Guide to Teaching Shakespeare?*" Trombetta hacked a phlegm-filled cough. "What the hell do you need that for, Charlotte?"

"I thought I might have time to look at it during lunch."

"God love you." Trombetta shoved the book back at Charlotte and shook her tight blonde curls. "Pssst!" she stage-whispered. "You're teaching *cosmetology* students, Charlotte. Nice kids, some of them, but idiots. They don't need Shakespeare."

Charlotte stirred the strawberries up from the bottom of the yogurt. It was near its expiration date, and the liquid on the top separated. "They're just kids being kids. Sometimes they may act like idiots, Bertie, but they're not."

"Casting pearls before swine," Trombetta said.

"You have some corn on your sweater," said Charlotte.

"Thanks," Trombetta replied. "Hey, Ted. Get this. Tinkerbell over here wants to teach Shakespeare to the great unwashed."

"That's not fair," Lagakis said. "You're being unfair to the kids."

Both Trombetta and Charlotte looked up at him in surprise. Defense of students was not to be expected from this quarter.

"Our kids are not unwashed," he continued, dimpling. "In fact, they're very well washed. They're washed, waxed, plucked, and polished. They *gleam* with grooming. And that's about it."

He took a napkin from the pile on the table. "Here, Bertie." He passed it to Trombetta, "You missed a spot."

"Thanks. Between you and Tinkerbell here, I should be okay." Trombetta brushed bits of corn from her breasts with a large but well-manicured hand.

"Tinkerbell," Lagakis said. "I don't think so. Not Charlotte. Much more of a Wendy, I think."

"Mother of Lost Boys?" Trombetta asked.

"Hello," said Charlotte. "I'm right here. In the room with you."

Lagakis dimpled again. "Mother of Lost Boys. Perfect."

The sounds of arguing voices floated in from the open door. None of the teachers looked up. Trombetta coughed again. "That's charming, Ted, but you're wrong. She's Tinkerbell. Wendy went home. She grew up. This one's still in Never-Never Land."

Charlotte wanted to retort that Never-Never Land was better than *Animal Farm*, but Bertie didn't give her a chance. Bertie said, "Know who I'd be?"

"In *Peter Pan*? Who?"

"Nana, of course."

There could be no response to that. Bertie did look very much like the large dog Nana. Charlotte felt uncomfortable, and so she decided to return to the previous topic.

"Don't you think our kids deserve to be exposed to real literature? This is their education, for God's sake. The only one they'll ever have, some of them."

"Kids whose main goal in life is to give somebody a manicure?" Bertie crumpled up the napkin and rubbed it on her hand. "*Out, damn spot.* Perfect for applying freckle cream or whatever they've got up there in the beauty shop."

Charlotte felt every muscle in her back tense and knot. She picked up her book. "I should be going."

"Relax. There's plenty of time." Still standing behind her, Lagakis placed a warm hand on Charlotte's shoulder.

She shrugged off his hand. "Don't."

"All right. I always forget that some people hate to be touched. Charlotte," he continued, "never try to teach a pig to sing. It wastes your time and it annoys the pig."

"I find that offensive," Charlotte said.

"See how she keeps me in my place?" Lagakis said to Trombetta.

"Fortunately, that isn't difficult," said Charlotte.

"Give him a break, Charlotte," Trombetta said. "He has a crush on you." She smiled, revealing bits of food in her teeth.

Charlotte shuddered. "Stop that. We're not high school kids. And what I teach—it works for me."

"Everybody's a high school kid. And I'm sure it *seems* to work for you," said Trombetta. She inhaled her fruit cocktail and started on the milk, sipping it through a straw. "Your course is what we used to call a gut course. No offense." A little gurgle sound signaled that she had finished the milk in a few swallows.

Charlotte blinked quickly. The back of her throat hurt. She took a swallow of tea, now quite cold.

"Look, Tink," Trombetta said.

Charlotte stiffened.

"Sorry. Look, Miss Bell, is that better?"

Charlotte shrugged. "My name is Charlotte. Just Charlotte."

Increased noise in the hall signaled the beginning of a fight. Lagakis's walkie-talkie crackled and he sprang to attention.

"L1 to D4—Fight on the first floor," he said into it. "Sorry, ladies." He took a final gulp of coffee, put his cup down on Trombetta's tray, and ran out of the cafeteria.

Trombetta continued talking. Her voice was menacingly kind. "Charlotte, then. Charlotte," she crooned. "I think I hurt your feelings just now. Are you about to cry?"

"Of course not," Charlotte said indignantly. *How had Bertie seen that?*

"Good," said Trombetta, in that same compassionate tone. "I'm sure you're a good teacher and all that. Kids will do anything for you, because you're pretty and you're an easy grader." She placed a heavy hand on the table and gathered up her cane. "God, I need a cigarette."

Automatically Charlotte picked up Bertie's tray and stepped over to the garbage.

"You did that so gracefully," Trombetta said. "The way you do everything." She gave way to another fit of coughing and then added, venomously, "You're light on your feet. A lightweight."

On that final bit of unpleasantness, Charlotte had glanced down at Bertie's thick ankles, emerging from black shoes that laced up the sides.

Now, just a few days later, she was bending over the woman's coffin. *My enemy is dead.*

෴

Valerie's Journal
DO NOT READ!
OMG ! Rohan Davis is back. See, I'm just walking

*to the store getting orange juice for my grandmother.
I have to pass this stoop where Antwan's crew hangs
out, and they always tease me, shouting out my name
and all, but this time they stood quiet, looking at
somebody behind me. Rohan. He got big, real big,
while he was inside. Like from working out. Trust me
this is weird, him being here, since Antwan's crew
took over his corner when Rohan went away.*

*It got so quiet you could hear my cell telling me I
had a text with that little ping it gives. Suzette, no
doubt. And then a couple blocks away a car backfir-
ing which always sounds exactly like somebody getting shot and sometimes it is. Finally Gareth, one of
Antwan's boys, goes, S'up, Rohan.*

*Rohan doesn't answer, which is a dis. Then Rohan
walks me to the store and waits outside, his back to
the glass window with the sign for cuchifritos, texting
somebody. When I come out, he reaches for the juice.
I got that, he says, and carries it, walks me back to
my house. And nobody on the street says one word. I
ask him if he wants to come up. I mean, his aunts and
my grandmother go to the same church and it was only polite plus I knew he wouldn't say yes. Next time,
he says. Got me some bidness to take care of. He says
bidness like there's little quotation marks around it. I
nod to show that I get it, that he's making fun of how
some people talk. Then he says maybe I'll see you in
school. I'm gonna start going. I couldn't help it. I
bust out laughing. Rohan stopped coming to school
regular back in sixth grade. In ninth he went to home-
room, but not to subject classes, usually. And then he
went to juvenile detention. Riker's Prep, some call it.
He turns a little red, which being darkskin looks burgundy on him and I realize that it's probably a parole
thing.*

*I bet you go every day, he says. School girl. I say
you know my grandmother. How she is. He gives me*

*this smile just like back in kindergarten when his
nickname was Kool-Aid he smiled so much. He takes
out a pack of Juicy Fruit and offers me one, which I
don't take, and puts the wrapper from his gum back
in his pocket. I used to be scared of your grandmother
he says and I tell him I still am. He nods, and I can
tell he likes that. He points to a car parked on the
street and I see the tat on his hand - just the letters
KA. For Kool-Aid, I figure. Like my ride? he says, real casual. And I see he's got a ticket and he don't
care.*

*The kids on the stoop are watching, like they're
watching TV. Then sirens again and everybody starts
running away from the stoop.*

*Little punks. Rohan steps on a cockroach that
crawls out of the bag and rubs his sneaker against the
step to get the bug off. He tells me to give him my
phone.*

*I'm about to say I don't have the phone with me
but it pings again. So I have no choice but to hand it
to him and he puts in a number. Call me, he says. Unless you already got a man.*

*Then he leans over and kisses me on the cheek. I
could smell the Juicy Fruit on his breath. I start to
wonder about mine. I had a hot dog for lunch.*

*First, I worry that I have bad breath. Then I worry
that he's going to get offended when I tell him to back
off. Even if people only think I'm his girl—well this
other girl I knew, Michelle, she had her throat cut
when her boyfriend couldn't come up with the money.*

*I hear the window open and without looking up I
know it's Grandma about to start embarrassing me,
her specialty. I mean, the woman doesn't care what
anybody thinks. I can't tell you how many times she's
come to school in one of her awful hats to make sure
I'm there. She has the blue one she crocheted herself
on now, just to open the window.*

You could hear her a block away. She shouts out my name. Valerie Martin. Get up here this minute. I say I'm coming, Grandma. Just talking to Rohan, here. She goes I told you to get juice. I didn't tell you to talk. Hello, Mrs. Martin, Rohan says. How you been?

So she tells him. How I been? I'll tell you how I been. I been watching you and I don't want you coming around my granddaughter. Bad enough her father's in jail, but I'm raising her right. You come bothering her and I'll have the cops on you. Hear me?

I think Rohan might get mad, but all he says is yes ma'am.

And Valerie, you're on punishment. Get up this house.

I gotta go, Rohan. Sorry it ain't gonna work out, I say real loud for the benefit of anybody listening. As I shut the outside door behind me, I see Rohan putting the ticket in his pocket.

Next day in school, I hear that Antwan got shot. People say it was Rohan called the hit.

CHAPTER 5

Trick or Treat

On the last day of October, Charlotte held the hand of a fifteen year old in labor.

Earlier in the month, at the faculty conference, Natalie announced that the state visit had been a complete success. The school was in absolutely no danger of closing. Charlotte herself had been observed and commended as a talented, enthusiastic teacher. When Natalie asked her to come forward to the microphone and take a bow Charlotte complied, reluctantly, to scant applause. To mitigate any resentment she insisted that the kids had done it all. A new student, Rohan Davis, had been especially helpful, raising his hand at just the right time. Charlotte saw that Lagakis, standing in the back, left the room.

Throughout that October, the autumn leaves remained green, clinging to the trees, until, on Halloween, a cold snap turned everything a withered brown with almost no burst of color.

On that final day of October, many teachers were absent, fearing gang violence. Charlotte was put in charge of the infirmary during her preparation period, an emergency measure because the aide who usually was there had called in sick. The school, festooned with plastic garlands and dotted with cardboard pumpkins and premature turkeys, had few students in attendance. One of the few was Caridad, a girl of fifteen, whose water had just broken.

When Charlotte called the child's home, no one answered.

"They're all at work," Caridad said.

The girl stood, one hand on the wooden desk, the other clutching her back. She was wearing a tee shirt that Charlotte recognized as one of Emily's which she had donated to the school's Good Will. The shirt did not cover Caridad's belly, and she looked like a brown egg on toothpicks.

"Caridad, why did you even come to school today?" Charlotte asked.

"My mother told me to. She had to go to work or they'd fire her. She said they'd take care of me at the school. It's my first," the child told Charlotte, one woman to another.

Charlotte sat with her, taught her how to focus on a cardboard jack-o-lantern and breathe.

When the EMTs finally came, the girl said, "What's your name, miss?"

"You know. My name's Mrs. Murphy."

"No, I mean, what's your first name? If it's a girl, I'll name it after you."

"My name is Charlotte, sweetheart," Charlotte said. "But, Caridad, you have a lovely name yourself. I know your name means love."

"Charity," the girl panted.

"It's the same thing. Just concentrate on having your beautiful baby and loving him or her. Good luck, Caridad."

The EMT gave Charlotte a look which said, *She'll need more than luck.*

❧❧❧

Soon after Caridad was wheeled away, school was dismissed early for safety reasons. Three cop cars were parked outside the school, and Lagakis was there too, chatting with the officers. As Charlotte exited the parking lot, she saw "wannabe" or interning gang members on the street corner, caps pulled over do-rags, looking for targets wearing the wrong colors. Her hands shook on the wheel. It was entirely possible that one would fire at her, shoot right at her red head through the windows of her car. It was Halloween, a Bronx Halloween, the day that more than one young boy would fulfill the initiation requirement of drawing blood.

It was just two o'clock as she pulled into the driveway that led to the back of the house. She remembered to stop for the mail. Someone had smashed the pumpkin on her neighbor Sally Bailey's porch. No pumpkins for the Murphys this year. Last year the jack-o-lanterns had rotted, forgotten, on the rarely used front porch, their once cheerful faces transforming into grotesque ones. Charlotte had placed a basket of rust-colored chrysanthemums near the mailbox. But now she saw that the basket had been overturned, the flowers uprooted. Mischief night. A Connecticut Halloween. She got out of the car and tamped the flowers back down with her bare hands. There was no mail.

As she continued down the driveway and made the slight turn to the back of the house, she saw Francis's red two-seater outside the garage.

Home at this hour? He had said dinnertime. He was not expecting her so early either, of course.

As she entered through the kitchen, she heard the door of the master bath on the second floor shut. Charlotte realized that she had tracked in some mud from outside. She took off her shoes and mounted the stairs in her stocking feet.

His laptop was open on the triple dresser, right next to a framed snapshot taken on their wedding day. Unusual. He was compulsive about putting things away—his socks and handkerchiefs rolled and folded just so in his drawers, his keys and change always in the same tray on his night table. A trait that made the loss of his ring even more out of character. Charlotte still wore her original ring next to the celebration sparkler. Her eyes fell on their wedding picture, standing on her dresser. She hadn't really looked at that photo for ages, just dusted around it when she tidied up. Now she examined their young faces, Francis with his arm around her as she held a rather large bouquet. Four months along, and just nineteen. Behind the bouquet was a bump that would become the twins. Francis looked like a tall little boy, a handsome little boy on stilts, dressed up in a suit that hung badly on his thin frame, his face tender and unlined. He had been standing very straight, very correct, looking not at his new wife but into the lens of the camera.

A very small wedding. Mother had called Charlotte a public sinner, only half joking in her Irish way, but she had liked Francis, in spite of everything. In the picture, Charlotte was leaning into him, so happy. She'd never expected to marry anyone so handsome. She'd been flabbergasted when he asked her out. At first, he'd been so ardent, so eager to get her into bed. But after she became pregnant, everything changed. That he proposed marriage was a happy surprise. But he rarely wanted sex after their wedding. She hadn't minded at first. There was the sleepiness and nausea of pregnancy. And then, no time, no energy, with two babies.

More than sex, Charlotte thought about affection, about the arms flung around shoulders that she saw with other couples like her neighbors, Jack and Sally Bailey. Sally once confided that she and Jack made love every night at nine. Charlotte kept her own counsel, did not mention that even when he was home, she and Francis lay side by side in their separate beds with one headboard. That when she slid her foot across the crack to touch Francis, he moved away.

At one point, she'd asked her mother, who told her not to worry about "that business." That Francis was a good man, a good husband. That she, Charlotte, had been lucky when he married her and saved her from disgrace.

As usual, Francis did not even glance at her, stripped to bra and panties, as he walked out of the bathroom. He lay on the bed and channel-surfed with the mute button pressed down. "I had quite a day. Don't you ever check your messages?"

Oh God. Her cell phone was turned off. In fact, it was still locked in the glove compartment of her car.

"I had a quite a day too. The health aide didn't show up. Half the staff didn't. I was in charge of the infirmary, and a student practically gave birth in front of me. Her mother sent her to school in labor. She was only fifteen."

He stopped channel surfing. "Why is that your problem? You should have stayed home too. I wish you'd quit. You don't belong there, poetry girl."

Charlotte wanted to cry, for Caridad, and for her own nineteen-year-old self in the same predicament.

But Francis had stepped up. He'd taken his medicine and married her.

Once more, she tried to explain. "Francis, I feel like it's the only place I *do* belong."

He nodded. "I know. And that's what I don't get."

The front bell rang for the first trick-or-treaters, the two little Baileys from the next door. Francis went downstairs to greet them along with Charlotte, and his mood changed. He even put his arm around her as, together, the Murphys made a fuss over the simple costumes.

Charlotte dropped a few wrapped candy bars into the plastic pumpkins the children held out wordlessly.

"Remember when we used to take the girls around?" he said.

She nodded. "It seems like yesterday."

He whispered in her ear. "I've got a treat for you."

Charlotte's heart skipped a beat. The twins were not due home for an hour. It had been months and months. Almost a year.

Back inside, he smiled at himself in the hall mirror and sucked in his stomach. "Here's your treat, poetry girl. A big raise. And a new title. You are looking at the *National* Director."

She hid her disappointment with a smile. "Great! Those

hours you put in! No one deserves it more than you, Francis. I'm so proud of you!"

"You should be. And just think. You'll be a California girl, pretty soon. So. Start packing. Bring lots and lots of summer clothes."

It took a minute for her to really hear what he was saying. California girl. And then it hit her. Charlotte saw her life moving away from her, her daughters in college, her students in New York, herself in the middle of nowhere.

"You're saying we have to move. Oh my God. To California?"

"Charlotte, I'll be getting in a month what you make in a year. No more schoolteacher unless you really want it. There are schools in California. And the kids can go to college wherever they can get in."

She gasped. "That's really—something, Francis. Such a lot of money." She pulled her hair back and twisted it into a bun.

"Really something? That's all?"

She reached across the table for his hand." I mean, *really* something. Maybe we could get away by ourselves this weekend?"

He gave her fingers a brief squeeze and released them. "I have to be in California. Why do you do that to your hair?"

Her hands went to the top of her head. "It's my Irish washerwoman look."

"This weekend get your hair styled. Go to that Spa Place. Go for the works."

"It costs—" She started to say *the earth,* but stopped. "What a crazy day this has been."

He got up and went to the sink for a glass of water. She wondered why he didn't use the dispenser on the fridge. There was lasagna for dinner because the twins had Princeton Review tonight. Dinner should be early. Princeton Review! College applications! Senior Year. It was impossible to move. Not now.

"We can't move," she said after a minute. "Not now.

They're in the middle of SAT prep. Abigail needs it so badly. And Emily—"

The sound of water running muffled his voice. "Emily will be fine. But you're right about Abby." He kept his back to her. "Say, how's this? What if—just for one year—we do long distance? I'll be flying back and forth all the time, anyway. I'll be here for Thanksgiving, and you and the girls can come out for Christmas. We put this house on the market in spring, and we sell after they graduate."

"Francis Xavier Murphy. How long have you been planning this?"

He turned to face her. "It's not the first time I've mentioned it. Do you even listen? I was hoping for Regional, but Rosemary kept hinting it was National, and I've been doing the what-ifs. I can't pass this up, obviously. But the girls…well, there's college applications and graduation and all that. They need to stay here."

"Who exactly is this Rosemary?"

"A VP, actually. Human Resources. She's been super helpful."

He wanted them to move. All those monologues about mortgages and interest rates had been leading up to this. Charlotte drew a deep breath. "This is a lot, Francis. It doesn't seem real. I need to think."

"It's real, all right. And I need to stop thinking. I'm going down to exercise—I'm wound up tighter than a drum."

Francis went to the elliptical machine in their basement and Charlotte went back upstairs.

As was her habit for happy occasions, she decided to find a celebratory poem to recite for Francis. She would find the poem about Icarus touching the sun. No, not that one. It ended badly, after all. Maybe Whitman? Whitman's *Song of Joy*. She normally consulted the anthology in the den, but Francis's laptop was still on the dresser, convenient for a quick search. She would just type in *Song of Joy Whitman*. She was no tech genius, but she knew how to use Google.

She passed her hand over the screen saver. A photograph appeared beneath Charlotte's hand and she drew back in surprise. It was unlike Francis not to close out his e-mail.

In the background—the ocean and a cloudless blue sky. In the foreground—Francis standing behind a woman in a jeweled swimsuit that surely never touched water. The woman's hair was perfectly highlighted and her even tan contrasted with Francis's reddened skin. His head was resting on top of hers, and his arms were wrapped tightly around her in an X, covering her breasts. Her breasts. Touching them. Close. The way he was holding her. That was the worst.

಄಄಄

Valerie's Journal
DO NOT READ
It was better than last year. Halloween. Except this kid on my block got shot. My grandmother said it was his own fault for riding his bike out on the street on that day. Everyone knows on Halloween you either stay home or take a cab or get a ride if you know somebody with a car. But anyway this kid didn't die but he'll be in the hospital for a long time.

Speaking of someone getting shot, now that they cancelled Christmas for Antwan, Rohan took back his old territory but him and Gareth are like big rivals now. In school they're both always hanging around the halls hardly going to classes. Only Rohan goes to Murphy's, which I'm in too, and he always tries to sit near me. You know it's not easy being friends with him because somebody from another clique might notice and take offense if you know what I mean. But he's super polite to me, and my friends. Like today, he offered to take me and Suzette home in his car, and Suzette was all for it, but I just said my grandmother

*said take a cab and he was cool with that. I'm pretty
sure he still likes me. One time he started to say
something and I just told him how it is. Every time I
see my mother, I know who not to take after, ever.*

*Hardly anybody came to school yesterday. I was
downstairs before in the principal's office because
Mr. Harney that drunk sent me to escort Monroe
there, like I was going to keep him from cutting out if
he wanted, but he went with me no problem. The
principal's secretary opened the door to the inside office to tell the principal we were there, and I heard
Ms. Albert say not to bother her now.*

*We had to wait a long time outside the office. I
think the principal is sick of seeing Monroe. If he
would even just open the book when they tell him to.
He's Special Ed but they mainstream him which
means he is a very smart SPED. I mean, there isn't a
lock he can't open.*

*It's like he has magic fingers. Anyway, me and
Monroe got to hang out in the waiting room for a
long time. The principal kept the door closed but we
could see her on the phone through the glass window
in the door. Then she put her head on her desk and I
swear she was crying. Her shoulders were shaking. I
hope it wasn't about Caridad. They say she went into
labor.*

*Then the bell rings and Ms. Albert comes charging
out with a face you don't want to know about and she
doesn't even look at us. You could see she could care
less about Monroe and no hello and no smile for me.
Now my grandmother is the head of the PTO, and the
principal always smiles and sucks up to me. Pretty
soon after that Lagakis gets on the PA and announces
school is dismissed like a kind of fire drill. Early dis-
missal, was all they said and we was all out in the
street like moving targets but a gypsy cab came by,
lucky for me and Suzette.*

PS. It wasn't Caridad. I heard that she's fine and she had a boy. She named him Charlie after Ms. Murphy.

CHAPTER 6

Half a Loaf

Charlotte locked the bedroom door and went through all his drawers, throwing his carefully folded underwear on the floor, even unrolling his socks, searching for clues. Calm. She felt as though she were on the ceiling, watching herself. *The feet go round a wooden way.* Those words of Emily Dickinson repeated in her brain as she searched his pants pockets, his jackets, the little velvet boxes where he kept his cufflinks. She found nothing. Nothing except his original wedding ring in the breast pocket of one of his suits. He only thought he'd lost it. Why? Because he'd taken it off.

The calm turned to rage. She wanted to kill him. Break all their dishes over his head. The rage turned to horrible imaginings. Over and over she pictured him with the woman in the picture, not just in bed, but walking with arms around this stranger as they never were around herself, until she was nauseous and threw up, barely making it to the toilet. She ran the water in the shower of the en suite bath to mask her racking sobs. Stripping, she stepped under it, as hot as she could stand. The shower felt like her mother's sharp fingers poking her in the back. As she cried, she heard the voice of her dead mother. *Leave it alone. He's a good husband.* She could not forgive him. She would *have* to forgive him, or lose her marriage. Did he even want to stay in the marriage?

Francis banged on the bedroom door. Was she through with the shower? She yelled out no and to use the guest bathroom. She ignored his pleas about clean clothes. Let him stink. When she heard the other shower running, sure he was out of earshot, she wrapped up in a warmed towel and picked up the phone.

"I knew it!" said Natalie. "As soon as I saw that ring. God. What a terrible day."

Natalie sounded upset for her, but did not stay on the phone long.

Emily actually came upstairs to see if Charlotte was all right. "I have a bad headache," Charlotte called through the door. That was no lie, for certain. "You'll have to deal with dinner."

"I'm on it, Mom," Emily said. "Take care of your headache." Her voice was soft, kindly.

Does she know? Am I the only idiot in the world who didn't know? Or maybe, maybe I did know. Charlotte covered her face with her hands.

೧෨೧

She didn't come downstairs until after the girls left for the Princeton Review. Then she found Francis watching TV in her den and told him to meet her in the kitchen. "Guess what, Francis? I found your ring."

"That's great. Thanks for bringing down my laptop."

She retreated behind the granite island, spun the ring across the counter at him, and watched his face. No sign of guilt.

Geese honked overhead. It was too dark to see them, but she could imagine the V formation, moving south. She held on to the island's ledge, and her fingers found a chip on the underside.

Francis cleared his throat. Twice. "That's great about the ring. Where was it?"

"Where you put it," she said. "When you took it off."

He acted shocked. "Oh, Charlotte. I would never deliberately—whatever you're thinking. Absolutely not."

She turned the computer's picture toward him. "Explain this. No, don't bother. I get it now. Why you never come near me." Tears came to her eyes.

His face grew red, but he gestured with the back of his hand, as though pushing away bad air. The new wedding ring glinted beneath the pendant lamp.

"Come off the stage, Charlotte. We've been married a long time. Do you expect me to chase you around the house like a teenager? I work too hard for that. Sex just doesn't have much appeal any more. But you're my wife forever, poetry girl. What about the ring I got you? Tiffany's." He seized her hand and she pulled it away.

"Natalie told me what the ring meant. And I didn't believe her."

"Hey. Don't be like that, Charlotte," he said. "I get it. You're pissed off about that picture with Rosemary. But don't you see? We have a few laughs. But I swear that's all."

"Were there others? Besides Rosemary? Tell me the truth."

He smiled a little smile and looked her full in the eye. "I am telling the truth. I work too hard for anything like that. Besides, I'm actually a pretty good guy. I've had plenty of opportunity. A lot of guys might cheat. But you have nothing to worry about."

She pulled a knife out of the block on the granite island, held it high above her head.

"What the hell are you doing?"

He stood up, took a step away from her. She saw a pulse throbbing in his eye. He put his hand over it, as though to stop it from pulsing.

She ran her finger along the blade to test its sharpness,

removed a head of garlic from the bin, and separated a clove from its fellows. She gave it a firm whack with the flat edge of the knife. A pungent odor permeated the kitchen as she peeled away the papery white skin and minced the clove fine. She made neat dice of a tomato, added olive oil, the garlic, and then smeared the lot on a leftover half of baguette. She sliced a red onion as well. Usually a piece of bread in her mouth kept her eyes from tearing, but she didn't have enough bread. Half a loaf is *not* better than none, she thought.

"A little treat for the girls." She sampled the bruschetta. "Otherwise, the bread is bland. Not *appealing*."

"Hey, forget I said that. I'm really sorry, Charlotte."

"About what? That you're having an affair? Or that I found out?"

"I am not having an affair. Nothing happened. Oh God, Charlotte, if you cry, I'll start."

"I'm not going to cry." She looked at him. Silent. Her teacher look. The way you looked at a kid who had not done homework.

"All right," he said. "Maybe we did a little flirting. That's all. No affair. Nothing happened."

She raised her eyebrows, continued to stare at him.

He looked down first. "All right. Maybe *something* happened. But it was *once,* Charlotte. Once in eighteen years. You weren't ever supposed to know. It was never going to hurt you. And it was a mistake. And I'm really sorry." He began to cry, tears like tiny seeds falling from his eyes.

She gave another garlic clove a whack. "This isn't like confession. An act of contrition doesn't make it all go away." She cut herself, a tiny scratch, barely breaking the skin, and pushed the released juice into her finger, felt the acid sting, knowing she was hurting herself but not able to stop. "And what was the mistake? Leaving your e-mail open?"

His voice became irritated. "You finding that picture—that was an accident. Snooping. That's outrageous."

She smashed her hand down on the counter. "Bullshit. There are no accidents. You wanted me to find it. You drew me a map. You fucking planned this."

"Language." His voice squeaked out in high register and he repeated the word in a lower tone. "Language, Charlotte. And I could say something like that too—but I never did. Not once. I never threw it in your face."

Charlotte sat on one of the stools at the island to keep her knees from buckling. She raised her chin. "You think I trapped you?"

"For God's sake, Charlotte. Even your mother knew that, God bless her. We understood each other. She gave us the down payment for the house and I married you. She was a wonderful woman and you are a wonderful wife. I would do it all over again. The sex is bad, but it's not that important."

His words sliced her. *Breathe, Charlotte. Deep breaths. Slow deep breaths.*

"Are you all right?" he asked. "I didn't mean for—"

"Am I all right? You go from nothing happened, to it happened once, and now you bring in my mother? And you finally get to it. I'm bad at sex."

"That's not what I said. You're making a big deal over nothing. Believe this. I want to stay married. I need you, Charlotte."

"What for? More convenient for your new job?"

His face changed. The anger in the room was palpable. "Be careful what you say, Charlotte."

She started to rub the garlic onto the scratch again. But then she got up to wash her hands, letting soap and water cleanse the wound so it would not fester.

"I called Natalie before. She gave me the name of her lawyer."

Francis turned white. "I can't believe you called Natalie."

"I can't believe you fucked Rosemary."

They looked at each other for a long minute. Charlotte raised her chin slightly, willing it not to tremble.

"Hold everything. Wait right there," he said and walked into the den.

She took the opportunity to wipe her eyes, not sure what her bluff had triggered.

He returned with a picture of himself and the twins taken a few years ago. He'd been coaching their softball team, and all three wore big smiles and backward baseball caps. The girls were looking at up him as though he were God.

"Remember this?" He looked into her eyes, a rare thing for him. "You know you don't want the girls to be without a father."

That was a direct hit. An intact family. The way it was supposed to be. The way it had never been for Charlotte and her mother. She kept her voice steady. "You realize you have to stop seeing her. That's a minimum."

"It's complicated, Charlotte. We work together."

"No. It's simple. Her or me."

"Okay, then. I'll stop seeing her. Not that I ever was. Believe me—I regret this with all my heart."

"How can I believe anything you say? You never meant for me to find out. The only thing you regret is leaving your e-mail open. You think I trapped you? And my *mother* bribed you! Where is the bottom?"

"Can we not go over and over everything again? I have a million things to do. I leave for California in two days. I'll be back for Thanksgiving. I hope we can work things out. Not for my sake. For the girls. To keep the family together. Will you try, Charlotte?"

She looked down at the diamonds on her hand. Very slightly flawed, the appraisal document said. Was half a loaf better than none? "I don't know, Francis. I just don't know."

ഇഇഇ

Valerie's Journal
DO NOT READ!

I felt so bad for Murphy to see me like this. She's not used to problems. But yesterday I had a meltdown. I don't know what happened. It was like that river we learned about that they dammed up and then they let the water run back in. I couldn't stop myself. I could feel it coming up through my toes. I took off my earrings and gave them to Suzette. I know how to fight. I was gonna take somebody out and it was gonna be Knudsen.

Blame it on the fact that I got no sleep last night with my mother in the emergency room. I get to school late third period, Mr. Harney was absent again, and they had Miss Knudsen covering his class in a skirt so short you can almost see the crack in her flat white ass. Knudsen stands real close to the blackboard, like new teachers always do when they're scared, so China starts getting loud. Saying stuff like Knudsen's trying to erase the board with her booty.

She ain't got a booty, Suzette yells out. Miss Knut—ee with no booty. It wasn't really funny but I just lost it and burst out laughing. All of a sudden, Knudsen's looking right at me and taking out a stack of referrals.

I guess Lagakis got the 411 to Knudsen about referrals. I can just picture him telling her how a teacher can write down what we do, even make up stuff about us, and write it on a dean's referral and then we have to go see Lagakis and listen to him call up our parent or guardian.

Suzette gets up to see what Knudsen was writing and yells out. It's for you, Valerie. Trying to say you're disrespectful.

Disrespect is one thing my grandmother will not tolerate.

So I got up but Suzette, Suzette, she saved me. She held my arms and pulled me back. She is strong. I almost broke away from her but I couldn't. So I said something stupid. I said something like I got friends in this neighborhood. Be careful, Miss Knut-ee. And I could see she went and wrote it down on the referral.

I don't know who called Lagakis. But when he came Suzette let go of me. Lagakis put his arms around me which being dean he is allowed to do, by the way, and soon as he touched me I started crying. Went right from mad to sad in a second.

Knudsen turned real red. I think she thought I was going to kill her. I think I would have. Nothing personal. But if I get even one referral my grandmother will put me on lockdown and take away my phone. No more texts from my friends. From my boy! Plus how would I know when my mother gets like that again. I shouldn't even care.

I was embarrassed to be crying like that. Valerie, Lagakis says. Come with me to the office and we can have a conversation. The class applauded as I left the room with Lagakis, but he shut them up with that cop look he has. By this time I wished he had gotten there earlier.

Let me know if you have any more trouble he says to Knudsen, and then he holds his hand, palm out, toward the door like he always does. I walked in front of him down the hall toward his office, and almost ran into Mrs. Murphy. And like I said, I felt bad, her seeing like this.

Murphy looks at Lagakis and he says, It's under control, Mrs. Murphy. Valerie and I are going to have a conversation.

I got in trouble, miss. Might as well tell her. Then Murphy stands up very straight, and except for the simple fact that she's so skinny she's looking like she could take on Suzette, even. I believe I'll join that conversation, she says. And Murphy walks down the hall with us.

Now Lagakis is pissed. This is none of your con-

cern he says to her. Murphy gets all emo. If I can't be concerned for Valerie, then who should I be concerned about? Can't we make an exception just this once?

I couldn't believe it.

Lagakis nods at her. We all have our little pets. But actions have consequences. This is my job, Mrs. Murphy.

Murphy takes out a tissue from her purse and looks at it and I'm almost afraid she's going to spit on it first, like my grandmother does, but she just wipes my face under the eyes and the tissue came out all purple from my eye makeup. Embarrassing.

Thanks, miss, I say. I know it sounds weird but it felt good, her doing that for me, even though the tissue smelled like peanut butter. I tell her. Something bad happened last night. In my family. I can tell she believes me. It's true, too, but it's still nice she believes me. Can't we make that referral disappear? she says to Lagakis. Lagakis starts talking to her like someone trying to reason with a psycho. Ms. Murphy, I understand what you want to do, but, you see—but Ms. Murphy ignores him and says to me. I'm so sorry, Valerie, about—your family problem.

I shake my head. I'm going to cry again. So she just nods.

Lagakis starts talking, his voice real soft. Valerie, you know I'm going to have to call your grandmother. Actions have consequences. Blah blah blah. He points to the discipline chart on the wall. You are in violation, and I am required by law to inform your grandmother. So call her I say. I didn't do anything but talk. Murphy says, Can't we make an exception this time? Wow. Lagakis actually hands it over and lets her read it. I'm sure that's against some rule or other. But Murphy reads it out loud. I got friends in this building. I got friends in this neighborhood.

Ms. Murphy puts it in the pocket of her skirt. I'll take it up with the principal, she said. I only hope that it doesn't get—misplaced—on my way down there.

Lagakis's face turns red. What the hell are you doing? I need that. You and your friend, he said. You and the principal. Two of a kind.

Murphy says Valerie go and sit outside in the waiting room. Close the door. So I sit on the bench outside and start texting. We're not allowed to have phones in school and if they catch me I'll get in trouble. But hell. I already am.

CHAPTER 7

Charlotte Stands Up

Charlotte closed the door. She could see that Lagakis was angered. It was not going to be easy, but she had to convince him. Charlotte had met Valerie's grandmother on Parent's Night. The woman promised she would "open up a can of whup ass" if Valerie got out of line.

"Charlotte, what the hell are you doing?" Lagakis kept his voice low. "You're trying to undermine my authority, and I can't have that. And a referral is a legal document."

"Plenty of legal documents never see the light of day."

"My God. You're as bad as your buddy the principal." He nodded a few times, his voice bitter.

"I'm trying to keep Valerie from getting a beating and some draconian punishment. I heard her grandmother say she hits first and asks questions later."

Lagakis frowned. "A *grand*mother? But if that's the case, file a child abuse report."

"Sure. Have her put into foster care. Or a group home." She eyed his half-filled coffee cup, picturing the brown liquid running down his face. Very tempting.

He held out his hand. "The referral. Please." He pointed to a manila folder on his desk, the blue ring he always wore winking at her in the sunlight.

She kept her eyes on the ring, willing him to agree with her. "Let's just lose this thing. I'll take responsibility."

"But what about Valerie? When does she get to take responsibility?" He extended his hand again for the referral. "You think you're being her friend, but you're not. Kids need rules. They need someone to say no."

Surely, Lagakis could be persuaded. Charlotte placed her hand on his arm and stared directly into his brown eyes. There was a golden rim around them. Tiger eyes, she thought.

"Charlotte. I know you mean well. That's why I—I admire you for it. But you're wrong."

My God. He was actually sincere. Wrong, of course, but sincere. She had continued to wear her rings. He looked down at her hand, diamonds still sparkling on it. "Mrs. Murphy," he said, emphasizing the *Mrs.*, and she blushed and pulled her hand away. "I'm sorry. Those are the rules."

Noise in the hall. The period was about to end. Charlotte heard the click of high heels in the outer office. The sound of the doorknob turning.

"What's going on in here? Why is Valerie sitting in the waiting room?" That well-known voice, that imperial stance. It was the principal, on her daily walk through the building. Management by Walking Around, she called it.

"Ms. Albert," Lagakis said. "Good morning to you too."

The principal ignored Lagakis. "Charlotte, what's happening?"

"Oh, Natalie," Charlotte said. "Maybe you can help us with this."

Lagakis sat down at his desk, his eyes two shades darker than they had been a moment before.

Charlotte produced the referral and let the principal see it. "I'm trying to convince Mr. Lagakis not to follow through with this. For Valerie—this is an anomaly for her."

"Once it's in writing, I have to act on it. She threatened a teacher," Lagakis said. "It's the rule."

"This is my building. I make the rules." Natalie read the

referral and then tore it up into little pieces. "Well done, Charlotte. I'm glad you caught this." She turned to the dean. "Mr. Lagakis. Valerie's grandmother is the president of the PTO. We do nothing to offend her. Nothing. Is that understood? And little Miss Knudsen? She does not belong in a classroom. Hopefully, she'll quit over this and I'll be rid of her."

Natalie threaded her arm through Charlotte's and walked out of the room. "Come, Charlotte. Tell me. How are the twins doing?" As they passed Valerie, she said. "My dear, I'm extremely disappointed in you, but we're going to let this go with a warning. Wait here until the bell rings and then go to your next class. And do give your grandmother my best."

As she walked out with Natalie, Charlotte could feel dark brown eyes on her back, and she tightened her shoulder blades, standing up very straight.

જાજી

Valerie's Journal
Ms. Murphy PLEASE READ!
Hello Ms. Murphy,

Thank you for being there for me. About the referral. Someday in the future I hope to honor you by being there for someone else or maybe even for you. I am also gonna use proper English, even quotes like you teach to show you respect. You can correct it if you want. And thanks again for buying us these journals and letting me take mine home. It is practically my only stress reliever.

Last night doing my homework, I decided I need to tell someone about me and J. Crew.

I was waiting on Fordham Road for the number 12 to go to the library thing you put me in when somebody said "Hello" in this voice I halfway recognized and you'll never guess who it was. It's the guy from the funeral, Ms. Trombetta's nephew or great nephew or something.

Now, I didn't mention it at the time but he had given me his phone number as we all were leaving the funeral but I got rid of it right away. I figured he wanted me to get him hooked up with drugs or something.

You don't see many types like him on Fordham Road. Most of them get right on Metro North and go home to their white picket fence. I wasn't going to say anything but when he said "Hello, Valerie." I had to at least be polite *so I just said, "What's up?" and then made believe to be looking at my phone.*

"You never called," he said but I didn't answer. Who told him to give me his number, I was thinking.

"Understandable," he said. Sort of adult like. You remember how he talks. And, "I really like what you're wearing." (I had on the purple tunic.) He said his name is Andrew but he goes by Drew.

I'm in the library writing this on my lunch now. I'll give it in later.

So I said I had thought his name was Crew not Drew, a little snotty in case he was playing, and he caught on right away and said he liked my clothes better than anything at J. Crew. So it was like, truce.

You remember that he had that blond hair falling in his eyes. I'd really like a chance to work on that cowlick. Blue eyes like you, miss. It turned out he was going to the same place as me. His English teacher at Prep—that's what he calls his school—was the one giving it and he was going there to help his teacher out. In case not enough people showed up for the library to run the workshop.

I felt bad for acting snotty so when the bus didn't stop and he said want to walk I said ok. It wasn't far but people were staring. Together? That's what they seemed to be thinking looking at us. We were walking past Fordham University, walking on the side of the street which I don't usually take. I normally cross after I pass Webster Avenue. On the other side of the street, my side, you see the White Castle and the old-fashioned high school building with a couple School Safety cars, and a mob of kids hanging out there at the bus stop. But we were on the side in front of Fordham U. On this side, there was this fence of iron bars and stone columns and behind that this big grassy field with trees and buildings made of the same stone as the columns. The top of the columns had names carved in them like in a cemetery. I never noticed them before. He told me they were the names of soldiers who got killed back in like World War I. I never knew that.

I was kind of glad when we reached the library to have somebody to walk in with. Everyone else there was like from Bronx Science or from Catholic School.

They read this poem "We Are Seven" by William Wordsworth and started talking about life after death. Really interesting. J. Crew had already read it. J. Crew wouldn't last ten minutes on the street but he could really rule at the library thing. I didn't say one word. I was so nervous. He told me later it was all BS. Talking about an unreliable narrator. Maybe sometime you could read that poem too, miss, to the class, and we could talk about it? Like before next week?

After the library thing was over, he waited for me. It's hard to tell if he was trying to talk to me or was just doing some kind of project for school. He was asking me all these questions like if I believe in God and why does God let kids get hurt? He's really a good talker. I thought it was interesting he brought it up because I always wonder about that too.

Anyway, this time I let him put my number in his

phone and he texted me already before I even got home. I warned him never to call but my grandmother doesn't understand texting. Please remember, miss, you said everything in this journal is private, and thanks for recommending me for the program and writing the letter to my grandmother on school stationery about it.

Hi, Valerie,
I am glad you like the library program. I will bring the poem but I can't comment on God or religion. Better tell your grandmother the truth about the boy. Thank you for trusting me.
Mrs. Murphy.

CHAPTER 8

Erasures

Apparently, Lagakis forgave her about Valerie's referral, because a few days later he stopped Charlotte in the hall. *Now what?* she thought.

"Look," Lagakis said. "I was going over some things in the office. Trying to make some space. There's stuff in an old locker that I let Bertie use. I don't know what happened to the key, but I got Monroe to open it. I was wondering, would you help me go through it?"

"Why me?" Charlotte asked.

"I have no one else to ask."

He and Trombetta had been friends. This would be hard for him, Charlotte realized.

And so she had gone to his office, begun the sad task with Lagakis standing behind her. There was the sweater with the button missing, an old wool hat, and a single glove. There were several umbrellas, an assortment of baseball caps taken from boys, who were not allowed to wear hats in class, a carton of Marlboro Lights, and a closed manila folder labeled *June English Regents*.

"I guess her family won't need these," Charlotte said, indicating the folder.

Just get rid of it was her first thought.

"I remember she made a bunch of copies in my office

last June. And she put them in a folder like this. Lots of copies," Lagakis said.

"You know the drill. Always make three copies of everything. Put them in three different places. Otherwise stuff might get lost."

"I should have done that before I gave you Valerie's referral to read."

"Lucky for Valerie, you didn't."

"Possibly." He smiled at her. Yes, he had forgiven her. His teeth were very white, she noticed.

"Here." He handed the folder over to Charlotte. "Hold onto these. You're the English teacher."

"Sure." She took the folder to her own classroom and locked it up, without looking at it, on a shelf next to the brown bag lunch she had brought from home. But it called to her all through the period as she taught her next class. She remembered how relieved Natalie had acted when Trombetta died, and how she'd insisted that Charlotte go with Lagakis to the funeral. *Bertie was always threatening to go to the media. There may be reporters.*

So when class ended and the students filed out, Charlotte went to the back of the room and opened the locker. She had to take her lunch out, anyway, and why not at least look? It was probably nothing but some notes about administering the Regents. Or about teaching a particular skill. It probably had no more meaning than the sweater, the collected caps, the umbrellas, the sad remnants of the person who was gone.

Still, she took the precaution of locking the door, shutting off the lights, and sitting in one of the student desks in the back, so she could not be seen by anyone who happened to look through the classroom door's window. Then, chiding herself for her own paranoia, she opened the folder. A pile of papers. On top of the pile, a blank sheet with inflammatory words in Trombetta's beautiful script: *Copies for the SCI*

The SCI. The Special Commissioner of Investigation.

Charlotte knew she should turn the folder over to Natalie immediately, sight unseen. But she could not.

With a badly shaking hand, she opened the folder. Copies. Copies of the multiple-choice grids of last June's English Regents. The multiple-choice answer grids. Of course. Always in pencil. So easy to change answers. To change them from wrong to right.

As Charlotte often told her students, a very strong multiple choice score on the English Regents could balance terrible essays, allowing the student to pass. An answer key had been stapled to the front of the folder, with students' names listed in red. Monroe's name headed the list. Suzette's was there too. Flipping through to Monroe's test, she saw circled answers next to an arrow pointing to the word "Erasures," penned in Trombetta's neat hand. Suzette's, like Monroe's, was dotted with red circles and that arrow pointing to the word.

Erasures.

Who had done this? Who had changed the kids' answers?

Why do this? Who would benefit? The kids, of course. Kids on that list would certainly feel that they had won the lottery—that they had been singled out for remarkable luck.

Who else benefited? And who had access? The principal.

Financial rewards for principals whose schools did well on tests were part of the accountability protocol. And Natalie benefited, with a hefty bonus. Last year the bonus had been $25,000. Add to that the $25,000 additional salary for taking on a failing school. But would Natalie change the grades, risk her position, for any amount of money? Surely not. There must be a reasonable explanation.

I have to tell her, Charlotte thought. But what would happen, if Natalie had not done it and Charlotte revealed what she'd found? Even without considering the bonus, Natalie had gotten a lot of good publicity from the Regents results.

Charlotte wasn't really sure how it worked, but she knew

that Suzette and Monroe were part of a cohort of students who were supposed to graduate this year. If they graduated on time, their success would bolster Natalie's position as principal.

Messengers had notoriously short lives. Perhaps she should keep it quiet. Lose the folder. Tell Lagakis there was nothing in it but some old essays. Keeping quiet was the least she could do for Natalie, whom she had known slightly in college. Her first college.

When she became pregnant, Charlotte had dropped out, and only returned when the twins were in school full time. It had taken her years, course by course, with a lot of help from her mother, who lived with them. She'd earned a teaching license. Then, when Francis's job was iffy, she'd gone to a job fair and Natalie had pulled her out of a line-up.

She owed Natalie, the one who had given her this job that she loved. She owed her, but she didn't belong to her. But surely Natalie had done nothing wrong and, as principal, deserved to know what was going on in the school.

Charlotte dithered and dallied, making a stop at the teachers' prep room. She locked the folder up securely. But eventually she walked down the stairs past the security guard and made her way to the office on the first floor where the principal was.

The principal's office was spacious, with a wall of windows facing the street. Across the length of polished hardwood floor, Natalie was seated at her computer, which was on a separate metal table perpendicular to her long wooden desk.

Outside, the wind grew stronger and the heavy glass windows rattled in their old wooden frames. Branches of the sturdy city trees outside the school shook off the last brown vestiges of autumn leaves and took on a silvery scrim of rain. Then the rain grew heavier, blurring everything.

The wind outside seemed to strengthen Charlotte's resolve. "Natalie," she said. "I need to talk to you."

The computer monitor morphed from a table of numbers into a screen saver of palm trees as Charlotte stood there in her gray skirt and sweater. She had pulled her hair into a ponytail with a rubber band, just to get it off her face, but now she undid it.

As her hair fell free, a few strands clung to the rubber band and she shoved it into her pocket.

Natalie swiveled her chair to face Charlotte and held out her wrists as if they were in imaginary handcuffs. "Take me out of this prison," she said. "I could use a vacation. How many more days till Thanksgiving?"

"Natalie."

"Yes."

"This is important. It's not good news."

"Is everything all right at home? Is it Francis? Acting up with Rosemary again? Are the twins okay?"

"Yes. They're—we're all fine. It's—I don't know how to say this."

Natalie's face showed concern for her friend. "Out with it."

Charlotte gulped and the words rushed out. "Okay. But don't kill the messenger. Somebody changed answers on the June English Regents. Interfered with the integrity of the test."

Natalie got up from her desk, walked over to Charlotte. There were bags like pillows underneath her brown eyes, which she fixed on Charlotte's face, searching. "A serious allegation. Very serious."

"Yes. I know it's serious."

"You have to have proof."

"Natalie, I found this folder. Trombetta made copies of the kids' original answers. She was going to go to the SCI."

Natalie clapped a hand over her mouth. She looked away. "You *found* it? How? Never mind. I need to look at this folder. Bring it to me. No, take me to it. Now." Then she paused. "Does anyone else know about this?"

"Lagakis. But he didn't see what was inside."

"Good. Don't worry. I'll investigate this. Just bring me to the folder." It was impossible to see out the window. The rain was, quite literally, a curtain. Natalie, in her high heels, stood almost a foot over Charlotte. She placed a hand on her forehead and shook her head. "I can't believe this is happening today."

Close up Charlotte could see the tiny puckers that were beginning to form on the principal's long neck.

"Why today, of all days, do you tell me this?" Natalie ran long red-tipped fingers through her hair. "But no, thank you for telling me. It's good to know I can count on your loyalty."

To Charlotte's surprise, the principal burst into tears.

"Natalie, Natalie," Charlotte went to touch her friend's shoulder, but Natalie pulled back.

Outside someone pulled a fire alarm bell and students' voices could be heard, whooping and laughing as they fled their classes.

Natalie closed her eyes and shook her head. "Not again. That's the fourth time today, and Lagakis doesn't have a clue who's doing it. Somebody also started a fire this morning on the fourth floor—set fire to the best bulletin board."

"That's such a shame."

Charlotte couldn't tell if Natalie was upset about the fire, or about the havoc to the bulletin board.

"No kidding. I had the police and the firemen here all morning, and of course someone pulled the fire alarm right in the middle of it all."

Lagakis's voice came on over the loud speaker. "Ladies and gentlemen, ignore the bell. Please go back to class." The joyful noises of the students subsided, but the wind continued to rattle the windows.

Natalie continued her litany. "Yesterday, Suzette beat up some ninth grader who looked at her boyfriend, and I have to deal with the ninth grader's parents and some educational advocate from Central. The guidance counselor reported a student that is being sexually abused."

"China?" Charlotte asked.

"You know I can't tell you that." Natalie nodded her head yes in tacit confirmation of Charlotte's guess. "I've got a conference call about that in thirty minutes. Visitors are here, snooping around every room the way they do. To top it off, I'm supposed to organize a memorial for Trombetta. The family's been calling me. They want to make some kind of donation to the school and I can't put them off, although it's really just a big nuisance. And now—this." Natalie wiped her eyes, and recovered her composure. "I need to stop crying and get that folder. Let's go. Now."

"If the grades were tampered with," Charlotte said, carefully using the passive voice, "it has to be reported. It's unfair to the kids who worked hard and passed on their own. And unfair to the ones who failed."

Suddenly the principal's tears were gone. Natalie drew herself up to her full, imposing height. Her voice was bitter, withering. "Did it ever occur to you that there's another way to look at that?" she said. "Maybe three or four different ways?"

"What do you mean?" Charlotte asked. How could there be three or four ways? Either the scores had been falsified, or they had not.

"Maybe," Natalie said, "someone was trying to do these kids a favor. Let's face it, the Regents isn't that hard. But after twelve or more years of school, some of these kids can't write a decent paragraph, let alone an essay. Maybe it's time to give up. They'll never pass the Regents on their own."

"Give up?" Charlotte was angry. Lots of kids passed on their own. Why cheat them of the ability to learn, to be challenged, to be tested? To fail, perhaps, but to try again? To learn from failure.

But then again, think of Suzette, whose essays consisted of brief, undeveloped chunks of clichés, no matter how hard Charlotte worked with her. Think of Monroe, who didn't even hand in essays most of the time. And think of Valerie, who gave her all and deserved to pass. Why should Monroe and Suzette get the same Regents credit as Valerie? Why should they walk in the graduation procession if they did not have the skills of a high school graduate?

Natalie's tone became brisk. Her jaw was thrust out like a lantern. "You know what a random act of kindness is?"

"I believe so. It's doing nice things for people you don't even know, without expecting a return."

Natalie laughed. "Close enough. Charlotte, what you say was done—if, hypothetically, somebody had done it— would be a kindness. We may never know who did that kindness. But those kids, Suzette and Monroe and a bunch of the others, will graduate, thanks to what— hypothetically—was done. They'll move on to get decent jobs, cutting hair or whatnot, and they'll contribute to society. They'll never pass that test on their own. It's too late to teach them anything. To keep them here and not let them graduate is just cruel."

Not let them graduate. Natalie needed her graduation statistics to go up. And why did she single out Suzette and Monroe?

"I think—" Charlotte began.

Natalie fixed dark brown eyes on Charlotte, as if to drill obedience into her. "Don't think. Just take me to those folders. Trust me. I will do a thorough investigation." She put a hand on Charlotte's shoulder and gave her a kiss on the cheek, and then tapped Charlotte's shoulders with sharp fingernails. "Let's go."

"You *will* investigate. You *will* make sure that everything is on the up and up?"

"Of course."

❧❧❧

Valerie's Journal
PLEASE READ, MS MURPHY

Thanksgiving Journal. I am thankful for many things. I am thankful most of all for my grandmother who is like the bane of my existence (like how I use the words you give us?) but even when she hits first and asks questions later I know she betters me. I am grateful for my friends I trust with my life like Suzette and Monroe and even China and I am grateful that I don't have a stepfather, speaking of China, and Rohan is in there too because being his friend has lots of bennies (benefits to you, Ms. M.) I am grateful that my mother has been ok recently. I am grateful that when I am eighteen in May I am gonna graduate and maybe get to travel upstate to see my father. Right now I am super grateful that I have a friend like J. Crew. You'll never believe this but he and I are meeting on the down low and what do you think we talk about? Books that he is reading in school and one I started is called The Bluest Eye *by Toni Morrison and it is the best book I ever read and he says it's the best book he ever read too. Could we maybe read that? And Ms. Murphy, I'm glad I have a teacher like you and if I ever have a kid I hope she'll have a teacher like you to guide her. Thank you, Ms. Murphy. Happy Thanksgiving!*

Happy Thanksgiving to you too, Valerie. I am thankful for students like you. I'd love to teach The Bluest Eye *but we don't have a class set. Perhaps you could borrow it from the school library and chat with me about it. Mrs. M.*

CHAPTER 9

Thanksgiving

Charlotte maneuvered the spatula under the thin crepe, but it broke. She sighed and began again, pouring batter into the non-stick pan.

She had taught all day. When she'd asked the students to write in their journals and then read aloud one thing they were thankful for, most said conventional things, like family, and God. One boy said he was grateful for the friendship of a young lady in the class, who blushed in pleasure. Later Charlotte saw that he'd also written, "I am thankful that I have a big dick."

Men. Everything a pissing contest. She laughed now, thinking of it.

"What's so funny?" both her daughters asked at once. They were seated at the kitchen table snapping the ends off green beans.

"I keep messing up," Charlotte replied, letting them think she meant the crepes. The assignment had been a mistake. Holidays were hard times for many kids. Maybe for her own.

She bent and then stood on tiptoe to stretch her calves, hearing the voice of her old ballet teacher. *Plié* and up. *Relève* and down. Mother had insisted on piano and dance lessons for Charlotte. She had wanted Charlotte to have the

best things in life, and thanks to Francis, Charlotte had
them, and so did her girls. *Count your blessings, Charlotte.*
Nobody has everything.

"It smells like Thanksgiving." Abby gestured at an array
of vegetables—sweet potatoes caramelized and drizzled
with orange juice, crunchy sprouts awaiting their sprin-
klings of bacon.

"You're making so much food, Charlotte," Emily said.

"You know your father loves the side dishes." Too late
Charlotte realized the double meaning of her words.

"What. Ever. I was wondering. Can Ryan come tomorrow? For Thanksgiving?"

The sound of the string beans snapping and thumping into the metal colander filled the kitchen as Abby continued to
work. Charlotte stared straight ahead, thinking. Another
face at the table might ease the strain, creating a social situation. But Ryan would be company. Francis would expect
to eat in the dining room, to impress the lone guest with
china and silver.

"Won't Ryan need to have dinner with his family?"
Charlotte asked.

"They eat early. In fact, they invited me to eat with them.
Can I?"

Abby snapped a bean so hard its inner seeds fell to the
floor. "Dad gets here around four thirty," she reminded her
twin.

"We'll be back in time for Dad. And Ryan thinks you're
so cool, going to the Bronx and all."

An eye roll from Abby, but Emily continued. "Please,
Mom?"

Mom? Emily must want this very much.

For Thanksgiving dinner, Charlotte selected a burgundy
knit which the saleswoman in Bloomingdales assured her
was fine with red hair, in fact, would bring out the rosy
tones in her complexion. The woman suggested a pair of
plain low-heeled pumps, burgundy suede, Italian leather,
softer than gloves, and they fit so well, like a second skin.

Charlotte signed the credit slip in a rush, never checked the price, and had no idea what she paid for them.

At four-thirty sharp, she dimmed the intensity of the Tiffany lamp over the dining room table. The twins were lounging in jeans and hoodies. Ryan wore a white shirt with pressed jeans, his hair freshly cut. Probably his mother made him dress up. The last time Charlotte saw him was on a lacrosse field, covered with mud, when she'd picked up Emily after a game. Emily sat beside Ryan on the sofa, their thighs touching. Charlotte sensed that if she left the room, they would start to kiss. Abby kept her back to them, practicing the piano across the room. Francis was late and the turkey would be overdone.

A little before six he walked into the house, pulling a carry-on and holding a bouquet of orange daisies. His eyes registered her new dress with a quick gliding motion.

His hair was different, sticking up, shiny with gel. The jacket of his suit was narrowly cut. Had he taken off a few pounds? He kissed Charlotte's cheek, hugged the girls for a long minute, and shook hands with Ryan.

"Good to see you, Brian. Heard so much about you."

"Ryan, Dad," Emily corrected him.

"Is that so? Charlotte, something smells good. I'll come in the kitchen and see what's cooking."

The twins exchanged glances.

In the kitchen, Francis brushed Charlotte's rear as he took ice cubes from the dispenser. "Excuse me," he said, polite as though he'd stepped on a stranger's foot. "I believe I'll have some vodka. Will you join me? Or would you like some wine? We have that zinfandel in the cellar."

"No thanks." She inspected the bird. "You're really late. I think the turkey's overdone."

"Blame the traffic. I need to freshen up before we eat."

He took a long swallow, said in a lowered voice, "I wasn't sure what you told the girls. Where do you want me?"

To mask her flushed cheeks, she opened the oven door.

It smells like Thanksgiving. She pretended that he was only talking about his shower. "There are clean towels in all the bathrooms. You have a choice."

Charlotte listened to his footsteps overhead, heard the squeaking door of the master suite's bathroom followed by water rushing through the pipes.

While they waited for Francis, Emily and Ryan disappeared to the basement recreation room, to play table tennis, they said. Abby remained in the living room, pounding the piano keys. Charlotte arranged the flowers in a silver pitcher on the sideboard in the dining room. Ugly plastic straws around the stems kept the blossoms upright. She removed the straws, and the flowers flopped loosely. She should have kept the straws. But they were so fake looking. Suddenly, arranging the flowers seemed important. Everything was so important. *Oh, please. Let me do the right thing.* Charlotte found a silver cord and tied them.

Francis returned, freshly shaved, the air around him exuding the scent of familiar shampoo. He had even changed into a sweater left behind when he went to California. He brandished a shopping bag printed with the word *Tienda* and joined Abigail at the piano bench, squeezing his daughter's slender shoulders. "How's school? Keeping those grades up?"

Abby barely looked at him. "School is—there."

"I come bearing gifts." He rattled the shopping bag. "Mexico this time."

"Can we open them later?" Charlotte asked. "Unless you want cold turkey."

His blue eyes met hers. "I'm good with cold turkey. Where's Emily? And Brian? I brought down a tee shirt for him."

Abby closed the piano lid with a thud. "It's Ryan. I'll get them."

Charlotte chose not to break the silence.

"That's a new dress. Nice," Francis said. "Not quite your color, though, is it?"

"I like the color."

The kids returned, Emily's hair slightly disheveled. The tee shirt for Ryan was from Cancun. There were silver filigree earrings for the girls and a diamond tennis bracelet for Charlotte, too large for her wrist.

"Maybe you can have it sized," Francis said, when Charlotte lowered her arm and the bracelet fell to the floor.

He knelt to pick it up and offered it to her as though proposing. "I believe you dropped this, poetry girl."

Charlotte could feel her daughters' eyes on her.

She accepted the bracelet from his hand and replaced it on her arm. "Thank you. It's—beautiful."

A communal exhale filled the room.

The table had been set since last night, and Charlotte allowed herself to admire the good china, carefully positioned on the lace cloth. She placed Ryan and Emily together, and she sat across from them next to Abby, so that the younger twin would not be alone. Francis, at the head, recited grace and then stabbed the poor turkey. Leathery drumsticks fell away from the carcass at a touch, and shards of dry white meat shredded under his blade.

Francis directed most of the conversation at Ryan, grilling the boy about SATs, college choices, even where his family would be spending Christmas, which turned out to be a ski resort Francis knew.

"How come we were never there?" Emily asked.

"Business trip," Francis explained. The Murphys would be in California, he told Ryan. "Got a place right on the beach."

The cranberry sauce became the star of the meal, trembling jewels of berries in the Waterford crystal bowl. Everyone needed extra to wash down the dry turkey. Conversation lagged.

"Hey, at Ryan's house we all had to say what we're thankful for," Emily announced.

Abby twisted her napkin on her lap.

"I think it's a lovely custom." Francis raised his glass as

if in a toast. "I am thankful for our daughters. Growing into wonderful young women. And for their mother. And our guest *Ryan*."

Everyone said Amen. Charlotte pressed her lips together. "What about dessert? I made the cherry crepes."

"Mom slaved over them last night," Abigail said.

Francis's hand suddenly went to his pocket. He frowned in irritation and moved his dessert spoon, aligning it more precisely within the pattern of lace.

"Gee, I'm stuffed, Charlotte. I think I'll take a little walk and have dessert later."

The room grew very quiet, and this time everyone could hear the phone vibrate. "Damn phone. I forgot to shut it off." Francis took it out of his pocket and shut it down with a decisive slide of his thumb. "No business this weekend."

"Who are you and what have you done with our father?" Emily said.

"I missed you. All of you." He looked at Charlotte. "I know what I have here, and—" He looked like he'd cry.

"Want some company on your walk? I'll come with you," Charlotte offered. "Maybe we can all go."

"Nope," said Emily. "Me and *Brian* here are going to the movies. You come too, Abby."

"Why do you need me?"

Emily waggled her eyebrows. Abby caught on. "Oh, right, I'd love to."

"Go ahead, kids," Charlotte said. "Dad will give me a hand with the dishes after we take a little walk. Only—" She extended one of her legs, showing off her shoes. "—not in these. I want to make a start on the dishes. Then change into sneakers. Do you mind waiting a few minutes, Francis?"

"Women and shoes." Francis winked at Ryan. "Sure, poetry girl, take your time. Take plenty of time. In fact, maybe I'll do that too. Go upstairs to change shoes. I'll wait upstairs. Have a good time, kids."

"I'll just get the dishes soaking."

This was it. He was waiting for her in the bedroom. The kids were gone. In the kitchen, Charlotte ran the hot water full blast, turned on the radio. She wrapped the leftover dishes in foil and stowed them haphazardly in the refrigerator. The china was hand painted and had to be hand washed. She gentled each plate into hot soapy water and kept the radio on. Loud. Enough to blot out everything.

He said he was good with cold turkey. She concentrated on that. That meant he had stopped the affair. She would forgive him. Wear the bracelet all weekend. They would reconcile. She could not catch her breath as she mounted the stairs and grabbed the doorknob of the bedroom they shared for so many years.

She waited, unseen, in the doorway. His eyes were closed and he was smiling, his handsome head framed by blue and white covered pillows, and he lay back on the special, new sheets that Charlotte had put on the bed *just in case.*

"You forgot the rules, Rosemary. I told you not to call while I'm here."

Then he opened his eyes.

"Hey, Charlotte—I'll be down in a second. Gotta go, buddy," he said to the phone.

Charlotte held tight to the downstairs banister and walked in a straight line toward the daisies, removed them from the silver pitcher, and threw them in the garbage. Her new bracelet dangled over the daisies, and she watched it slide into the trash with them.

She plunged her hands in the soapy dishwater. Grease had made little bubbles under the suds, and it filmed her wrists as she opened the drain. There was the sucking sound of fat going down the pipes. She wiped the residue from the sink with a paper towel and ran the hot water again, full throttle.

Her hands painfully red, she shook them in the air to cool them and plunged them again and again in hot water, although rubber gloves were right there, waiting. She

soaped and rinsed, soaped and rinsed, and the china dried as
soon as she placed it in the draining rack.

Her legs cramped, and she shifted her weight, *Relève and
down, plié and up,* in her soft new shoes. She turned from
the steaming water, and suddenly Francis was behind her,
wearing a college sweatshirt and sweatpants.

"Almost ready, poetry girl?"

"I'm not going anywhere with you, Francis."

His jaw dropped in a good imitation of surprise. "Is
something wrong?"

"You can stop pretending. I heard you on the phone."

There was just an inch of vodka left, and he poured it into his glass. "A business call. You're mad? I don't blame
you. These guys have no sense of family." He moved to
throw the bottle cap in the garbage and saw the daisies.
"Charlotte. You threw these out already? What did you—
oh, shit." For a tall man he had slender hands and feet. He
once told her he used to be short, that he grew twelve inches
in eighth grade to his present height of six four. Now he
took her yellow rubber gloves, hanging like a bunch of ba-
nanas from the faucet, and stretched them over his long fingers. "Do you realize what this thing cost?"

"Do you realize I don't care?"

He extricated the bracelet, covered with greasy food, and
peeled off the gloves. When he went to the sink to wash it,
she didn't bother to warn him, and hot water burst out.
Good. He adjusted the faucet, scrubbed his hands thoroughly. Pontius Pilate. Lady Macbeth. The bracelet went into his
pocket.

"That—call. Charlotte, it wasn't what you think."

"You forgot the rules, Rosemary," she quoted.

He shrugged, smiled, held up two hands in a surrender
gesture, a little boy with his hand in the cookie jar. "Okay,
okay. I know how that must sound. I'm sorry."

"How can you smile?"

"Because it's funny. I mean, you think this is important,
and it's not. Trust me. It's nothing."

"It's not funny, Francis, and it's not cute. It's time to stop pretending. I think we should agree on something."

To her surprise, he nodded. "*Now* you're being sensible. This really doesn't have to be so hard. Here's my plan. Come to California at Christmas. We can be a family again. You'll love it. Trust me."

She drowned him out with the voice she used in the classroom. "Let me be clear. I do not trust you. And I never will again."

"You're not being reasonable."

"I am, actually. Eminently reasonable. We can work out something for Christmas. The girls get out of school before I do. Let them spend a week with you while I'm at work. They both want to see California. To shop on Rodeo Drive. I think that maybe the best thing is for them to go. I can fly out later, spend Christmas with them."

He seemed to drop the mask, to look at her as an equal, almost a friend.

"Very sensible. So we can come to an arrangement?"

Rage made her strong. "What? Me looking the other way while you—"

"You're not seeing the big picture. Can't you be adult about this? We're not in one of your storybooks. I love our girls and I would never hurt them. I take good care of you. And consider your own interests. You're sneering now. You think you know how to be poor, don't you?"

"Absolutely."

He pointed to her new shoes. "Not any more, you don't."

❧❧❧

Valerie's Journal.
DO NOT READ!
Thanksgiving break sucked.
My grandmother makes this sweet potato pie and it's delicious but I know why she does it. She is think-

ing of my father. "He never even wanted to bother with the turkey," she says. "But he couldn't get enough of my sweet potato pie."

I still remember what it was like when he was still here. I was seven when he was arrested. I saw it happen. I was playing on the stoop of the house we lived in where my mother in fact still lives. He always used to come home and hold out his arms and say to me how's my little princess but that day he didn't.

When I was a little kid, I had absolutely every toy you could ever think of, and the nicest clothes of anyone. I used to think it was because I was tall and God could see me better than other people. But then I guessed that God couldn't see me anymore because all of a sudden my father was gone "on vacation" is what they told me at first, and my mother was sick. Then I was living with my grandmother and a bunch of other little kids and well, end of story here I am.

Anyway the day after Thanksgiving she goes on the bus from Manhattan to visit him, my father, but she can't take anything with her to eat. All she can do is buy food from these vending machines they have up there. So she's always holding on to her change so she'll have enough.

She won't take me with her. It's like a five hour trip to the middle of nowhere, she says, and she needs me to baby sit the foster kids. She always takes up my school pictures though. She says maybe when I'm eighteen, which is in May I can go.

I had to watch the foster kids by myself for an entire day. It was like so good to be back at school. Plus, when I got up to Murphy's class all the lights were off and she was showing a movie. She said she'd be showing it all week! I mean, there is nothing in this world better than having movies in your English class.

It's Macbeth by William Shakespeare, but that's

cool. You can always go to sleep if you don't want to watch, what with the lights not on.

Murphy got Monroe to set up the movie, which for some reason she can't do herself, and just slumped down in the seat and didn't much say anything. But I asked her hey what is this gonna be about and she kind of roused herself and handed out this printout thing of what was happening in each scene. I bet she was gonna forget to give it to us.

It was a good thing she did or I wouldn't have understood a word.

So after class I went up to her and said, miss, everyone is going to sleep and she looked back at me and I could see she had been crying big time. But she like pulled herself together and said, sorry, she'd do better tomorrow.

I mean, what does she have to cry about? First of all, that lady has the dollars. Her kids they go to school where they don't have to worry about getting shot at or raped or anything on the way there or even in the building. She's got this big house, judging by the picture on her desk. And her husband is good looking in that picture. Which, by the way, is off her desk now.

But, hey, you never know. People in Africa or someplace could say what do I have to worry about, with plenty of food to eat here in the Bronx.

So I kind of patted Murphy on the back which I wouldn't normally do but she just sat there and let me. I sort of think she needed someone to touch her. Like Ms. Trombetta used to. So I got an idea. And I said sorry for your trouble and maybe you should come up to the shop. Looking good can get you to feel good. You know, like put your best face on stuff. Our teacher in the shop says that what cosmetology is for. Helping people look better and feel better.

And she smiled at me and said, "Assume a virtue if

*you have it not," sounding a little bit like Murphy
again. I asked her was that a Macbeth thing and she
said no, Hamlet. She said something about remembering rosemary. But then she thanked me. Even
stood up and gave me a hug, which was a little weird
but I let her. But when I stood away I saw she was
crying again.*

CHAPTER 10

Sex Education

Francis had been away traveling so much during their marriage that Charlotte sometimes forgot, now, that they were separated. She would wake up in the morning, and it would take a few minutes before she remembered. The girls, busy with their friends, seemed not to notice. But at odd moments, a deep sadness came to Charlotte, and thoughts of her lost marriage, her *failure* at marriage, caused unexpected crying jags. After it actually happened in school, she tried behavior modification. Whenever she thought about Francis, she snapped a rubber band on her wrist. Hard.

Winter was nearly here. Through the windows of her classroom, Charlotte could see the tops of trees, nearly leafless now, and two small black birds perched on the wires that hung between telephone poles. The high-ceilinged classroom, crowded with many more desks than were needed, was stuffy. She made her way to the wall of windows, pulled a tall pole from its hook place on the wall, and affixed the hook on the end of the pole to the ring on each of the windows, opening the windows three inches from the top, as directed by school rules. She had to weave her way through the desks, tearing her tights as she walked. It was impossible to remove the excess furniture from the room—

more school rules—but she wished she could chuck half the desks out the window into a big dumpster. She walked to the chalkboard and block printed: *MACBETH: ACT II SCENE ii* in yellow chalk on the green board, making her lettering clear and easy to read. Monroe could not understand script.

As soon as all the students had entered and were seated, she drew herself up to her full height and made her voice loud and British, imitating the cadences of Shakespearean actresses she had listened to on CDs. She felt the unaccustomed confidence fill her body as only happened here, in the presence of naïve children who would not know when she made a mistake. To them she was an expert, knowledgeable, a connoisseur of Shakespearean drama. She did not know how she summoned it, the presence, but it always came. It had to do, somehow, with taking leave of everything but the present moment, everything but the now. It had to do with making eye contact with every single student in the room, making eye contact and holding it with a fierce intensity. It had to do with letting go of fear and shame and any thought of how the students might perceive her.

She had prepared to dramatize this scene, in which Lady Macbeth smears the king's guards with his blood, by mixing dishwashing liquid with food coloring to make fake blood. She dipped her hands in the "blood" before the students entered and practiced the line she would ask them to discuss: "My hands are of your color, but I scorn to wear a heart so white." Later she would hold forth on the symbolism of color. She held up her hands as she said the word *hands*, and allowed the red liquid to drip on the floor. She *was* Lady Macbeth. Her husband's betrayal, her worry about her daughters, her suspicion of Natalie, all of this and everything else ceased to exist.

The class entered noisily, but began to quiet when they saw her standing near the basin of blood. She pointed to the board silently with her gory hands, deliberately allowing red drops to fall on the green board. One by one, she stared the kids down; one by one, their heads dipped to the floor to remove the texts from their backpacks. When all was completely silent, she dipped her hands once more and intoned the line. If she'd had a crown nearby, she would have set it upon her head.

The class sat stock still, shocked by the blood and by the nearly insane vehemence with which she spoke the lines. But then, out of the corner of her eye, Charlotte saw Lagakis and the guidance counselor Kevin King waiting outside the door. Lagakis was holding a large red box. Oh, God. Where was her brain? She had forgotten that they were scheduled to usurp her class time for mandated Sex Education. She would have to do the scene tomorrow.

"Come in, gentlemen," she said, pretending that she'd known they were coming all along. They must think her as mad as the character she'd been playing. In a way, she had been, but madness was part of the magic. The magic, the stage presence, deserted her when she was not alone with her class.

Lagakis bounded into the room, clapping loudly. "You are some actress. I was impressed before, but now I'm really impressed. I never realized. You're wild!"

"You don't understand," she said.

"Oh, I'm beginning to. I think it's great." But then he looked down at her hands. "Who did your manicure? I hope you didn't tip. What happened to your wrist? It's bright red."

Mr. King was staring at the two of them. Charlotte extended her hand for him to shake, and then realized that it was still wet. "Good morrow, your majesty," she punned on his name. "Welcome to Inverness Castle." As she spoke, she wiped her hands on the paper towels she'd brought. The color was still there, of course. *All the perfumes of Arabia.*

"What?" said King.

"Just my little joke."

King looked at her as though she were from another planet and rolled his eyes in sympathy at her class.

Watching the three teachers talk to each other, the class became restive.

Quickly, Charlotte improvised, told the students that she'd just given them a taste of the scene, but that today was dedicated to mandated sex education. To her immense satisfaction, they actually groaned. The sound of their disappointment was a balm to her hurt mind, she thought, borrowing Shakespeare's words. If only Francis knew what she could do behind the closed door of her classroom. No! She must not think of Francis! She pulled on the rubber band again. Snap!

Kevin King began pacing the front of the room like Chris Rock on his HBO special. "I know that y'all will be happy you don't have to do Shakespeare today."

Again there were more murmurs of dissent. Mr. King seemed nonplussed.

Now Valerie was speaking. The girl was dressed, as usual, in shades of purple. Today she had draped what might have been a blouse over lavender leggings. Her hair was a mass of soft curls tied up in a lavender scarf. She was lovely.

"Shakespeare's cool," Valerie said. "How come *we're* not supposed to like it?"

Charlotte felt a thrill of vindication at Valerie's words. Lagakis stood so close that he was touching Charlotte's shoulder. He bent low, and warm breath brushed her ear. "I guess they do need Shakespeare," he whispered.

She stepped away and walked to the back of the room to avoid him and also to avoid distracting her students from King's presentation.

The view from the back of the room was so different. Charlotte read the inspirational motto plastered across the top of the blackboard: *Failure is not an option.*

King was dressed like many of the students, in jeans, sneakers, and a tee shirt with a logo. He was well built, very handsome. Half the girls were in love with him. The boys loved him too—called him Kev and engaged him in elaborate handshakes when they passed him in the halls. However, Charlotte knew that the principal was unhappy with the popular Mr. King, thought he was too familiar with the students. Natalie was also after him to wear shirts with collars and to lose the jeans. But if it helped him to win the kids' trust, what did his attire matter?

King continued to pace around the room while he talked to the kids. Charlotte was again reminded of Chris Rock marching back and forth on the stage as he went through his routine. In a way she and King were both entertainers, she realized—she as Lady Macbeth, and he as Chris Rock. *Whatever it takes*, she thought.

Now King walked over to Valerie's seat. "What's cool about Shakespeare, valley girl?" King asked.

Valley girl! The kids gave Valerie that name when they thought she "acted white." Valerie shrugged off the insult with impeccable dignity.

Unbelievably, Monroe raised his hand. Charlotte could never remember his doing so before.

"Yo, Kev, I like Lady Macbeth," Monroe said. "She's a strong black woman."

The class exploded in bursts of laughter, and attention immediately shifted from Valerie to Monroe. Charlotte saw Lagakis's shoulders shaking at Monroe's remark, although he turned aside to hide his face. But still...

Support for Shakespeare from Monroe! Although, Charlotte realized, the support was really for Valerie. The two sat side by side, and, from the back of the room, she saw Monroe's hand reach for Valerie's and give it a squeeze. How easily he touched Valerie, how easily he signaled his friendship, or perhaps more than friendship, with touch, and how easily Valerie accepted his gesture. Charlotte had seen other couples do this, not only teenage lovers, but even long married adults. Snap! Snap!

Was it possible that Monroe had a crush on her prize pupil? It never failed. The smartest girls attracted the...well, Monroe was not exactly dumb, but he was no scholar. Charlotte wondered about Valerie's feelings. Would she settle for a Monroe? And if he were able to comfort her with touch, was that really settling? Did men have to be taller, stronger, smarter, richer? Snap!

It was time to lend a hand in getting the class focused. "This lesson is important," Charlotte said. "Even more important than Shakespeare."

"Thank you, Ms. Murphy. Settle down now," Lagakis said to the class, making his eyebrows form a straight line across his forehead. When he frowned like that, Charlotte thought, he looked like a Neanderthal, only less intelligent. Still, the frown had its effect. When they had quieted, he said to the guidance counselor, "They're all yours, Mr. King."

And King proceeded to hand out slips of paper on which students' names were written. Each student got the name of a classmate. He made Charlotte and Lagakis take slips of paper too, and he took special care with Charlotte's. Charlotte looked at it and saw that she had drawn Zamar. She sighed, hoping that Suzette would not consider this worthy of an explosive episode.

"All right," King said. "One of y'all has drawn a name with an X on it. Who is it?"

China raised her hand. "Here I am, *mi amor*," she said to the guidance counselor.

"No," Lagakis said. "Do not call him that, China. He is Mr. King."

King laughed it off. "They ain't gonna fire me for that. Stand up, China."

China was sitting in the front seat, and as she got up, she wiggled her hips slightly. She turned around and waved at the class. Her hair was blond this week, and she was wearing a low cut pink blouse and tight jeans. A necklace that spelled out her name grazed the tops of her breasts.

King walked over and put his arm around her, and she put her arm around his waist. He held out his hand for the slip of paper, which he displayed to the class. "Now that X means—" He paused for effect. "—that you got an STD. Maybe AIDS. Maybe genital warts. Take your pick."

The class went into an uproar. China's face and neck were splotched a bright red.

"Get the fuck out, China," someone said.

"Okay, y'all. Language. Keep it clean," King said. "We're just playing here. But at the end of this period, I want you to think about it. How somebody told China to get out."

The class fell silent. King continued his pacing around the room.

"Next—who got China's name on their paper?" Zamar raised his hand reluctantly. "Well, stand up Zamar, that slip means you had sex with China. You got what she got."

Suzette half rose in her seat, but Zamar said, "Easy, baby. Just let Kev do his thing," and she gave him the finger and sat down.

"Okay," King said, "Who got Zamar's name?"

Charlotte rose. "I do," she said, and the class went wild. Even Suzette laughed.

"Ms. Murphy, now you got it," said King. The class whistled and stomped. "Settle down. Who has Ms. Murphy's name?" When a shy boy named Hector reluctantly raised his hand, King made him stand up. "You had sex with Ms. Murphy. Now *you're* HIV positive," he said. "With warts."

"From Ms. Murphy?" Lagakis said, in mock horror. He was obviously doing this to help King make a point. Charlotte wanted to kill him, but she bore it like a good sport. *It's for the kids,* she told herself. *They need to know this stuff.*

"That's the deal," King said. "You can catch this stuff from anybody—from the last person you think might have it. Ain't nobody safe."

King continued to call names, and soon half the class was standing. A few boys had drawn the names of other boys, and a huge commotion ensued over that. King ignored the class's reaction and calmly cited statistics. "Some of y'all are gay on the down low," he added. "One in ten are playing for the other team." The class was giggling and pointing at each other, but there was an undercurrent of tension.

By the end of the period, every single student was standing. And King said, "See? You can have sex just once with one person and you've had sex with everybody they were knocking boots with. Right now, it's like you've had sex with everybody in this room."

Lagakis came forward and placed the red box on the desk. "Of course, the only sure way to be safe is abstinence," he said. This was greeted by boos. "All right," he continued. "In this box—" He opened the lid dramatically. "—*if* you are sexually active, here's how to protect yourself and to protect your partners." And then he opened the box and showed the class a pile of condoms wrapped in all the colors of the rainbow. "These are free," he said. "I keep the box in my office and anyone who wants them just come to me. No questions asked. Everybody can have them free. If you don't believe me, look at the sidewalk outside the school." He caught Charlotte's eye and winked, too quickly, she hoped, for anyone else to notice. "Smart people use them. I want you to be smart, and safe."

"They got drugs for AIDS now," someone shouted. "And warts? It ain't nothing."

"Yeah, but not everybody can take those drugs," King said. "There's side effects. And you really want warts you-know-where? Better wear a glove. Repeat after me. No glove, no love."

Suzette ran up and grabbed one of the condoms. She ripped it open and started blowing it up like a balloon. "It tastes like feet," she said.

Lagakis ignored her and drew a banana from the box. "I'm gonna ask for a volunteer," he said. "I want to show you how to put on a condom." He looked at Charlotte, and actually dimpled discreetly, but she did not meet his eye.

She could never! And certainly not as partner to Lagakis. He was behaving acceptably in front of the kids, but she could just imagine how he would leer at her in the teacher's room later if she agreed. She also did not want to betray her ignorance. Catholic Francis made a point never to wear condoms.

China came forward. "I'll do it," she said. "But not with you, Lagakis. With *Mr.* King." She gave the counselor his title quite deliberately.

"You got it." Lagakis handed the banana to Mr. King. And then slowly, drawing it out as long as possible, King made a ceremony of unwrapping the condom, and drawing it up the banana, which China held.

"That's a pretty small banana," someone shouted.

"China's a chicken head," someone called out.

"Let's see her eat the banana," someone else said.

Charlotte was terribly uncomfortable. This was all for a good cause, but the scene was too graphic for her. Still, Shakespeare was graphic too. She wondered how she would rekindle interest in Shakespeare after Lagakis and King left. Perhaps she could pursue the blood theme? Tie it in with the exchange of fluids? In spite of her qualms, she knew it was so important for kids to have this information. She decided to share that thought, feeling modern, open-minded, and decidedly cool.

"This is important," she said. "Even more important than Shakespeare."

King shot her a look of respect. "That's right, Ms. Murphy. You're all right." And then he said, "One thing. These things don't work if you don't use them. Every time. Every single time."

Valerie raised her hand. "But they'll be no children, then. What do people do if they want to have children?"

Lagakis stepped up to the front of the room. "If we want children, we have to get tested," he said.

"Oh, you're shooting blanks anyway, Lagakis," Suzette called out. "How come you ain't got no kids?"

Lagakis turned bright red, but recovered. "Everyone who is even considering having sex needs to get tested. And I was getting to that. The Red Cross is running a blood drive on Monday. We need *everyone* to donate blood. And when you donate blood you automatically get tested. If there's a problem, you'll get a call-back—"

King interrupted. "But even if the test comes up negative, you still need a condom," he said. "For six months. It can take that long for the HIV antibodies to show up in your system for the test to be accurate."

An undercurrent again. Murmurs of "You get AIDS when you give blood," and "They want to get in our business."

"It's safe," King said. "They use a different needle for every person. And it's strictly confidential. And we ought to do this. Give back to our own. There's a shortage of blood in the hospitals in our community."

"And if we give blood, we automatically get tested," Lagakis said.

"We heard you the first time." More mumbling and protests came from the class, but no one raised a hand.

"Any questions?" King asked. Still no hands.

"*I* have a question," Lagakis said. "Ms. Murphy, I'm gonna ask you, in case a girl doesn't want to talk to me, or Mr. King, can I give you some condoms to keep here?"

Charlotte had not expected this, but she agreed immediately. He really had given her no choice, asking in front of the students.

"Of course," she said. She hesitated, unwilling to touch the condoms, then reached in, took a pile from the box, and placed them in her desk drawer. If he knew, Francis would not approve of Charlotte distributing condoms. He would go through the roof if either of their daughters even saw the condoms. She started to snap the rubber band on her wrist.

And then her heart began to pound. Francis! For so long she had been smugly secure, confident that Francis and she were both faithful, that monogamy had protected them both.

But that was not the case. Charlotte began counting on her fingers—she and Francis had not had sex for...how long? Not since he had had too much to drink at Jack and Sally's party. When was that? Almost ten months ago. But he'd admitted Rosemary had not been his first affair. And suddenly Mr. King's lesson hit home. She, Charlotte, had had sex with them all, with all of Francis's partners. *My God. I need to do this,* Charlotte realized. *I need to get tested.*

"What about you, miss?' Someone called out. "You giving blood?

How glad she was now, for all the nights Francis had lain far away from her on his own side of the bed. How glad she was that he had never accepted her covert invitations, her foot touching his, her casual brushing up against him. He had actually been protecting her, whether he meant to or not.

"Oh yes," she said. "I'll be giving blood. Definitely." If she did not get a call-back, she would be clear, she thought.

Her hands still had several bright red spots. She pulled out a bottle of hand sanitizer and began to rub them vigorously.

කමක

Valerie's Journal
DO NOT READ
Well, I couldn't give blood, being I'm not 18 till May, but I got to help out, handing out cookies to the people who donated. Nothing good, just the cheap kind you get in the supermarket. Murphy didn't even take a cookie, and she's losing weight, she could have used a couple calories. Lagakis took three, greedy old man.

Anyway, soon it was almost Christmas vacation, and me, Monroe, and Suzette were in charge of a gift to Murphy from the cosmetology class. It's like a promotion the school has—a complete makeover. We usually charge for it, but for Murphy it was on the house. I mean, she needs something, you can tell. We came in before the start of regular classes, even Monroe. We were in the Christmas spirit.

Miss Murphy has good nails. "Miss, your nails are beautiful," I tell her.

I wasn't just gassing her up. Her nails are strong, and with real half-moons. "It makes the job so easy when you have good material to work with," I say.

Now Murphy's mouth turns up a little. "You did well on your essay, Valerie," she tells me. "As usual."

"Hold still. How did I do?" asks Suzette. Suzette is cutting Murphy's hair. I could see Murphy getting nervous and I don't blame her. Suzette is failing English.

"I didn't get to yours yet," Murphy answers Suzette. She closes her eyes.

"That means I failed," says Suzette. "As usual." There are tears in Suzette's eyes, I swear. Murphy looks really nervous now.

Suzette says, "It's all good, miss. I wouldn't take it out on your hair."

Like hell, she wouldn't.

Murphy tries to see in the mirror but Suzette turns the chair around. Murphy starts to say something but stops. I notice Suzette looking at an old article about Beyoncé in People magazine. Murphy's hair is thick and holds a curl, so Suzette goes a little scissor happy.

Now Murphy is sitting in the green chair in the back for the simple fact that the cushion on that chair is only ripped a little. Her hair is wrapped in a black towel to protect it from cream smeared on her face. Our cosmetology teacher was downstairs in the cafeteria for coffee. She's supposed to stay with us but if

*another teacher is there she's like, bye, see you. She
never does anything anyway. We run the shop our-
selves.*

I pull on Murphy's fingers to stretch them first.
"Forget the essays," *I tell Murphy.* "You're too
tense. Relax."

"Teepee, wigwam," *she says. There goes the
mouth again. Laugh lines.*

"Excuse me, miss?"

"Teepee, wigwam. Two tents. Too tense, get it?"
She is a little corny. It's part of her job.

"Just a joke," *she says.* "An English teacher
joke."

"You have great cuticles," *I say to calm her down.*
"Do you want a design? I can do a snowflake. Or
even Santa Claus. I've been practicing."

"NO!" *Murphy says, real loud. I didn't know she
could get that loud.*

"No snowflakes," *Murphy says in her regular
voice.* "No design. And don't you have a lighter col-
or? Maybe just some clear polish?"

*I bought the cranberry polish myself in CVS. The
school just has this really old junk.* "This color, miss.
For Christmas."

I start to rub cream into her hands. "Make her
take her rings off," *Suzette says.* "The shea butter is
getting them all dull."

*Murphy took kind of a sharp breath and looked
down at her hands.* "Is that necessary?"

"No, miss. But it would be better."

*She waited another beat, and then starts tugging
them off. She probably never even took them off before since she said I do. She probably kept them on
even when she did dishes. I swear she practically
cracked a knuckle, because she looked like she was
about to cry or something. But she just put them in
her purse and held out her hand again. Except she*

was pretty clumsy, and knocked her purse over. Some stuff fell out—her wallet, like 20 pens, and an envelope from somebody named R. Gordon, Law Offices. So. Murphy has a lawyer. A plane ticket too. I made sure that purse stayed in her lap the whole time. I mean, none of us would rob Murphy, but this is the Bronx. I could just see those diamonds sparkling in somebody's teeth. There was a little red circle, like a dent, where the rings had been. I put some extra aloe on and more shea butter.

"You should take your rings off when you do housework, miss," I tell her. "That little red circle needs air."

Meanwhile Monroe was working on Murphy's legs and feet, massaging heavy cream into them, rubbing the cream in and around her toes like they taught us to. Murphy had her usual long skirt, and it was funny to see how she tried to keep it tucked up around her knees like she never even had a pedicure before. You could see she was embarrassed, but Monroe just kept working it in. He's the best with the leg and foot massage and of course was strictly cool about it. He had tied his dreads back into a ponytail, and was wearing black nail polish, done by me, and it looked great. I could imagine him one day as a stylist to the stars, if he ever got it together. But I could see it was tough for Murphy, having a student rub her legs, and a guy student at that.

"Just relax, miss," I say. "Breathe. Make believe you don't know us. We're professionals. We do this every day. Close your eyes and pretend you're on a beach or something."

Murphy closes her eyes and pretends to pretend. You could tell she hated it. But Monroe is really good, with strong fingers. Some things you need a guy for. He's working her calves, rotating her ankles. He moves her toes back and forth.

The cream smells really good, like peaches. I think Murphy is getting into it. She lets out a sigh when he finishes.

"That's it, miss," I say. "Let it all out. Teepee whatever." I give her the snowflakes and she doesn't say anything. She keeps looking down at her hands. "You can put the rings back on in ten minutes," I tell her. While the polish dries, Suzette works on her face, covering up the freckles, making her eyelashes and eyebrows darker. Finally, she blows out the hair and does the ringlets, fussing with the curling iron for ages. She gets it so Murphy looked like a movie star.

There was a little drama when we turn the chair around. I tell Murphy to close her eyes. Okay, now. Open them. Ta da! The new you!

Murphy doesn't say a single word. Her mouth falls open. We're all waiting, for like ever.

Finally, she says, "This is incredible."

"But do you like it?" Suzette says. "I worked hard on those ringlets."

"Of course I like it." She doesn't look anybody in the eye, but keeps staring down at the manicure. Maybe I shouldn't have done the snowflakes. I'm about to offer to take them off, but she kind of nods and smiles. "It's great. Really great. Thank you, all of you."

"So it's okay?" I realize I'd been holding my breath.

"It's...life changing. I feel like a different person."

"Don't forget your rings," I remind her, but she shakes her head, all solemn.

"No, Valerie. You are absolutely right. That little red circle needs air."

CHAPTER 11

Caffeine before Christmas

A different person. An ugly, clown-like person, with heavy make-up and wild ringlets in her hair. She glanced at her hands. Already the red dent seemed lighter. State monitors were in the school again. She could be observed, even questioned, about her teaching at any time. She had to be at the top of her game, but all she wanted to do was wash her face, sit quietly, and stare at her left hand. The naked ring finger of her left hand.

She craved a cup of strong coffee, not school coffee, but industrial-strength Dominican coffee. Coffee would help her think. She had a few minutes before the start of her next class, and, not bothering with a coat, she walked across the street to the bodega. Beginning flurries of snow swirled around her, and she crossed against the light, too cold to be law abiding. In the Bronx, traffic lights were only a suggestion.

The crowded dark store was decorated with twinkling Christmas lights. A short-order cook was tending garlic and peppers on a stove in the back. Bags of potato chips and fried pork rinds dangled from clips on a stand in the middle of the room, and a few skimpy ham and cheese sandwiches, wrapped in plastic, sat on a tray on the counter, competing for space with lottery forms and advertisements. She probably should eat something. But all she wanted, all she could manage, was coffee. The store was warm, but she was shivering.

"*Buenos Dias, senorita,*" the little woman behind the counter said.

Senorita. She should be *senora.* But no, her rings were off.

"*Buenos Dias. Un café, por favor,*" Charlotte said, and the woman turned and poured steaming black coffee from a carafe behind the counter into a Styrofoam cup.

The woman placed a glass shaker container full of sugar on the counter, along with a wooden stick, and Charlotte poured a full measure. Strong and hot, the coffee warmed her fingers as she curved them around the cup.

"Nice," the woman said, pointing at Charlotte's manicure.

"*Gracias,*" said Charlotte.

Her hands looked so strange, tipped in cranberry and silvery snowflakes. Ringless. A radio playing in the background announced that the airport was still open, but a storm was predicted. Perfect. She would miss her plane. She could not endure a pretend family holiday. Better to get used to being alone.

Let the snow be her excuse to the girls. She doubted Emily would mind, and Abby would only worry if Charlotte flew in bad weather.

She pulled out her purse to pay, saw the envelope with the separation agreement, and knew for sure that she would sign it. She gulped the coffee, enjoying its heat at the back of her throat, and finished it quickly. "So good," she said to the woman, pointing at the coffee. "*Muy bueno.*"

Someone entered and walked to the back, leaving the door ajar. It was hypnotizing to watch the snow cover and transform the dirty street. Even the tall green bags of garbage looked festive and Christmassy. Everything white and pure. Sparkling. She ordered another cup to take back with her into the school and hurried across the windy street.

As she scooted around the scanning machine in the front entrance, George, the security guard, said, "They're looking for you upstairs, girly. They been calling your name. Best stop by the principal's office."

On the first floor, she saw Dean Lagakis walking in the hallway, wearing a Santa Claus hat. He gave a low wolf whistle when he saw her.

In case she had missed the point, he whistled again. "What have we here?" he asked, looking at her hair and make-up. His black eyebrows arched so high they touched the white fur of his cap.

"The cosmetology kids gave me a makeover. Christmas present. Don't even think about giving me a hard time. I'm in no mood."

"To tell the truth, you looked better without all that stuff on your face."

"Thanks a lot," she said.

"It's actually a compliment. To a naturally gorgeous woman."

What a jerk. A walking sexual harassment. He never missed an opportunity.

"So gorgeous I almost forgot to tell you," he said. "They're looking for you."

"I know."

He raised his hands, palm out, in the classic surrender gesture. "Hey, I'm only the messenger. But there's somebody downstairs with a lot of feathers in his bonnet."

Charlotte took a big gulp of her second coffee and climbed the marble staircase that led to the main floor, where she saw the principal. Natalie was standing at the top step, dressed in a red suit. It was the second time Charlotte had seem this outfit. Christmas color? Or power suit? Both, Charlotte decided.

"Charlotte, thank goodness. Where have you been? I've been paging you for ten minutes."

"I needed coffee," Charlotte said, pointing to her cup.

"You know I have coffee in the office," Natalie said.

"How ridiculous to go outside. You'll be sick for California."

"I'm not going, after all," Charlotte said.

"I don't blame you, in this storm. The girls?"

Charlotte shook her head. "Already with Francis."

Natalie nodded. "I think you're doing the right thing. You'd be stranded in the airport for days, with the snow they're predicting. Why not come to my house for Christmas? I don't want you to be alone."

"Thanks, Natalie. Maybe I will."

"Listen, an important visitor is here and he wants to talk to you."

"The monitor wants to talk to me?"

Natalie shook her head. "God help me. Not just the regular monitor. That would be nothing compared to this. Someone from the Special Commissioner of Education. Today of all days. Right before the vacation. Unexpected. Like the Spanish Inquisition," she said, referring to an old Monty Python episode.

Charlotte smiled in recognition of the quote. "Nobody expects the Spanish Inquisition," she said. "But why me? Why do they want to talk to me? Did you tell them I was the one who gave you the Regents folder?"

Natalie raised her dark brows. Wrinkles like ripples in sand covered her tanned forehead. "Of course not. But as to why they want to speak with you, I'm not entirely sure, Charlotte. Did you ever..." She hesitated, choosing her words. "...have a conversation with anyone about that, um, folder?"

"Not since I showed it to you," Charlotte replied truthfully.

She had spoken about the folder to Lagakis, but that had been before showing the folder to Natalie. Natalie looked directly into Charlotte's eyes. Charlotte glanced away and looked at the main bulletin board. *EQUIVOCATION IN MACBETH* was written in large cardboard letters that Charlotte had purchased privately at Staples.

On the bulletin board, Valerie Martin's Macbeth essay had pride of place, with Charlotte's handwritten comments praising the essay for "exceeding state standards." Valerie had written about how the forces of darkness equivocated to twist the truth. The only problem had been that Valerie, as always, had written in purple. Natalie had made the girl write it over in blue ink, to impress the monitors.

Equivocating. I am equivocating, Charlotte thought to herself. Why am I doing that?

Natalie's eyes were deliberate, probing darts. "You didn't say anything about the folders, did you, Charlotte? To anyone? You're quite sure?"

Charlotte nodded, hesitantly. She didn't like the direction of this conversation.

"Excellent, excellent." Natalie took a deep breath and appeared to relax. "And will you promise not to mention the folder? Can I count on your support?"

Charlotte widened her eyes even as Natalie narrowed hers. "What do you mean?"

"You know perfectly well what I mean, my friend."

This conversation was a land mine. Charlotte had to be very careful.

Now Natalie was explaining, sort of. "Somebody— tipped them off about the folder."

Charlotte turned her attention back to the bulletin board. Equivocation.

"Charlotte," Natalie said. "Wake up! Did you hear what I said?"

Charlotte jumped when Natalie said "Wake up." Then she took another sip. "Somebody tipped them off?"

Natalie began fidgeting with her necklace of green and red beads. Her voice was a low whisper now. "It was Trombetta, probably. Wrote the state a letter before she died." Natalie shook her head at the perfidy of it. But then she looked up and smiled. "But without the folder you found there's no proof. If the monitors ask you, just say you don't know anything about it."

"Why?" Charlotte asked. "There was a folder. I found it. Lagakis saw it too."

"You told me he didn't look inside it," Natalie said.

"Well, I gave it to you when I found it. I can't answer for what Lagakis did. Look, the students' answers were changed. Natalie, I thought you were conducting an investigation. A thorough investigation. That's what you told me."

Natalie rolled her eyes and groaned. "I love you dearly, Charlotte, but sometimes you are *impossible*. Come down out of the ivory tower, won't you? This is no time to be disingenuous. Too much is at stake."

A shiver went down Charlotte's back. *This is important. Charlotte! You need to think. Concentrate. Concentrate.* She took a long deep swallow of the coffee in her cup. The feeling of alertness, of power, flowed through her veins.

Thank God the bell rang. Charlotte had a class.

"I have to go teach," Charlotte said.

"Don't you think I thought of that? Your class is covered."

A strange man in an elegant blue blazer poked his head out of Natalie's office. "Ms. Albert? Did you find Ms. Murphy?"

"Oh yes," Natalie said to him sweetly. "She's right here. Please just excuse us one minute."

She pulled Charlotte into a room marked Women Teachers. They were alone in the small, airless bathroom, and Charlotte realized that she had to go. It had been freezing outside and she had had the coffee. She automatically walked into a stall, but was pulled out by Natalie.

"Charlotte," she hissed. "I need you. Don't. Fuck. This. Up."

"Why me?" Charlotte asked. "Why do they want to talk to me?"

"Because," Natalie said. "Because your initials are on the exams as a rater."

"On t—the changed grades?" Charlotte asked. Her stomach began cramping.

"Of course."

"I have to go to the bathroom," Charlotte said, placing her coffee on the small ledge of the sink and entering the stall.

Natalie practically followed her in until Charlotte looked pointedly at the door. When Charlotte finally had a modicum of privacy, she found she was too nervous to relieve herself.

"Do you mind stepping outside, Natalie?"

"Yes, I do mind. I'm in deep shit. Deep. Help me, Charlotte. They're waiting for you, and you're going to go in there and tell them that there never was another set of scores. Never was a folder. That you wrote your own initials on the exam."

Charlotte sat on the toilet, facing a tattered green flyer that read: *If you sprinkle while you tinkle, please be neat and wipe the seat.* Wipe the seat. Wipe the slate. A clean slate. That was what Natalie was requesting. When she had marked Regents Exams, she had been scrupulously careful, as fair as she could be. Word was out that, in future, all Regents Exams would be sent from schools, to be graded by strangers. Perhaps that was best. It was hard to be objective about one's own students. But last June she had tried to grade fairly.

Charlotte finally succeeded in emptying her bladder by flushing the toilet first to mask the sound of her own stream. She flushed the toilet again and then walked over to the sink to wash her hands. If only she could wash them, figuratively speaking. Charlotte looked at herself in the cracked mirror over the sink and pursed her lips. Whistle blower.

There were no paper towels. Of course. At least there had been toilet paper. She walked back into the stall and pulled off a few sheets to dry her hands. She rubbed them slowly, playing for time. Out, damn spot.

She turned and faced Natalie, who was looming behind her in her all-red power suit. "You're asking me to lie for you."

"Not lie. Just to keep a secret. We're friends." Natalie's tone was bewildered, hurt, but her eyes were hard.

"Friends don't lie to each other. Friends don't forge friends' initials."

"Friends are loyal," Natalie answered.

An expression of weariness suffused her face. The blue tones of the fluorescent light revealed marionette lines leading from the principal's nose to her chin. Charlotte watched Natalie's mouth move up and down, up and down.

"Don't be an infant, Charlotte. You don't realize what you're doing," she said, placing a hand on the wall next to Charlotte, effectively trapping her. "Look, when are you going to figure out that nothing is just black and white? Sometimes there are—good lies. Necessary lies." Natalie was standing very close. Her perfume was overpowering in the small room. "Listen to me, Charlie. You're not helping anyone if you tell what was in that folder. Do you know what you'll do? You'll hurt yourself. You'll hurt the school. You'll hurt me. And most of all, you'll hurt the kids."

Charlotte could feel the ghostly touch of her mother's fingers, poking at her back. "Stand up straight," her mother's voice said.

Charlotte drew herself up to her full height and looked directly into Natalie's eyes. "You lied to me. You said you were investigating. And if there's one thing I learned from this whole mess with Francis, it's this—I'm sick of lies."

There was lipstick on the principal's teeth, something Charlotte had never seen before. Charlotte touched her own teeth and nodded. Natalie looked in the mirror, saw the lipstick, and rubbed it off with her bare finger. "Thanks," she said.

"Natalie," Charlotte said. "Maybe there's a way to finesse this. Use the passive voice. Just say, mistakes have been made or something similar."

"There is only one way to finesse this," Natalie said. "It's for you to get on board. So, as far as you're concerned, there is no folder."

Equivocation was not enough, apparently. Natalie wanted full out mendacity. Charlotte's thoughts were swirling around her brain. She had to concentrate.

"You're scared, aren't you? Don't worry. I'll protect you. The only thing to be afraid of is if they find out about the folder." Natalie's voice was calm, assured, but she kept twisting her beads, twisting, turning, so hard that the strand broke. Charlotte bent to pick them up and Natalie said, "Oh forget the beads. They're just some cheap junk I wear to look like it's Christmas." Brightly colored globes were rolling all over the floor now, and Charlotte kicked the ones she could reach into a corner.

"Someone could trip on these," she said.

"Will you forget the damn necklace?" Natalie said.

Charlotte could not take her eyes off the beads on the tiled floor.

"Look at me," Natalie said. "Not the beads. This is really important. Sometimes I have to wonder how such a smart woman can be so stupid. You've been in the classroom with the kids too long."

"Funny. That's what Francis used to say to me," Charlotte said.

Natalie smiled at Charlotte, a superior kind of smile. The kind of smile that says *I am a smart person and you are not.*

"Francis is an asshole. But even a broken clock is right twice a day," Natalie said.

"Are you saying Francis was right?"

"Of course not," Natalie said, too quickly. "But—how about, when this is over, I get you a little job that takes you out of the classroom for a while? You can edit a school literary magazine or something. No teaching, just a nice little office and whatever else you want."

"Natalie, I enjoy teaching," Charlotte replied.

Natalie spoke with exaggerated slowness, as though to a child. "Look, Charlotte, some of those kids *cannot* pass the Regents. We need to change the whole school, attract new kids, better kids, kids we can work with. I've started an articulation program that will do that. But you know damn well that first I've got to get rid—graduate the ones who are here."

"I think they can learn," Charlotte said. "I think they deserve to be taught, at least."

The principal leaned back against the tiled wall, her eyes raised as though trying to summon patience from the ceiling. Then she spoke again. "Charlotte, I have never once stopped you from teaching. Interfered with what you're trying to do. But you haven't been successful with all the kids, have you? If those scores don't go up, they're going to close this place. If I could just get my numbers up, I know things will get better with the incoming freshmen. Remember the story of Hans Brinker and the Silver Skates? Well, that's what I feel like. The little boy who plugs up the hole in the dyke with his finger. I've got my finger in the friggin' dyke."

Natalie said this last sentence at full volume just as the doorknob rattled and Miss Knudsen, the teaching fellow assigned to Renaissance House, walked in. She looked from Charlotte to Natalie. Natalie motioned the young teacher to leave. "Give us a minute," she said, and the frightened girl scuttled away, no doubt wondering what she had interrupted.

"Natalie, I'm not going to lie for you."

"It's not lying! It's just shutting up. But one more thing. You think you enjoy teaching? Do you think you'd enjoy five periods a day teaching the Renaissance Kids? Let's see you manage the thugs and gang-bangers."

"Are you saying that you'll change my program if I don't lie?" Charlotte said.

Natalie did not answer the question. Instead, she started to pick up the pieces of her broken necklace from the floor. "I guess you're right," she said. "Someone could trip over these."

Charlotte bent to help. The beads made a loud ping sound as the women threw them into the metal wastebasket.

"I'm not a monster, Charlotte. I'm not threatening you. I'm saying that the whole school will be one Renaissance House if you don't cooperate. They'll send in somebody else who won't take care of things the way I do. You're being very foolish, Charlotte. You're upset and you're not looking at the big picture. Don't throw everything away just because Francis left you."

Charlotte flinched, but she would not cry. She took a last sustaining swallow of coffee. It was ice cold now. She threw the paper cup in the wastebasket and went in to face the man in the blue blazer.

જજજ

Valerie's Journal
DO NOT READ
Murphy looked good today thanks of course to the hair and nails done by me and Suzette. Good but kind of tired. She had that old rubber band around the hair again and I made her take it off before Suzette got there. Murphy understood and she let me do a quick touch up. Suzette spent a lot of time on Murphy's hair and I knew she'd have a fit if she saw that messy bun thing Murphy puts it in with a rubber band.

Murphy wears them like some kind of jewelry, the rubber bands I mean. Always one or more on her wrist. Sometimes you see her snapping them. I know she'll put one of them back in her hair first chance she gets and never think about the damage she's doing to herself. I taped a coated elastic band in her Christmas card. Hint.

By the time we had English, half the school was absent. The Spanish kids never even came to school being they had to go to the DR for Christmas and other people were just too depressed. Most people left after lunch, which was pretty bad, by the way.

Lagakis came in and almost killed himself there was so much food on the floor. Plus, it started snowing and people had to get home before the buses got too crowded.

Just because it's Christmas, and most of the class skipped, didn't stop Murphy. She had her little Christmas lesson all ready. I swear if the trumpet was blowing the end of days, she'd still put that journal assignment on the board and make us read something before we went off to the Heavenly Kingdom.

She had candy for us too—you could see the little packages all wrapped up on the chair behind her desk.

I hope it stops snowing because I'm going to meet J.C. in the diner on Jerome Avenue after school. I'm kind of scared that my grandmother might find out that there's no workshop for writing in the library to-day. If she finds out, you can really cancel Christmas for me, but I'm excited to see what kind of present he has for me.

It might be he didn't get me anything but I doubt it. He's been giving out these little hints.

Rohan was there today. He gave me a present, in fact. It was kind of good to see him, being we go back since kindergarten.

It's actually better to do some work than just sit around and BS like we did in most classes today.

Anyhow, Murphy gave us this story and everybody got into it, even Rohan. He's a pretty good reader, and Murphy made him read the whole thing out loud. It was this story about Langston Hughes being a passed around child, and when we finished reading it, Rohan asked if he could keep the copy. Murphy said we all could keep it, and then she gave us the candy. I'm not exactly a passed around child but I know what it means.

Murphy gave us the extra candy she had in case

the whole class showed up, as if she really thought they might. I took some for the foster kids.

Merry Christmas and Happy New Year to me! I've run out of room in this notebook. I won't be writing for a while.

CHAPTER 12

Breakdown

As a child, Charlotte had dreaded holidays spent alone with her mother. Her father had disappeared before she could remember, and it was just the two of them. Things got better once she had Francis and the kids, but this Christmas would be the hardest of all.

After she had spoken to the monitor and taught her last class of the day, Charlotte lingered at her desk, straightening piles of papers, tidying a drawer, moving books from one closet to another. The custodial staff was patient with her, cleaning other classrooms first, but finally she realized that she was keeping them from their homes and families. The streetlamps were already on, creating blue shadows on the snowy sidewalk. Looking out the window at the beam of light directly under the streetlight, Charlotte saw that snow was still falling lightly, but snowplows had been out, destroying the purity of the earlier vista.

How would you identify the strengths of this school? What are its weaknesses? The monitor had been soft-spoken and considerate, had wished her a happy holiday. He didn't want to hear the truth.

Where were her tights? She'd left them in the cosmetology room after her pedicure. That room was locked now. Oh well, she'd get her feet wet anyway as she walked to the parking lot. As she moved through the darkened hallway of the school, she noticed that even the principal had gone home.

Natalie had probably needed a stiff drink. Did Natalie know what Charlotte had said to the monitor? Not possible. Charlotte herself hadn't known what she would say until she looked into his eyes. Only one light was on in the dim hallway—Lagakis's office. Charlotte hurried by, hoping to avoid him. But he emerged just as she passed his doorway, as if he had been waiting for her. He loomed over her with his large frame, standing too close, as usual. Peering past him inside the room, Charlotte noticed that his desk was also unnaturally tidy.

"Leaving so soon?" Lagakis asked. "Let me walk you out to the parking lot. It's pretty dark already."

"I'll be fine," Charlotte said.

"Please. I won't be a minute. I would prefer it."

Lagakis wore no overcoat, just a tweed sports jacket. He took a scarf from his closet, wound it around his neck, and grabbed a few Christmas cards the kids had given him. One card had a candy cane taped to it. He broke the candy cane in half and offered a piece to Charlotte.

"From Valerie?" Charlotte said, indicating the card where the candy cane had been.

"Of course. I guess she gave one to every teacher in the school. She really is a nice kid." He fell into step behind Charlotte.

The custodian, old Mr. Kirby, nodded approvingly at Lagakis. "It's good you're walking her down," he said. "I was gonna do that if you didn't."

"Merry Christmas," said Charlotte. "Have a wonderful holiday."

"Oh, it ain't no holiday for us," he said. "'Cept for Christmas we'll be here just about every day, getting ready for y'all to come back. When you come back, this floor will be shining like glass, and the desks will be clean as they were in September."

"Take care Mike," Lagakis said. "Happy New Year."

"God," Charlotte said. "I didn't realize those guys don't get a vacation."

"Hey, don't feel sorry for them. That Mike, he makes more money than the principal."

"What? A janitor?"

"Not a janitor. A custodian. An independent contractor. He gets a budget, and then he gets to decide how much to spend and how much to keep. And he knows how to keep quite a bit of it."

As they walked the short half block, Charlotte's feet, clad only in light loafers, were ice cold. As they entered the parking lot, Lagakis took a few steps ahead of her, went to the trunk of his own car, and removed a snowbrush.

"I can do that," Charlotte protested as he started cleaning off her car.

"Just get inside and turn the engine on. Your feet have to be freezing. You're not even wearing stockings."

"You don't have to." *Why did he have to notice everything?*

"Will you just let me? I want to. And—it's Christmas."

"Well, thank you. That is so nice of you."

"I'm a nice guy."

She opened her car door and something seemed wrong. The light that usually illuminated the dashboard had not come on, she realized. She inserted her key in the ignition, turned, and heard nothing but a click.

Lagakis was already dealing with the snow on her windshield, pulling the windshield wipers up, removing bits of crusted ice from them with his bare fingers.

"What's happening?" he said. "Turn on the engine and set the heater on defrost."

"Nothing's happening." Charlotte stuck her head out of the car. "I think the battery's dead."

"Unlatch the hood."

Charlotte fumbled around, not sure where the latch was.

Lagakis did not wait for her but reached across her lap

and found the latch of her car, accidentally brushing against her bare legs. "Excuse me," he said.

Once the hood was open he took a look inside. "God, Charlotte, how does your husband let a woman drive around with such a corroded battery? This thing is filthy. No wonder it's dead."

This could not be happening. "Oh God. What do I do now? I could call Triple A, but I know they'll be an hour at least." Across the street was a store called Fix-a-Flat, but it was already closed. Snow was swirling around the car, heavier now.

"Don't worry," said Lagakis. "I'll just give you a jump. Won't take a minute."

But when Lagakis hooked up his cables to her battery, nothing happened. "It's not your battery," he said.

"Is it the alternator?" Charlotte asked.

"Probably the alternator," he said. Then he looked at her. "How did you know that?"

"It's always the alternator, isn't it?" she said.

"Look," he said. "I know a guy. Gus. My cousin. He owns a garage. He'll know what to do. Just sit in my car—warm up, and I'll make the phone call."

He opened the door of his car for her, turned on the engine and the heater, and then left to continue cleaning off the windshield of her car. She sat in the passenger seat, noting the lack of dust on the dashboard. There were no crumbs on the console either.

Surprisingly, there was not even a heavy cigarette smell, as there had been last time. Perhaps it was because of the air freshener dangling from the rear view mirror.

The heat heightened its sweet vanilla smell, making her think of flowers. California flowers and California sunshine. Probably flowers and sunshine surrounded Francis right now, as she sat freezing in a darkening Bronx parking lot.

"Oh, poor me. Poor little Charlotte. Stop that," she told herself, and she snapped the rubber band on her wrist. "It doesn't help."

She watched Lagakis as he methodically cleared the windshield and then brushed snow off the roof. His face was serious, intent on the job. Soon what looked like mini-avalanches fell down the sides of the passenger window to the ground. When Lagakis had finally cleared all the snow from her car he returned to his own, simultaneously talking into the earpiece of his telephone. His face retained the same purposeful look.

When he had finished, he joined her in his car. "He'll be here in about ten minutes, my cousin Gus. He has a friend who has a friend. He'll be right over."

"How can I ever thank you?" As the words left her lips she thought, oh no, here it comes. What a perfect opening for him. But he surprised her.

"Don't worry about it." He looked over at her. "Last time you were in this car—" He paused.

"We were going to Bertie's funeral," Charlotte finished for him.

Lagakis looked straight ahead. "Yeah. That was rough."

Charlotte was silent.

"I've been meaning to ask you something," he said. Here it came—another one of his little remarks. She didn't think she could handle it today, after all that had happened.

"Let me stop you now," Charlotte said. "You know I'm married."

"Yeah, yes, I know that. Mrs. Francis X. Murphy, right? He's a lucky guy."

Again Charlotte was silent.

"Look, I know what you think of me, and I don't blame you, but that's not what I was going to say," Lagakis said.

Oh God. What was wrong with her? Always thinking the worst of the poor man. And after he'd cleared off her car and rescued her from being stranded in the Bronx in a snowstorm.

"I'm so sorry," she said.

"I don't blame you. I know I'm an asshole sometimes. I wouldn't blame your husband if he took a shot at me."

Charlotte was silent, conjuring up the image of Francis and Lagakis engaged in a duel. But would Francis fight for her? Highly doubtful. It was eighty degrees in Beverly Hills, she had heard on the weather channel this morning. Francis was undoubtedly lounging by some pool. The kids would be with him, soaking up the sun.

She stared at the lighted dashboard. Rear defroster, she read. A little symbol showed that heat was directed to the floor of the car. She felt her feet beginning to thaw. They hurt. Her throat hurt too, the way it did when she was about to cry. The wipers flicked bits of snow off the windshield, making a steady, clicking noise. She reached once again for the rubber band on her wrist, but did not snap it.

Lagakis turned to her. "What I was going to say—oh, never mind," he said, looking at her eyes, which had started to tear. "I'll ask you another time," he said. "It's not important."

Suddenly Charlotte understood why he had waited to walk out with her. He wanted to know about the visitor, the monitors. Did he also know what was in the folder?

"You wanted to know if I talked to the visitor."

He nodded.

"Yes," she said. "I talked to him. For almost half an hour."

His eyes looked searchingly into her face. "And did you tell—did you tell what you saw?"

He knew. He knew about the copies of the original grades that were in the folder. Bertie must have told him. And strangely, what Charlotte felt was relief.

After the crazy day, the day of having her nails done and her legs massaged, the day of her last day of class, the day before the terrible lonely Christmas she would spend, the day of her car not starting, the day of cold feet finally warming up in the heat of a warm car, Charlotte began to cry.

Lagakis leaned over the console and awkwardly placed an arm around her shoulders, and instead of reaching for the rubber band, to her surprise, she put her head on his large chest and sobbed.

"Hey," he said, "It's all right, sweetheart. It's okay. I don't care what you did, Charlotte. I truly don't care."

She sobbed even louder then. He stroked her hair. "Charlotte, Charlotte." He wiped a tear from her cheek with a gentle forefinger. "It's going to be all right."

"Sorry," she said. "It's—it's just been a hard day."

"I'm sorry." He drew her closer to him and kissed her cheek where the tears had been.

He smelled like a candy cane, nothing like the cigarette smell she thought he would have. She almost turned her mouth to his mouth, but at the last minute she kissed his cheek, just a quick peck on his soft cheek. There were still crystals of snow in his hair. His arm tightened around her.

The sound of someone tapping on the window brought her back to herself.

Gus, as it turned out, did not have an alternator, but a tow truck.

"Sorry, miss," Gus said to Charlotte. "I can't do anything tonight. Everything's all fucked up with the snow. Oh, excuse me. Sorry for the language."

"The one time Gus was ever early," Lagakis said, removing his arm from around Charlotte.

"Where can I rent a car around here?" she asked.

Lagakis shook his head. "Forget it. Not around here. I'll drive you home. You can deal with renting a car tomorrow."

She leaned back in the passenger seat and hugged herself, rocking back and forth.

"I told," she said. "I didn't have to. He didn't ask. But I told the monitor."

He nodded. "You did the right thing."

CHAPTER 13

On the First Day of Christmas

Night had fallen. The sky was black. It was the darkest evening of the year, and she had miles to go. Gus and a helper were easing her car onto a flatbed trailer. It looked as though the snow had stopped, but then, under the orange lights of the tow truck, she spied tiny flakes still falling.

"I don't want to talk about the state guy anymore," Charlotte said.

"Okay. Here," Lagakis said. "Listen to the radio."

He pressed a few buttons, and Christmas music poured out of the burled wood console. Charlotte had a memory of sitting in the den with an arm around each of her daughters. She wrapped her arms around herself, remembering.

She closed her eyes, picturing the twins as little girls in nightgowns. She sensed, rather than felt, Lagakis's arm steal around her. But when she opened her eyes, she saw that his hands were folded in his lap. She had imagined it, she realized.

She moved a little closer to the door on her side, pretending to look out the window.

"I think Gus needs me," Lagakis said. "Just sit here, relax, and listen to the music. I better give Gus a hand getting out of the lot."

As he opened the door, the cold air chilled her. She watched him pull his jacket closer around him. The block was deserted. Outside, Gus honked the horn of the tow truck.

Lagakis stepped into the street—stood there, in the middle of the street—his scarf blowing back in the wind. What an idiot, Charlotte thought. He'll get himself killed. He motioned to Gus to pull out of the lot and held up a hand to stop an on-coming car. He should have let the car pass, she thought. This isn't a school safety drill. "Oh God, be careful," she breathed. She could almost read the headline: *Teacher killed by hit and run on school street.* But no, the car was stopping a safe distance from where Lagakis stood, and the tow truck slowly negotiated the turn out of the parking lot, orange lights sparkling on the snow. Soon the truck had disappeared, taking her car wherever it was going. She saw Lagakis wave his cousin off with a raised fist. It was a victorious kind of wave, a conquering hero kind of gesture.

"On the first day of Christmas my true love gave to me..." More holiday music. Everywhere you went you heard it—the malls, the A&P, the commercials on the television. They made you listen to it no matter what. She fiddled around with the many dials, trying to find the off button. Lagakis got back into the car, removed his scarf, and threw it into the back seat. Then he stepped back out and took off his jacket too.

"Too warm in here for that. Here's Gus's card. Call tomorrow," he said, finally settling into the driver's seat. "He'll give you a good deal, whatever the problem is. He's family."

"Thanks," Charlotte said.

"My pleasure."

"And a partridge in a pear tree."

Lagakis adjusted the volume. "Don't you love it? That's my favorite song."

"Oh, well then, let's listen." It figured he would like that endless repetitive song.

"You don't like it, do you?"

"Well, no actually, but that's okay."

He pressed a button and the car was accusingly silent. "You've suffered enough today. I'm sure I'll have another chance to hear it."

"I'm sure you will," she agreed.

"Don't patronize me. I get it. The song is overplayed. But maybe there's a reason for that." He sounded angry.

She was a terrible person. After all he had done for her. But it *was* an annoying song.

"I'm sorry. I have a headache." As she spoke, Charlotte realized this was true. She also realized that she'd given him an opening with that clichéd punch line.

He did not disappoint. "Not tonight, dear, I have a headache?" he said. "You sound like my ex."

His ex? Charlotte had never thought of him having an ex.

Lagakis said. "Here. Drink some of this." He pulled an unopened bottle of water from the cup holder, opened it, and offered it to her. It was still ice cold despite the warmth of the car, and she shivered as the water touched her teeth.

"That's a good girl," he said. "You need to stay hydrated. Now, where to?"

He pressed another button, and a GPS screen rose up from the center of the dashboard. Again, she had the sense that he was showing off his toy for her. "Where to?" he repeated. "I know you live in Connecticut."

"I'm taking you way out of your way."

She would owe him forever. He would drive her home, see her dreadfully dark, empty house. It would be freezing there, since she had turned the heat down this morning. She would have to invite him in, make some excuse about Francis and the girls.

"I'm happy to do it. Let's call it my gift to you for Christmas."

"I really should just rent a car." What was the name of that company? Expedia? No, Enterprise. "Enterprise will pick me up anywhere," she said.

"By the time they get here, I'll have you home," he answered. "Now, where to?"

There was no choice. She told him her address.

He nodded. "Westport?"

"You know it?"

"My uncle owns the fur store there.

"I thought he owned a florist."

"I have lots of uncles. We're Greeks. Flowers, fur, and food. That's what we do."

She thought he would mention the fourth F-word, as before. But he did not.

CHAPTER 14

Arabian Night

The traffic was moving very slowly on the Bronx River Parkway. A large arrow flashed a warning: *Accident Ahead.*

"Shit," said Lagakis. "I should have taken the Hutch. Or gotten straight on 95." He poked a few buttons on his elaborate radio, and six lords were leaping. He quickly changed the channel.

"Please. Listen to it. I'm sorry I was so awful about that song before."

His jaw was set. He was still offended, she saw.

"By the way," she said. "It's okay if you want to smoke."

"Okay. Look. I really don't smoke any more. I just did it to stand outside with Bertie. Otherwise, I was afraid someone would take a pop at her."

"I thought you were friends."

"We were, in a way, but I haven't had a cigarette since the day of her funeral."

They rode on in silence, while she cast about for something to say. But he began with what he probably regarded as harmless small talk.

"So, Charlotte, what are you doing for the Christmas break?"

"Oh, nothing special," she replied. That was no lie. Her mind frantically sought about for a plausible explanation for the empty house as she asked, "How about you? Going away?"

"I'd like to," he said. "But Yiayia would have a fit. We always have Christmas at home."

"Yiayia? An unusual name."

"It's Greek."

"Is she your girlfriend?"

He shot her a quick glance and then grinned. "She thinks she is, and I let her think it."

Lagakis with a girlfriend. In spite of all his innuendos and insinuations, he had some little Greek girlfriend at home. Men! But at least Charlotte had found a way to direct the conversation away from her own situation.

"Tell me about her," Charlotte said. "About Yiayia."

"What do you want to know? I don't know how to begin."

"Well, what does she look like?"

"Look like?" His eyebrows rose. "Oh, I see." When he smiled like that, he was almost good looking.

"Um, she always dresses in black."

Charlotte pictured a woman with enormous breasts in a tight black sheath. Low cut, if she knew Lagakis. Stiletto heels too. Very subtle.

"Tell me more. I suppose she's a good cook too?"

She was *Scheherazade* in reverse, and Lagakis was spinning his own tale.

A small red car attempted to merge into the middle lane, which was the only one showing blacktop. My God, was that Francis? In a split second, Charlotte imagined that Francis had changed his mind and was driving home to Connecticut.

Of course, it was not Francis. Francis was gone. That part of her life was gone. The driver cut Lagakis off and gave him the finger. Lagakis did not reciprocate or even honk, but applied the brakes slowly, allowing the other car access. "Gotta love those red cars," he said. "Always the worst drivers. What kind of jerk drives that fast in snow?"

The jerk I married. Snap. She pulled the rubber band on her wrist and let it hit her flesh hard.

Back to the present, to the here and now. Earth to Charlotte. Concentrate! Her car had broken down in the school parking lot. Lagakis was driving her home. Just keep Lagakis talking about himself. Think of the advice in *Cosmopolitan*, the bible of her single days. Well, of her first single days. She held out her hands and stared at them. Unadorned except for the nail polish. So strange.

Lagakis noticed her wrist snap. "Hey, what's going on? Are you all right?"

"You were telling me about your girl. Yiayia. Tell me more. Can she cook?"

"What?" said Lagakis. "My girl Yiayia?" He looked over at her. "Oh. Yes. Yiayia cooks. In fact, she's a great cook. Made me gain too much weight at one time. I was close to 300 pounds in high school. I have to watch myself around her."

"You've been together since high school?"

"Even before that." He let that sink in for a minute. Then he relented. "Yiayia is the Greek word for grandmother."

"You tricked me!" She burst out laughing, and he joined her. It felt good. "Your grandmother!" she marveled.

"Couldn't resist," he said. "You really didn't know that Yiayia meant Grandma?"

"I never heard of it before."

"Amazing. I thought it was common knowledge. I guess when you grow up with something, you think everybody knows it. Had you going there, didn't I?' he said, proudly. "But I have to admit, I wasn't sure how you'd take my little joke."

Was she that humorless? No wonder Francis had left her. No, wait. She was bad at sex.

Aloud she said, "No, that was great. After this terrible day, I needed a laugh. Why would you worry about that?"

"I don't—I don't know, Charlotte. I do stupid stuff sometimes. Say stupid stuff. It's like I don't know how to talk to people—women especially. Beautiful women most especially."

"You're doing it now. Stop, okay?"

"Doing what?" But he smiled.

The red lights ahead began to move. The heated back of the seat soothed her sore muscles, weary from the tension of the day. She must not relax. She must be *Scheherazade*, but in reverse. Keep him talking about himself.

But Lagakis steered the conversation. Rohan was the first topic. Did she know that Rohan Davis had been in the building that day?

"Yes," she replied, "He actually came to my last class. He's a sweetie, isn't he?"

Lagakis's hearty laugh filled the car. "You've got to be kidding. What ivory tower are you in, Charlotte? Don't you know who he is?"

"I know he's a good reader. What else is there to know?"

"Only that he's one of the biggest gang bangers in the Bronx. One word, no, one nod, from him and you could get cut, beaten up, even killed."

Rohan? At the head of a gang? Rohan, hurting her? Impossible to reconcile this sweet and soft-spoken boy with the criminal Lagakis had just described.

"But he's a great reader. I think he's really smart."

"I don't doubt it," Lagakis said. "Leaders of gangs usually are. And at least he's sane. Not like Gareth."

"Gareth? I've never met him. What a beautiful name, Gareth. Sounds like something out of King Arthur and the Knights of the Round Table."

"Be glad you haven't met him. He's nuts. *Certi-fi-able.* Got a wild look in his eyes. But a bunch of kids follow him. He's trying to challenge Rohan, you know."

"Challenge Rohan? Like in a joust?"

"You're not far off," Lagakis said.

"Rohan read today in my class. He really seemed to like

the story I gave—asked if he could keep it. It was about being a passed-around child—a kid brought up by relatives."

Lagakis kept his eyes on the road and said, very softly, "Passed-around child. You're good. Holidays are tough for our kids. For lots of people, I bet."

"Don't I know it," Charlotte replied. "That's why I always give them little holiday gifts. Just candy or cookies, but at least they'll have *something*."

Lagakis said, "Kids tell me you're a great teacher. I can see why."

Charlotte hugged those words to herself. "Thank you for telling me that. But I give so little—and they give me back so much. I feel guilty sometimes, that they think so well of me for the little I do."

"It's the truth, that's all," he replied.

"Thank you, Ted." It was the first time she had used his first name.

"Do me one favor. Don't call me Ted. Or Teddy. Never Teddy."

Charlotte intuited that his ex had called him Teddy. Maybe even Teddy Bear.

They passed a sign: "Connecticut welcomes you," he read.

"God, we're in Greenwich already. Traffic has really let up. Anyway, what do you want me to call you?" Charlotte asked. "Do you have a street name?" she asked facetiously.

"People who know me call me Theo."

"For Theodore? Theodore Lagakis," she said, pronouncing each syllable carefully.

He nodded. "It sounds good the way you say it."

He became very quiet and Charlotte did not break the silence. They were in Norwalk already, passing the sign for Stew Leonard's. That was where they had always bought their Christmas trees, she and Francis and the girls. Stew Leonard's, the store with the freshest trees, the sweetest fruit, and the entertaining animal puppets that burst into song to delight the children. It was probably jam-packed right now with families. No, not tonight in this snow. Families would be home, wrapping presents and making cookies.

Snap!

"It's the next exit," she said. "Not this one."

"We're coming to Westport now. Exit 17. The exit for Longshore, right?"

"Yes. But for my house you take the second exit in Westport. Exit 18. How do you know Longshore? From your uncle? The uncle on your mother's side?"

He smiled. "Yeah. You got the right uncle this time. Longshore. That's where I got married. My big fat wedding was there. My very own Big Fat Greek wedding."

"You're married?"

"Was." He shrugged. "Oh, it was a beautiful wedding. Everybody said so. The happiest day of my life."

"You're—not together now."

"That's why I call her my ex," he said shortly. Then his tone softened. "Sorry, Charlotte, I didn't mean to be sarcastic."

She looked over at him. His face, illuminated by the light of the dashboard, was impassive. The dimples were gone.

"Where to now?" he asked as he negotiated the slippery exit ramp. He slowed, making allowance for the ice.

Apparently, the conversation about his marriage was over. "Turn in here," she said, as they got to Greens Farms Road.

Christmas lights illuminated all the other homes. Marie across the way had a full display on the lawn: Santa and eight reindeer. Charlotte's next-door neighbor, Sally Bailey, had hired someone to wind lights around the giant pine tree that stood on her front lawn. Its colored lights created rainbows on the snow.

"I love your rainbows," Lagakis said.

"I love them too, but they aren't mine. It's the fourth house on the right. The dark one. Would you like to come in? Have a drink after the long drive. I have some brie in the fridge, and there's wine."

He shook his head. "Driving."

"Some coffee, at least? I have a *tarte tatin*."

He laughed. "You sound like Yiayia." But he kept the engine running and his hands on the wheel. He ran a hand over his forehead, pushing his hair back. He must be tired, she realized. He'd been driving for over an hour.

"I never realized you'd been married," she said.

He nodded. "I don't broadcast it. I got burned pretty bad."

"Honestly I wouldn't have guessed."

He shrugged. "You didn't have enough interest to even wonder." He took a deep breath, as if to say, here goes. "Speaking of wondering, Mrs. Murphy. Your house is dark. If you were my wife, I'd have a timer so the light came on when you pulled in. You never even called your husband when you thought you were stranded. And something else." He held out his own left hand and tapped his ring finger. "No rings? Is that something new?"

"My God, you notice everything."

"Certain things."

She squared her shoulders and got it over with. "I was planning to tell people after Christmas. My husband— Francis and I—we've agreed to separate." She stole a look at him and found his face unreadable in the shadows. "We've been apart since—since Halloween. He's in California with our daughters this vacation."

"I see."

There was a long pause. Charlotte heard the sound of an ambulance. Someone had had an accident. An emergency. They would be spending Christmas in Norwalk hospital. At least they wouldn't be alone. Stop that! She went to snap the rubber band on her wrist.

"Separated? Are you getting a divorce?"

She shook her head. "I don't want to get into it. I don't want to talk about it."

"All right, Charlotte. I won't bother you. Believe me, I know it's tough. I've been there." He opened the door on his side of the car but left the engine running. "Let me help you up those steps. They're kind of icy."

"I'll be fine. Are you sure you won't come in? Use the bathroom, at least, before your drive back?"

"Better not. Besides, I'll probably stop at my uncle's. My cousin Gus will have told him where I'm going. The Greek grapevine. I won't hear the end of it if I pass his house without stopping."

Be careful what you want, for surely you may get it. She hadn't wanted him to come in. She had been worried about the awkwardness of just this moment all the way home, and now it turned out that he didn't even want to come in. Anticlimactic, she thought. A good vocabulary word for the students, if she could keep them from laughing at the word climax. Irony would work here too.

"I'll wait here till you turn on the light inside."

"Good night, Theo. Thanks again."

She opened the kitchen door and turned on the light. She went to the window, pulled back the curtain, and waved. He waved back and drove away.

CHAPTER 15

Just Charlotte

L agakis's car made its way down her driveway, now illumined with the outside lights she had turned on for him. Soon the red tail lights disappeared, and she was alone.

She called Francis in California, to let him know that she wasn't coming. Snow, she told him. Her flight had actually been cancelled, so her decision was easy to explain.

What now? She was not in the least hungry. It was so quiet. Not a creature was stirring, she thought. Not a sound. Not a soul. Not even a mouse. She went into the little den off the kitchen, switching on lights as she walked through the house. This was the room that was most entirely her own, furnished with remnants of her mother's home. Charlotte fell onto the plump old sofa, its frayed chintz soft and welcoming. Her fingers found the hole in the armrest, an old friend. Needing background noise, she turned on some music at high volume, and soon Mozart—clear, unemotional, not a note wasted—filled the empty house. She should eat something. The freezer was well stocked, but she lacked the energy even to microwave a frozen dinner. In the end, she settled for some very stale Girl Scout cookies and a glass of milk.

She ate on the couch in the den and then went back into

the kitchen and placed her empty glass in the dishwasher.

She was freezing. She was tempted to wrap up in the throw that always lived on the sofa, but no, if she went to sleep now, she would be awake all night. Instead, she made herself get up off the sofa and walk into the living room, where she turned up the thermostat, lowered that morning to conserve energy. As the old boiler fired, she realized that the hot water would be at its very best. It seemed like a long time since her morning shower. It was an ideal time to take a bath.

The master bath was an anomaly, a modern room in an old fashioned home. She had liked the graciousness of their old house, with its high ceilings and fieldstone fireplaces, but the baths had needed to be remodeled, and here Francis strongly favored modern convenience and clean modern lines.

They had taken a long time over the many choices: whether to pick porcelain or marble for the wall tiles and floor, chrome or nickel for the faucets, pure white or cream for the sinks and tub—but somehow, the finished room looked to Charlotte more like a spa in a luxury hotel than a bath in a family home. She had wanted to soften it with a few plants, but Francis had protested. Why bring dirt into the place where you go to get clean?

She had then proposed hanging a museum print of a nude bather that had caught her fancy. She had purchased the print, which depicted a slender young woman with long red hair, years ago in the gift shop at the Metropolitan.

But Francis acted somewhat shocked, and Charlotte felt embarrassed even to have thought of buying it, let along displaying it. In the end, she had agreed with Francis that the print was out of character with the rest of the room and not appropriate with children in the house. The print was relegated to the closet, facing the wall.

Now that Francis was gone, she would hang it, she decided, turning it face up again. Why wait? She took it out of the closet and brought it into the bathroom. She hung it somewhat unevenly on the hook where Francis used to keep his robe.

In the closet was a white robe still wrapped in tissue paper. It was too nice, she had always thought, to actually wear. But tonight she took her usual pink bathrobe from its accustomed hook and replaced it with the luxurious white terry cloth one. She turned on the water in the tub and looked at herself in the mirror above the two sinks. The light was usually flattering, but she looked horrible.

Her lips! She ran a finger over them. They were chapped, with flakes of dry skin, still coated with Valerie's cranberry lipstick, clinging to them. Her pale skin was made even paler by foundation applied to conceal her freckles, and the blusher meant to highlight the apples of her high cheekbones stood out sharply in contrast. Her eyes were the worst, reddened with the irritation of unaccustomed make-up. And the tears she'd shed earlier had turned Suzette's carefully applied mascara into raccoon rings.

She turned on the faucet in her sink and reached for the soap, but realized she had to get something gentler to remove the makeup or her eyes would get even redder. She had to get it off. But how, without rubbing her face raw? She seldom wore any foundation and didn't use any creams or cleansers on her face. Her skin was clear, if freckled, and she didn't know how to use makeup the way her daughter Emily did. Emily was always bringing home this or that product from the mall.

She walked through her bedroom, down the long hallway past the hall bath, and into Emily's room. Charlotte skirted tufts of clothes on the floor and rummaged around on Emily's dresser top, where bottles and tubes crowded each other. Aha! Clinique! Emily had apparently caught a Clinique bonus. Charlotte looked through the bag, methodically removing every tube and bottle. Sure enough, there it was, a cleanser designed to remove makeup, appropriately called *Take Off the Day*. There were also, she discovered, condoms.

Good. At least her daughter was protecting herself. Charlotte placed the condoms back where she'd found them. She should have spoken to her, of course, and had not. No wonder the girl wouldn't call her Mom.

There was a scented candle on top of Emily's dresser. Charlotte paused to inhale its fragrance. Hyacinth, the label said. The smell of spring.

Why not, she thought, and grabbed the candle and some matches and retreated to the master bath. She lit the candle and set it on the tiled shelf that surrounded the tub. Then she applied the makeup remover, rubbing the delicate tissues under her eyes carefully. She bent over the sink, soaping her face well with her normal unscented soap and rinsing with plenty of warm water. Much better. By this time, the tub was nearly full, and Charlotte organized her shampoo and washcloths on the ledge next to the tub. The candle had a wonderful scent, reminding her of the corner of the garden where old perennials still bloomed.

If thou of fortune be bereft
And in thy store there be but left two loaves
Sell one and with the dole
Buy hyacinths to feed thy soul.

John Greenleaf Whittier wishes you a merry Christmas. "Have yourself a merry Christmas, Charlotte," she said aloud. "Half a loaf is not better than none, but you have hyacinths."

She lay back in the warm water, trying to quiet her mind, but thoughts persisted. Francis having an affair. Something Natalie had once said made Charlotte giggle. Francis was such a stiff, Natalie had maintained, that his Native American name would be Rod Up His Ass. And yet he had seemed so happy to be holding the tanned woman in his arms. "Rosemary." Charlotte made herself say the name. Natalie had laughed at the woman's name too. Rosemary for remembrance.

Natalie. In so many ways, Natalie had been a good friend. It was she who had offered Charlotte the job. She had been supportive and kind when Charlotte had had to stay home when the kids were sick. She had been entirely sympathetic and discreet when Charlotte had explained that Francis had cheated. Just that afternoon she had invited Charlotte to her home on Christmas Day.

I can't go there now, Charlotte thought. "You're on your own for Christmas, Charlotte my girl," she said aloud.

Oddly, saying it made her feel better. She could face it, she decided. She had damn well better. She had made her bed by telling the monitor about the folder.

The room was warming up. The water was wonderful, almost but not quite too hot. She soaped her legs and lifted them above the water like a star in an old movie. Her polished toes shone likes jewels when she rested her feet on the ledge above the faucets.

Natalie. Her job. Francis. The twins. All lost. *Nought's had, all's spent, where our desire is got without content.* The lament of Lady Macbeth. But what did she, Charlotte, desire? More than what she had. More than this.

She soaped her body and submerged entirely in the tub, plunging herself into this new reality. She could hardly remember the last time she'd taken a tub bath, always opting for a quick morning shower. Sybaritic, she said to herself. This is a sybaritic experience. Another good vocabulary word for the students.

The students. Always, her mind fled to the students. Surely, she could take a bath without them there. "Get out of this tub," she said out loud.

The students. And Francis. And the girls, of course. But now it was just her. Just Charlotte. She soaped and rinsed and soaped again, trying to organize her thoughts. Her job was safe—the man in the blue blazer had assured her of that. Natalie might make her miserable, make her want to transfer, but could not fire her. She was licensed, tenured, in a shortage area.

She had a sheaf of glowing evaluations in her file. She could always work.

Francis? She must stop thinking of him. Scorched earth policy, she thought. All thoughts of what they had had, or what she had fantasized they had had, must be obliterated. It was a matter of survival. She let the water run out of the tub and began rinsing her hair with the hand shower. She took a towel from the warming rack and gently patted herself dry.

The twins. Francis was their father, and the girls loved him. But this was their last year in high school. They were on their way to lives separate from her, from Francis, even from each other. It was painful, but there was no help for it. The family she and Francis had created was broken. She needed to step back. They would return to her, she hoped, as good friends, as best of friends, once they had finished their task of separation. But that was years away. It was time to say goodbye to the past, to begin again.

Charlotte wrapped herself in the white robe and looked at herself in the mirror. This time there was no surprise. It was just Charlotte.

Suddenly the bathroom lights above the mirrored medicine cabinet flickered, came back on, flickered again, and then went out. "Oh no," she said, still speaking out loud. The music stopped and the candle was her only source of light. A power failure. Sometimes they went on for days. It must have something to do with the storm. Where were her flashlights? Her candles? The battery-operated radio?

Holding the candle, she made her way to the stairs, taking slow careful steps around the darkened shapes of the furniture, shining the beam of light. She was stranded, she realized, with no power, no heat. Her car was in the Bronx somewhere. The SUV the twins drove was parked in long-term parking at Bradley International Airport in Hartford.

Downstairs she located matches, flashlights, and extra batteries and set up a flashlight in every room. She put the candle down on the coffee table in the den. The phone! She picked up the phone and yes, there was a dial tone. She checked her cell phone and saw that she was fully charged. She could get help if she needed it. But whom to call? The Baileys were next door. If she needed help, they'd be there for her. But she didn't want to bother them now.

She put on the portable radio. Christmas music. Another damn partridge in the miserable pear tree. With a snap, she turned that off and found a local station. Over three hundred homes were without power, she learned. Staples High School was designated as the emergency destination. Good luck getting over there with no car.

Should she build a fire? Wait a little while. The power might come right back on.

Was it still snowing? She went to the window and pulled the blinds. Yes, in fact, the snow had gotten deeper, with drifts creating hills and valleys on the lawn.

Wait. Lights in a power failure? She peered out the window and saw two headlights coming up her driveway. It was a large car, a dark-colored car, almost invisible in the night. It was him, she realized. Lagakis.

⚭⚭⚭

Valerie's Journal
READ IF YOU WANT
    I got to write after all. When I got home after the last day of school and opened the present Rohan got me, guess what? It was a book. A book to write in. Not from Staples or the dollar store of course. Rohan has class. It's big and comes with its own pen. And it's purple. And the cover is made of genuine purple suede leather. I told you. He has class.
    I didn't have anything for him, but he said that was ok, that he could buy anything he wanted except one thing, and he gave me this look and I knew he meant me. Kind of romantic, but scary. And if he ever knew about J. Crew and my relationship, I think may-

be it wouldn't be so healthy for J. Crew and maybe not for me either. No present yet from J. Crew. He said something about getting it engraved.

Anyway—I'm busy reading Middlemarch *by George Eliot. I took out the oldest book in the school library to get some privacy. Grandma likes to watch me read it with the dictionary looking up every word. She won't let the foster kids go near me when I'm reading that book.*

There's a doctor in the book who's in trouble because he won't give people this medicine that they don't need. His name is Dr. Lydgate. Anyway, they call it strengthening medicine and he's telling the women in the story that it's not helping them and they're looking around for other doctors. Maybe it's like drugs today, making people feel strong. Feel better about everything. Maybe he should just give it to them if it's not hurting them and makes them feel better. I know. The deal is he's lying, which being a doctor is not good. But sometimes you have to lie, right?

CHAPTER 16

Comfort

Holding a flashlight, still in her bare feet, she waved to him from the screened porch, which adjoined the garage. Through the windows of the porch she could see the wind kicking up wildly, blowing snow across the lawn.

"Are you all right?" he said, as he entered the porch. He stamped his feet, releasing bits of snow. "When the power went off, all I could think about was you all alone here. No car."

"You came all the way back?"

"Just from my uncle's house. He's not too far off. I knew you had no car," he said again. "I figured I'd check on you."

"I'm fine."

He ran his flashlight over her. "If you could just see yourself," he said

"I was just getting out of the tub when the lights went out."

He looked down and noticed her bare feet on the green outdoor carpet of the porch. "For the love of God, get back in the house. It's cold as a witch's—it's cold out here."

She beckoned him with her flashlight. "Come inside. Watch—there's a little step up. I'll close the garage door."

He came into the dark kitchen and set a silver package

on the table. She had flashlights lined up along the counter and had placed extra batteries next to the box of cookies.

"Looks like someone was a Girl Scout," he said.

She nodded and then realized he probably could not see her. "Yes," she answered. "Always prepared."

"Good to know. Was that your dinner?" he looked at the cookie box.

"Yes," she confessed. "I just wasn't hungry."

He beamed one of the flashlights on the foil-wrapped package. "My aunt. She always sends me away with care packages. That's for you, if you haven't eaten. It's actually still hot."

"She knows you're here?"

"You don't understand my family or you wouldn't ask that."

"Thank her. And thank you," Charlotte said. "But you could have just called."

"I don't know your number, or even if your phone was working."

"Thank you." It felt like all she was doing was saying thank you.

"Well, enjoy the moussaka. It's good cold too, but better hot. I guess I better get started back to my uncle's house. Here's my number." He handed her a slip of paper. "You can call if you need anything."

"Are they expecting you to come right back? Your aunt and uncle?"

He hesitated.

"Why don't you stay a while, at least until it lets up? Keep me company."

"Better not, I think. I'll stop back tomorrow. Give you a lift back to Gus's place if you need it. If your car's ready, that is."

She could not face an evening alone with the portable radio. "Wait," she said. "Do you know how to start a fire? I know the fireplaces were cleaned last summer, but I haven't actually lit them myself."

"Here I thought you were a Girl Scout. Just kidding. I'd be happy to. Just point me in the right direction. I'm an expert." He pulled his shoulders back as he said that.

"There's a den off the kitchen. Supposed to be a library, really. That's the little room where I live."

She led him into her lair, her feet grateful for the rug. Charlotte placed her flashlight on the coffee table and sat down on the sofa, her legs tucked behind her. She saw his gaze fall upon her bare ankles, and she closed the opening of her robe more securely.

"You look like the Christmas angel in that white thing," he said. "The light shining in the darkness. But you ought to put some warm clothes on. This place is going to get pretty cold if the power doesn't come on."

"I'll stay like this until you've got the fire going," she said. "You may need me here to help you find stuff."

She didn't want to go upstairs in the dark. And she didn't want to change. The robe was so soft and warm and it was brand new. She did not want to put on anything that wasn't brand new. He walked over to the fireplace and poked around. He was the kind of person who could not be still for very long, she thought.

He picked up the old clock from the mantle. "Nice," he said.

She almost said, "Be careful," but she did not. "It was my mother's. There's a picture of her on the bookcase. I'll show it to you when the lights come on."

"Oh, I'll probably be long gone by then. Just hold the flashlight over here."

She came up behind him and ran her beam over the mantle, a simple piece of gray stone, which held the clock. It chimed the half-hour—just one ding. The long evening stretched far ahead.

He startled when the clock chimed, jumped back a little, nearly stepping on her foot, but she moved away in time.

"I don't want to crush you with these size twelves," he said. "Sit back over there on the sofa."

"I'll be fine," she protested, but she sat down, drawing her feet up under the robe.

Outside, the storm was still roaring. The sound of the windows rattling broke the silence, and then all was still. She could no longer see the beam of his flashlight, but her own, which she had set on the coffee table, gave a little light.

"Matches," he said, like a surgeon calling for a scalpel. He turned sideways to look at her and ran light over the fireplace. "I see you've got some wood, and kindling, but where are your matches?"

"Here," she said, pointing her own beam on the little metal box on the wall. "Plenty of matches."

"Hold the flashlight over here so I can see. No, stay on the sofa," he told her. "Just direct the beam."

"Yes, sir."

"Sorry. I don't mean to give orders. I just want to get your house warmed up for you."

"Don't worry about it. I'm just glad you're here."

"I'll have this going in no time."

He removed his coat, placing it on the arm of the sofa, and went about the task she had set for him. The jacket was still warm, and she moved down, pulling it over her cold feet. In a relatively short time, he had the beginning of a fire started. She could see his broad back silhouetted against the glowing wood.

His cell phone rang. He took it from his pocket and looked at the number. "My uncle." He turned his back slightly to her, and began speaking in Greek. He laughed once, harshly, and then said in English, "See you at Yiayia's," and hung up.

Charlotte said, "Does your uncle know where you are?"

He chuckled. "Like I said before. You don't know my family. Once Gus got a look at you, there was a telephone call from one aunt to the next. Theo driving with a woman to Connecticut. Who is she? What does she look like? Where does she live? About a dozen cousins got in on the

act. They know who you are, where you live, and where I
am."

"Sounds like a great family."

"Pain in the ass," he said. "But, yeah, they're okay."

"You told them you're all right?"

"Actually, my uncle said it's turning into quite an ice
storm. He said the roads have slicked over. I'm sorry, Charlotte, but I may have to stay here tonight."

❧❧❧

Valerie's Journal
DO NOT READ!
*I wish I had invisible ink, only one day I'm proba-
bly going to want to read this entry over. At least I
hope I'll want to. It calls to mind this poem we had in
class, "The Road Not Taken." This is strictly personal and confidential and when I finish I'm planning to
fold the page over and staple it shut the way you said
we could, Ms. Murphy. Just in case, you made a mistake and you are reading this. DON'T!*

*Well, anyway, I've made up my mind and I'm go-
ing. Going to meet my boy and just tell my grandmother I've got to go to the library for a paper.*

*I got the idea from watching this teacher Ms.
Knudsen who drags this fat book around with her,
underlining stuff in yellow highlighter. She has to do
a paper. I wish I could get one of those highlighters in
purple but it's a library book. So I got some Post-its
at the dollar store. You know what color—and told
Grandma I have to do a paper.*

*But my grandmother would take me out this life if
she ever knew. I mean, Murphy had to personally
write her a note on school stationery before she even
let me sign up for the library workshop program. So
how to get protection?*

J. Crew and me. I guess this is it. It will be my first time. Ms. Trombetta's apartment is empty and if I meet him there—it's in Riverdale—we can finally be alone. That's how he put it.

First, I was suspicious. Suzette would tell me I told you so. Boys only want you for one thing and all that. But I think I love him. I can talk to him, and he tells me stuff too. The way I figure it, I might be in love and you should probably do it with the first guy you're in love with.

But no baby. That's my line in the sand. I've got to make sure. I'm embarrassed to ask Lagakis or even Murphy. I don't like to walk in that aisle in the drug store. But you know the saying, No glove, no love. That's going to be my motto.

It kind of began to get serious a while ago, in fact, but I had to cover it up. Sometimes I feel that my whole life is a cover up. But what else can I do?

If I asked China, it will be like taking an ad out in the newspaper. And Suzette—she'd kill J. Crew before she let me go there.

I figured if anybody saw us together in Riverdale we'll just say we met at the workshop, and of course the funeral, and just keep walking.

But guess what he's coming to my school for a memorial for his aunt and then we can start to act like we actually know each other. My grandmother is coming to the memorial too being she's head of the Parents Organization.

Anyway, thank God for the phone because I really look forward to his texts and I'm keeping my grandmother happy so she'll let me keep the phone. I'll make up something.

J. Crew knows about my mother's drug problem and my father in jail, and he says I'm like a hero to him. It's funny because so many other kids in my school have the same thing going on even worse. I at least have my grandmother. Maybe that's what makes him special to me—that he thinks I'm a big deal just for handling my regular life.

CHAPTER 17

Comfort and Joy

The wind was howling. A tree branch fell against the window and then crashed to the ground.

"You may get some tree damage tonight. What do you have, about an acre?"

"More. A lake too."

He inclined his head toward her and took a breath. "What *is* that?"

"Just bubble bath stuff. And a candle. Hyacinth."

"That's like Cynthia backward, that word. Well, I took a shower too, at my uncle's. I was starting to smell like cat piss."

Charming. He was pacing around the room. She patted the sofa cushion next to her.

"I'm no good at sitting." But he joined her on the sofa, leaning forward, feet braced on the floor, hands on his knees. His back was a broad dark outline against the firelight.

"You should put something else on, Charlotte. Something warmer."

She ran her hands over the soft fabric of her robe. "I'm comfortable."

He got up again. "Makes one of us. I need to move around."

"You're impossible."

"No, Charlotte, that would be you," he said. "I'm going to get the moussaka."

He grabbed the flashlight from the coffee table where he had placed it, upended, like a little torch.

"But I'm not hungry."

"You will be. Stay," he commanded.

He made for the kitchen, and she stared into the fire, listening to him opening cupboards and rattling things. She hoped he wouldn't break anything. "Knives and forks in the drawer next to the sink," she called out.

"Right."

Francis would have expected her to fetch the dish. She placed her wrist to her nose, inhaled the scent, fading already. *Buy hyacinths to feed thy soul.* Francis had wanted to get rid of them, old flowers in a forgotten corner of the property, missing more petals each spring, but she had saved them.

"It's actually still warm." Lagakis had returned, balancing the flashlight, an aluminum foil casserole, and some utensils. He set the dish on the coffee table and peeled back the foil. The aroma of cinnamon rose up from it, and she realized she was starving. He chuckled as she took a bite, and then another and another.

"Guess you didn't like that."

"I'm sorry—I hardly left any for you."

"I had plenty at my aunt's."

He was walking around again, holding the flashlight to books and photographs on the built-in shelves.

He paused at a picture of Francis with the twins. "The kids are beautiful. No surprise there. Look at their mother."

"Cut it out."

"Hey—what did I say? They're nice looking kids. And they do look like you."

"What about you? Do you have any children? "

"None that I know about." Then his tone changed. "There I go again. Asshole of the month." He sat next to her on the sofa, hunched over a little. Flickering light from the fire settled on the ring he wore on his left hand. "Charlotte. I'd have loved kids. But we couldn't have any. Bad swimmers."

"I'm sorry," she said.

"Me too."

He turned to face her. "Say, Charlotte can I ask *you* something?"

"That depends."

"I thought kids usually stay with their mothers. Why are you all by yourself here, without your daughters? Don't you want them for Christmas?"

She considered making up a story. But she found herself answering truthfully.

"Theo, Christmas this year is really hard. The kids are upset. I thought they needed to do something different. Maybe we all did. So they're with Francis and maybe even—" *Say it.* "—the woman he left me for."

He let out a low whistle. "He left *you?*"

She was able to speak quite normally. "In a manner of speaking. He cheated on me. He claims he doesn't want to break up."

Lagakis shrugged. "That's different. He'll be back."

"I don't think so."

"I'd bet money on it," he replied. "And you'll take him back."

"You'd lose both bets. You probably think I'm not a very good mother. Letting the girls go to him."

"You wouldn't know how to *not* be a good mother."

Suddenly, he reached over and hugged her to him, pressing her face into the buttons on his shirt and taking her by surprise. She tensed, and he withdrew his arm. "Excuse me. I always forget and hug people."

"And I don't know what to do when people hug me."

"Well, you can't help it, being Irish," he said. "It must be hell."

"Being Irish?"

He laughed. "That too. Is it me, or is it warming up in here?"

"I'm warm," she said, "but my feet are freezing."

He grabbed one foot with large warm hands. *Thank you, Monroe.* At least her feet were smooth and soft.

"Go get some socks. Your feet are ice cubes." He put his hands in his lap. "I'm sorry. You probably think I'm coming on to you or something. But I plan on being a perfect gentleman."

"Are you?" She stretched her feet out on to the coffee table and closer to the hearth. Firelight caught the design Valerie had painted on her toes.

Theo's eyes followed her movement. "I bet Valerie gave you those snowflake things. I'd love to have seen your face when she did."

"Not my usual style," Charlotte admitted.

"You have style?"

"That's rather harsh. Yes. I have style. It's called the librarian look."

He gestured at her robe. "Tonight you look like an angel without wings. But those outfits you wear at school." She sensed him smiling in the dark. "I bet the boys in your class are always asking you to write on the board."

"How did you know that?"

"'Cause that's what I would do. You have a gorgeous ass."

She punched his arm hard, making no impact.

"Charlotte I used to think you were a goody-goody. Until that day when you pocketed Valerie's referral."

"Then what did you think?"

"I thought you were a *pain* in the ass."

She imagined his dimples as he smiled at his own joke. "Theo, Valerie didn't deserve that referral. Why did you want to let it stand?"

"She threatened a teacher. Yeah, she's a nice kid, but the rule is there for a reason."

"And you always follow rules?"

"I see I'm not going to win this argument." He rose and walked over to the sheer curtains on the window. "I'm going to close your drapes, if you call these things drapes. But they're so thin. It's hardly worth it."

"Not practical, but I like the light in the morning."

He closed the thin curtains and sat back down. "I guess you're not practical. Maybe you never had to be. But you were brave today. Blowing the whistle on good old Natalie."

"Brave? Or stupid? And she asked me to go to her house for Christmas."

"You are in deep shit," he said. "And it's my fault."

The wind moaned a little louder, and something thudded against the windows. He had both his hands over his face.

"Your fault? You knew what was in the folder?"

"Bertie dropped hints."

"I see. And all the while I thought you just felt too bad to go through her things."

"Oh I did—that too." He sounded miserable.

"But you wanted *me* to be the one to handle the folder."

"Believe me, I'm not proud of that. So, Charlotte, do you hate me? I fucked up your little deal at school."

"I fucked it up myself. And I'd do it again. And, no, Theo. I don't hate you."

He drew a deep breath and released it. He grasped her hand. "Thank God. I've been feeling like a shit all day. I'm a shit and, Charlotte—" The wind was rattling again. "What about upstairs?"

For a moment, she thought he wanted to go up to the bedrooms with her. But then she realized that he was talking about the drapes.

"We have—there are thick drapes upstairs. I'm sure I closed them when I took my bath. But I'll go check. I'll put some socks on too."

"And put some clothes on. Have a little mercy on a poor sinner like me."

He went to the window to check the storm, closed the

sheer curtains again, and took the Moussaka off the coffee table. "I'll bring this back."

"Don't bother. I'll take care of it later."

"I need to move. I could sure use a glass of cold water," he said.

"Do you want something stronger?"

"Water's fine. I'll get it."

She was afraid he would hurt himself, fumbling around for a glass. She followed him into the kitchen, but he did not hear her bare feet. As he turned around, starting back to the den, they collided like two magnets in the dark room. She pretended to trip and he caught her by the elbows. She stood there, almost but not quite, in his arms.

There was a horrible crack and crash. He rushed to window. "Oh shit, Charlotte. It looks like one of your trees came down."

He was blocking her view. She tapped him on the shoulder. "Did it hit your car?"

"No. Don't even think about that. But your driveway appears to be blocked."

"Let me see."

He took a step back to let her stand in front of him. As she stared out at the snow, she thought he kissed the top of her head.

"I think you're trapped here," she said.

"What a horrible predicament," he whispered. She could feel him behind her, definitely aroused.

Charlotte fought a duel with her brain and lost. She turned and put her arms around his neck, pulled his face down, and kissed his lips. They were soft and full, and she was surprised at how well they fit her own.

He won't want you after tonight, her brain said. *So what,* she answered it.

He kissed her hair, her forehead, her cheeks, and her chin. He kissed her lips lightly, soft short kisses and then a long kiss.

He was a good kisser. A very good kisser. A+, she

thought, and then realized she was putting a grade on his kiss. She wondered what he thought of hers.

It felt like forever since she had been kissed. She did not close her eyes, but he did. But then he stopped kissing her. She took his hand and led him, guided him, back into the den and onto the couch.

"So much for being a perfect gentleman."

"A perfect gentleman is not what's needed."

"I'm scared," he whispered. "I'm probably an idiot. Mr. Rebound."

"I'm scared too."

"The only thing you have to be afraid of is me following you around school like a puppy. A very large puppy!"

All the while, his fingers were working on the double knot of her sash. He untied it and pushed her robe aside. His hands were reading her like braille.

He can't really see me, she thought, with my stretch marks and scars and freckles and flaws. I'm invisible. It's dark and I can be the perfect woman he thinks he wants.

He was kissing her throat. It felt wonderful. It was going to happen. It had to happen. It had been so long. She didn't want to think about anything but this tenderness of touching, of being touched in the dark.

"Like silk. I knew you would be. Skin like silk." And he kissed her cheeks and her lips again.

There was the crackle of the fire, there was the wind rattling the window, there was this sensation of being caressed in the dark. She breathed deeply, opening herself up to the light pressure of his hands. How had she lived without this for so long? *Why* had she lived without this for so long?

His hand lowered, stroked her backside and thighs. "Your skin is so soft. You're so soft."

Oh God. He stopped.

She ran her hand along his erection. "You're not," she said, "so soft."

Don't stop, Theodore, she thought. Put your hand back where it was. Don't ever stop.

But he had stopped. "We should," he began, and she thought of the condom in Emily's room. Of the ones in her briefcase, now far away in the Bronx. But she could not bear to stop.

"It's all right."

"Are you sure?" he said.

"Oh, Theo. I am so sure."

CHAPTER 18

Aubade

And now good morrow to our waking souls,
Which watch not one another out of fear.~ John Donne

Our waking souls. Charlotte woke, his knees against the back of hers, his arms around her arms. Sunshine penetrated the light draperies, its brightness heightened by the snow. Aubade. Aubade, a love poem in which a lover tells the sun not to rise. Poems flew in and out of her brain, and she understood them all after last night.

But she really, really had to pee.

She tried to slip away from his arm, and he merely tightened his grip. He was naked under the throw that had covered them both. She looked down and saw that his arm was covered with dark hair. She stroked it. He did not awaken. He was warm and she did not want to leave, but the pressure on her bladder was insistent. She elbowed him in the ribs, and he woke up fully, his arm now a steel cage.

He pulled her even closer, kissed the back of her neck. Golden sunbeams danced before her. *And all at once I saw a crowd, a host of golden daffodils.*

"Let me up. I have to go to the bathroom," she said.

His arm loosened and she sat up. She found her robe and put it on, and she tucked the throw they had been sleeping under around him.

"Look at you this morning," he said. "How are you?"

"I have to go to the bathroom. And I'm thinking about this poem," she said. "'Daffodils.'"

He pulled the throw closer around himself. "English teachers."

She left the first floor powder room to him and went upstairs to the master bathroom. After the relief of emptying her bladder, she washed herself. The water was cold. When she looked in the mirror, she saw that her face was flushed, her lips dark pink and swollen from kissing. *Look at you this morning.*

This was the good morrow. She wanted to think about last night. She wanted to think about poems. She wanted a cup of strong coffee and a big chocolate donut. She wanted to make love again. And again.

On her way back downstairs, she paused to look out the window on the landing. Dazzling. Fairyland. The snow had stopped falling. The sky was already that extraordinary electric blue of certain winter days. The apple trees in the back yard were coated with ice, and crystal drops hung from them, sparkling in the sun.

In the yard next door, Kai, the Baileys' dog—part Husky that he was—frolicked in the snow, his upwardly curved tail waving madly at several brown birds perched on the feeder.

An icicle fell from the overhang of the Baileys' porch and Kai barked at it. The beautiful night, the beautiful morning, this dazzling new day, slipping by, minute by minute. She hurried downstairs.

He was waiting for her in the kitchen, an anthology from her bookcase in front of him. She was disappointed to see him dressed already, but it was freezing. He looked out of place, too large for the smallish kitchen chair. He closed his eyes and shook his head.

"What's the matter?" she asked.

"I hate this stuff," he said. "Poetry. You are going to be a pain in the ass." He patted her ass to emphasize his point. "Nice," he said and pulled her onto his lap.

"I feel so sorry for you," she said. "Having to read poetry."

"Me too," he said, pulling her close, kissing her neck.

After a minute he continued, "The poem. Is this the one?" and read, "'I wandered lonely as a cloud.'"

She nodded. "That's right," she said. "'Daffodils,' by Wordsworth."

"I think I get it," he said.

"Isn't it beautiful?"

"This part? The *pensive mood*. Are you pensive about your husband? I'm guessing he'll call soon, on Christmas, probably. All ready to come back. And you'll go back to him. And I don't blame you."

It was true. She had fantasized about Francis calling, renouncing Rosemary, begging her forgiveness, asking to come back.

"But if you do," Theo continued, "that's it for me. I never went to kindergarten and I don't share with others."

She turned and put her hands lightly around his neck, pretending to choke him.

"After last night? Go back to Francis? Never! You, you are so thick sometimes," she said. "You don't get it at all. Listen.

'They flash upon that inward eye
Which is the bliss of solitude?
And then my heart with pleasure fills
And dances with the daffodils.'

"Don't you see?" she said. "Listen to the words."

"I hear them," he said. "But I know he'll call," he persisted. "And then what will you do?"

"It's *nothing* about him," she said. "The poem."

"I'll have to work on that one," he said.

"You don't get it at all. The poem says that—something beautiful, like daffodils in spring, or the way you made me feel last night—I'll always remember. Thinking about last night will keep me going when I feel lonely or pensive."

"As in, we'll always have Paris? Only for us it's daffodils?"

"More than that."

The light in the kitchen was extraordinary, with beams of
sunshine dancing all over the kitchen tiles. Outside, the
noise of snow plows and ordinary traffic.

"Last night," she said, turning around on his lap to poke
a finger in his dimple.

"For me, too, sweetheart."

"It reminds me of another poem, 'The Good Morrow.'"

He smiled his Steinway smile. He sat up straight. "Do I
have to read that too?"

"Oh, yes."

He raised his eyes to the ceiling as though addressing
God himself. "English teachers. You gotta love 'em." His
brown eyes beamed with golden light as he continued to
smile at her. "Which, obviously, I do."

CHAPTER 19

Back to the Bronx

Charlotte finally went upstairs to get dressed. Shivering, she layered a thick gray sweater and wool slacks over silk long johns bought for a ski weekend, flinching when the garments, icy cold from lying in the unheated dresser, touched her body. She started to put the robe away, changed her mind, and carried it back downstairs. Theo stood in the doorway that connected the kitchen to the den, watching as she draped the robe over the sofa where they had made love.

Unshaven, looming over her in an awful plaid shirt she had not noticed last night, Theo resembled a repairman on a lunch break. A sexy repairman.

"Any regrets?" he asked softly when she came to stand near him.

She reached up, kissed his cheek. "Absolutely not."

He did not return her kiss, kept his hands in his pockets. "Not yet, maybe."

"What's the matter? Are you having regrets?"

"Truthfully? Yes."

She looked into his eyes. Their expression was unreadable. "Already?"

His face assumed the smirk he usually wore in school. "Yes, Charlotte. I regret having to read poetry."

"Be serious."

He bit his lip. "I'm seriously hungry. Any white bread and mayonnaise around?"

"I'd rather have leftover moussaka," she said, and his expression softened.

"So would I, sweetheart."

In the kitchen, they sat, knees touching, and shared the remains of his aunt's dish in silence, spooning cold layers of eggplant straight from the casserole. "You were joking, weren't you? About having regrets?"

"Your power's back," he responded.

"My power?" She was so caught up trying to understand his behavior that she took a few seconds to realize that he was talking about the fact that the lights had blinked on and strains of Mozart were coming from the CD. Not her power over him.

He turned in the direction of the door, tapping one foot. He couldn't leave yet. There was the blocked driveway. She hoped the tree guy was too busy for her. But they were on a preferred customer list. Francis paid a fortune to be on that list.

"Coffee? Would you like me to make coffee?" she offered.

"Coffee? You are a goddess." He smiled, but began to crack his knuckles. His eyes kept moving toward the door.

Charlotte measured out Francis's favorite French roast, defrosted an apple tart in the microwave, poured cream into her favorite little pitcher with the blue and white flowers. Theo stopped cracking his knuckles, thank goodness, but instead stirred his coffee incessantly, absently, letting it spill over the cup into the saucer.

When he finally stopped and sipped the coffee, Charlotte heard scraping noises of snow shovels, and then, the whirring of an electric saw.

Instantly, Theo was at the back door, peering through the window but keeping well back behind the cheerful country curtains. "There's a guy out clearing the tree. When did you call him?" He kept his voice conspiratorial, almost a whisper.

She came to stand in front of him as she had the night before, but he stepped away from her, out of sight. The morning sunshine had disappeared, and the curtains framed an expanse of gray sky and white snow.

"Why are you whispering? They work for our arborist. We're good customers."

"*Our arborist?*" His laugh was a snort.

She turned to see his lips curved once more in that familiar smirk.

He sat back down at the table, traced large stubby fingers over the blue and white floral placemat. "Fancy." He reached into his pocket, pulled out his phone. "I better check in with Gus. See how your car is doing."

He turned from her and began speaking in Greek, his voice low. She strained, trying to decipher meaning from unfamiliar sounds. She heard laughter from the other end. Theo listened for a while, and then said something that brought the conversation to a close.

He put his phone in his pocket, placed both hands on the table in a motion that nearly upset the coffee cups. "You're all set, Charlotte. The car is ready. We should go now, so you can drive back before this stuff freezes over."

Charlotte nodded. Apparently, she would be driving back alone. He checked his pockets. "Don't want to leave anything behind," he said.

She heard her voice stiff, offended. "I do work with you. You'd get it back."

"That's not—I just mean no incriminating evidence."

"Is this a crime scene?" she asked.

He did not reply. He returned to the couch, folding the robe she'd left there and handing it to her like a flag to a soldier's mother. "You should put this away."

"It's staying there," she replied. *And so am I,* she thought. Whatever happened with Theo, she would not return to the bed she had shared with Francis.

Charlotte tidied the kitchen, washed coffee cups and the moussaka dish, wiped the counters, rinsed the sponges, and wrung them out thoroughly, the familiar tasks incongruous with the fact of Theo on her sofa.

"Want me to help you?"

"I don't mind this kind of work."

"You look like you've had some practice."

"A cleaning woman taught me."

"That figures."

She felt the need to wipe that smirk off his face. "A cleaning woman known as my mother. That's what she did for a living. I used to go with her sometimes. She had high standards."

"I would never have guessed."

"That she had high standards?"

"That your mother . . . and now you have all this."

"Does that make a difference?"

"I don't know. I'm sorry. Am I being an asshole?"

"You know you are. The question is why."

Theo didn't answer. Instead he found his tweed jacket, draped carefully on a kitchen chair, and put it on. "I better check out my car."

"Wait. I'm coming with you." She went to the closet and pulled out the coat she'd been wearing the day before. In silence he followed her out the back door and waited while she locked it.

The workers had been thorough. Not only had they cleared the tree, they'd plowed the driveway, shoveled the back steps, and cleaned most of the snow from Theo's car. After settling Charlotte in the passenger seat, he got in and started up the engine. Cold air blew in immediately.

"It will warm up in a minute," he said.

She nodded, shivering. *I hope you do too*, she thought.

Abruptly he popped the trunk and got out. He walked around the vehicle as though inspecting it for damage. He took a roll of paper towels from the trunk and rubbed some condensation from the side mirrors. He also took an envelope from his pocket and scribbled something on it. Finally he got back in the car, clicked on his seat belt, and steered slowly down the long driveway.

Charlotte's neighbor Jack Bailey, on a walk with his dog Kai, stood at the Murphy mailbox, which was nearly buried in plowed snow. He waved, indicating they should stop.

Charlotte opened her window. "Hi, Jack."

"I see you got cleared," Bailey said. "I need the name of your guy. Ours won't be here for days."

"We use Norris," Charlotte said. "But he's not taking any new customers."

Jack was eyeing Theo's license plate. "Visitor from New York?"

"My colleague," Charlotte started to explain, "Had a breakdown and—"

"Jack Bailey," Jack introduced himself to Theo, who stared straight ahead.

Not knowing what else to do, Charlotte said, "Jack, This is Theo Lagakis."

Theo nodded and revved the engine.

Jack's blond eyebrows rose to the top of his navy blue watch cap.

"We're in a hurry. He's giving me a ride back to the garage," Charlotte said.

"Drive safe," Jack said. "Hi to Francis."

Jack's wife Sally, clad only in a warm-up suit despite the cold, came out on her front porch, and waved across the snowy yard. From the passenger seat, Charlotte waved back automatically.

"Nosy neighbors?" Theo asked as he pulled away. "I think she wanted to get a look at me."

"Just friendly," she said. "You were very rude."

"They'll chalk that up to the New York license plate," he said. "They saw the car here all night. That's not good. It's better to have neighbors who mind their own business."

Charlotte refrained from talking about good fences. "What are you worried about?"

"Don't play naive, Charlotte. I've been through a divorce. It's tough, especially for women. You need to avoid even the appearance of impropriety."

"You sound like something out of the nineteenth century. Don't worry. Sally is a friend. A good friend to me."

"Yeah. Like Natalie."

She reclined her seat. The warmth of the heater after the cold house, the motion of the car, the need not to think about what had just happened, put her to sleep.

"We're here," he said, startling her.

The car had stopped on a narrow one-way street. A nearby overpass afforded a glimpse of cars and trucks driving very fast on a highway. On the sidewalk, the snow was piled up in mountains, already grimy. Next to the passenger door, a narrow path led to a low building: GUS'S GARAGE. The letters of the sign, once a dark blue, were faded into near invisibility. Adjoining the garage was a parking lot protected by a high metal fence, with barbed wire circles on the top. It was filled with cars covered with snow, except for one, facing in the direction of the locked gate. Her car looked as clean as if it had just emerged from her own garage.

The street was too narrow to admit more than one car. Cars were backed up behind them, honking vociferously. A man wearing a hooded jacket got out of his car and shook his fist. Lagakis put an arm up in an apology wave and said to Charlotte that she would have to get out and go into the garage by herself.

"I can't park here," Theo said. "But I called Gus just now. He's inside waiting for you."

"Does he know? About us? Last night?"

"Of course not."

Charlotte had no choice but to believe this. How else could she walk into the shop alone?

"I'll drive around the block until you come out. Will you follow me to my place?"

The relief of it. He looked as though he feared she might

actually say no. "Thank you," she said. "I was afraid...not of being here, but that you were finished with me."

"My God. Can't you fucking see I'm trying to take care of you?"

"Then drive slowly. I always lose people when I have to follow them."

The honking was insistent.

"You would need a knife to cut me loose. A very large knife. But just in case, here's my address," and he withdrew the scrap of paper from his pocket. He'd scribbled an address on it. He lived in Riverdale.

Her car turned over nicely. Charlotte paid, using Francis's American Express card. Gus took the card without comment.

From outside, Theo honked the horn twice, paused, and hit it twice again. He had already made the journey around the block. Gus came around from behind the counter and stopped the traffic while she pulled out of the lot. When she thanked him, he merely smiled and waved her off. She was very glad to leave that block.

Theo drove slowly, making sure she was behind him as he negotiated the narrow streets. He seemed to know which streets would be plowed and which would not.

It was a relief to reach Riverdale, the nicest neighborhood of the Bronx, plenty of stately houses, even more clusters of apartment buildings. There would be no place to park, with the piled up snow hardening into ice mountains, and cars that had yet to be dug out. He led her to a parking garage under his apartment building, indicated a space where she should park. "Keep your car in my space. Then we can ride around and figure out where to put mine."

The space he found, finally, was a few blocks away. Once again, she did not have the proper footwear.

"Don't you own a pair of boots?" he said.

"I didn't realize I'd be walking."

At one point, he picked her up to carry her across a muddy crossing.

"Sir Galahad," she said, into his ear.

"It's faster this way," he replied.

"Are we in a hurry?"

"I am."

∽ↄ∾ↄ

The apartment was dreary, situated on a low floor, and she got a quick impression of all-purpose white walls and neutral beige carpet when he unlocked the door. But once again he picked her up and he carried her to bed, like a romantic hero on a long awaited bridal night. A laundry packet of shirts was sitting on top of a snack table, one shirt taken out. It was probably the one he'd worn to school yesterday. The rest of the room was messy and crowded, with newspapers and books spilling everywhere. Nothing she would ever want to read. Thick history texts. Biographies of politicians. A worn *Physician's Desk Reference*. No fiction at all. It was hard for her to even picture him reading anything. Still, he must have been to college somewhere.

On a cheap folding snack table next to the bed was a radio, a cell phone charger, and a picture of a family of four. She recognized the young Theo immediately, a chubby little boy with dimples and huge tombstone teeth. He stood in front of a tall woman, presumably his mother. Her hand was on Theo's shoulder. An older boy, definitely a relative— possibly, Charlotte thought, his cousin Gus—stood beside Theo in front of the father. Theo saw her look at the picture but did not comment. Instead, he invited her to sit on his bed, took off her shoes and socks, and simply held her feet with hands that were miraculously warm.

She leaned back on soft pillows and drew him to her.

"Christ, it's good you're here," he whispered.

That he could be so tender and yet so eager pulled her body to his with an electric charge she had not known could exist. She put her arms around him. And it was even better than the night before. A series of tiny explosions, like a string of firecrackers, and then sheer loveliness. Rainbows.

"This is trouble, Charlotte."

"I don't care."

☙❧

Valerie's Journal
DO NOT READ!

When it snowed so hard I figured the plan would have to be cancelled and I wasn't really that upset because believe you me I was scared. But no—the library was open the next day and my boy sent me a text that all was go and I decided to just find some drug store in Riverdale and buy my own condom. Nobody over there would know me. And I didn't want to ask J if he had them because what if that wasn't what he had in mind? I don't want to give him ideas, although I'm pretty sure he has them.

Anyway, J. met me at the bus stop. He doesn't even wear a hat and his ears were all red. I couldn't stop at the drug store and I figured what the hell let's just see what happens and we started walking through the snow and the slush and I'm looking around just to make sure there's nobody who knows me. It's mad hilly in Riverdale and we were walking up this place he calls the terrace. And then it was like a nightmare I heard my teachers' voices. And there they were. Murphy and Lagakis. And he was carrying her I heard her say, "Are we in a hurry?" and he answered "I am."

I got scared then, and I said to Drew, "Oh my God I'm busted those are my teachers" but he said "Don't worry, they're in their own world can't you see?" And it was ok.

Then I thought I saw somebody from Rohan's crew

then, and who knows maybe they're up here in Riverdale too, so I pulled J. into a drug store. And who do you think was in the drug store but Mr. Eugene the assistant principal but he went out right past me and I don't think he even saw me.

Well, I figured I better say something. I remember what our counselor said. You could die of embarrassment. So I said to J, "Do we need protection?" and I swear he didn't even know what I was talking about for a minute and then his ears got even more red and he said "Not to worry." Then we went up to his aunt's place and the rest well it's embarrassing but we were just mostly talking. We talked for like four hours and he read stuff to me out of the books his aunt had there.

That place had more books than the library and he said when he was little he used to go up there and his aunt which is our Ms. Trombetta of course used to make him read to her. He said she was a special person in his life. So just when it was almost time for me to leave he leaned over and kissed me. I swear that's all. I had remembered to write a lot of stuff in my notebook for after when my grandmother checks it. Trombetta actually had some book about Middlemarch with notes and I copied that.

So nothing happened which is cool. Suzette always says it's only sex. China says she's in love. Me, I'm more mixed up than I ever was.

Chapter 20

Halcyon Days

Afterward, when Theo went to use the bathroom, Charlotte surveyed his apartment, wearing the shirt he had just taken off. She sniffed under the arms, liking the smell. His bedroom was small, dominated by the large bed. She peeked through cheap plastic blinds on the single window. A family of four was entering a minivan, the children wearing bright knitted caps. One of the children dropped a mitten in the snow. Charlotte wanted to weep, remembering mittens and being a family of four.

Theo tapped her shoulder and turned her around. "I've got the shower running. Heat, hot water, and light. The better to see you, my dear," he said with a leer, waggling thick eyebrows.

"That makes me nervous," she confessed. "The moment of truth. Not dark like last night. You looking at me."

"Are you out of your mind?" He slipped his shirt from her. "You must know you're beautiful. And besides. You're Charlotte."

"Look at these," she pointed to silvery stretch marks on her breasts and belly.

He kissed the places she pointed to. "Even more beautiful for that. These are badges of honor. You gave life. I can't."

"At least we don't have to bother with those repulsive condoms. Do we?" she asked.

"I guess," he said. "We kind of skipped that step last night. But I gave to the Red Cross at school. I'm clean. And, Charlotte, it's been a long time."

"A long time for me. I'm sure you could tell. And I gave blood too. No, no call back."

The bathroom was tiny. A framed diploma hung over the toilet. She leaned forward to inspect it. A masters. All teachers had to have masters. Hers was in English Education. His was in Administration and Supervision.

"In case I run out of toilet paper," he said. "Come on in. The water's fine."

She gave herself a quick shake and entered the shower. His lemon soap made the small area smell like a citrus grove. Under streaming warm water, she soaped his furry chest and drew a heart in the suds. He put his hand over hers. "Don't break it."

For their dinner, he defrosted still another of his aunt's care-packages, a lemony chicken dish, enough to feed four people.

"Why does she give you so much food?" Charlotte asked.

They ate at a card table in a small dining ell off his living room, sitting on unmatched folding chairs. He explained that when he'd gotten divorced he and his ex had sold their home and all its furnishings.

"Did your ex get along with your family?"

"Who do you think set us up? Greek on Greek. Let's compare bankbooks and make a deal."

"Are all of your family in some kind of business? I remember you once said flowers, fur, and food."

"It's a big family, Charlotte. Some of us went on to college, others didn't. All types of people—rich and poor—and everybody knows everybody else's business."

She recited a bit of childhood doggerel: "'Rich man, poor man, beggarman, thief—doctor, lawyer, Indian chief.'"

"That's about right. Everything but the Indian chief," he said mischievously.

"That would be politically incorrect."

"Yeah, I'd never want to be that."

"We'll call it a Native American chief, then," she said and told her teepee wigwam joke.

He groaned and asked what she would like to drink. When she suggested wine, he took a bottle of champagne from the refrigerator, opened it, poured her a glass, but did not take any himself.

"This is delicious," she said, sipping it. "Aren't you having some?"

He took a swallow of water. "That wine was a present when I retired. I was saving it for an occasion, which this is. I don't drink. You're not driving tonight. Go ahead, if you enjoy it."

"Is there a reason why you don't drink?" she said.

"If I tell you, I don't want you to feel sorry for me. I'm fine now."

Charlotte wondered if he was a recovered alcoholic.

"I made a resolution. I always want to be able to react on time. To drive, if I need to. Drinking slows your reactions, dulls the senses."

She put her glass down.

"No, go ahead. Enjoy the wine. There's another reason I don't drink. I don't like to think about it. I don't like to talk about it."

And then, after a pause, he told her about the Christmas he was nine. A car crash. His father had been driving drunk. "Careless bastard," he said. "Taking chances with her. With my mother."

She picked up her glass, took a deep swallow. "Did they..."

"Both," he said. "She was killed instantly. It took him longer, the son of a bitch."

He said the words without expression. He pointed to the ring on his pinky. "This was hers."

She started to cry. "And you act like such an—"

"Asshole" he finished for her.

She felt an overwhelming tenderness, an urge to make it up to him, to compensate, somehow, even though nothing could. She came up behind him and rubbed his back and shoulders, occasionally brushing her lips across the nape of his neck where babies are kissed. As her fingers dug into the tense muscles, she willed every drop of kindness she possessed into her hands. She thought she could feel him absorbing it. He breathed deeply, slowly.

"Thank you," he said, after a few minutes. "I know you want to be good to me, but—having you do that actually makes it harder. That's the reason, I guess, they keep feeding me. My aunts. They feel sorry for me. I don't want that."

"I'm not planning to add to your store of silver packages. But can't you allow somebody to feel kindness toward you?"

He took her hand, kissed her palm, and got up. "End of discussion."

And then he pulled still more aunt-generated food from the freezer, frozen pastries this time, and she made coffee while they heated in the oven. "This place looks a lot better with you in it," he said, as she stood at the counter, pouring water into the coffee maker. She was wearing one of his tee shirts, which fit her like a dress. "That's the librarian look I like," he leered. While the coffee percolated and the pastries scented the air, she felt the need to offer a part of herself, as well as to lighten the conversation. And so she confessed her ruse to lure him into staying over the night before—was it only last night?—told him that she really had known how to build a fire all along. He laughed and said the phone call from his uncle was bogus. He'd simply arranged for his phone to ring. "I knew you wouldn't send me out in the storm," he said.

"Is that why you came back?" she said. "Did you think we would…"

He was shocked. "Oh no," he said. "What do you take me for? Some kind of predator? I was worried about you." But then he smiled. "But after about one minute, let's say, I was hoping. When I walked into the house you seemed awfully glad to see me."

She rolled her eyes and pretended to be offended, glad to see him jocular. "Don't be obnoxious. And you acted pretty standoffish. Was that for show?"

He flapped his folded arms in imitation of a bird, looking so ridiculous she had to laugh.

"Chicken," he said. "Approach avoidance."

He laughed at the surprised look on her face. "Yes, I am marginally literate," he said. "Occasionally use them big words.

"I see you have a master's degree. You want to be a principal?"

"My ex's idea," he said. "First, she didn't want a cop. Then, she didn't want a teacher. Bottom line she didn't want me."

"She left you?"

He shrugged. "What happened—that's between her and me," was all he said.

If he didn't want her to feel sorry for him, he was not succeeding. Perhaps not sorry for him. Tender. Maternal, even. She resolved to ask no more questions. Yet...

She poured his coffee, and as she stood near him, his arm automatically circled her waist as if to hold her fast. Later, he held her hand across the table. It was almost better than the sex.

Her father had left when she was too young to remember him. Mother expressed love with corrective pokes in the back: *Stand up straight, Charlotte.* For Francis, affection was an avenue to sex and dwindled correspondingly. Her daughters had been loving babies and children. But now they were too big to sit on her lap, although Abigail was sweet and indulged her.

Theo never passed her without a pat or a touch. These

were her halcyon days, warm days in the middle of winter. She slept in his arms that night, and the next, wonderfully tangled, and woke to his kisses. All day they talked, exchanging lives, stopping at intervals to make love. She asked him why he'd become a cop, and he told her what she'd already divined, his need to protect, to keep people safe. As for why he left the force—he said he'd served with the bravest yet most cynical people he'd ever known. "It was all about collars," he said. "Make arrests and get ahead. This one time when I was walking a beat, I caught this six-teen-year-old kid who was fucking shoplifting. I was supposed to arrest him. That's what a good cop was supposed to do. I couldn't hack it, Charlotte. He was a good kid who wanted stuff. That's all. I should have made him give it back and let him go. I knew it. I could feel it. But I made the arrest, and he went to jail. I never felt right since. So I put in my twenty years and got out."

After that, Charlotte didn't have to ask him why he became a teacher. In her turn, she told him about her life as the poor person at the party—the girl in a private school whose mother cleaned the other girls' houses. She held nothing back, telling about Francis—explaining her shotgun marriage and the role her mother had played. She hoped her frankness would encourage him to talk about his own marriage.

But Theo listened, stroked her hair, and said nothing more about his ex. Finally, she probed. "Why did you marry her?" she asked.

He drew a deep breath. "All right. One time. We talk about this one time. And no more."

"Why did you?"

"She was the smartest woman I ever knew. Maybe the smartest person."

"Smarter than me?"

"Don't start, Charlotte. You're different, thank God."

"Good answer. So. She's smart. And that's why you married her?"

He shook his head. "At one time, I had something she needed. Charlotte, I was an idiot. Let's just say she *used* me." He said the last words through tight lips and she knew to stop asking.

Christmas day arrived. He was going to visit his grand-mother, he said. His family gathered on December 25, although for Yiayia the important celebration would be on January seventh, Orthodox Christmas. He invited her to join him, and she quickly refused. She could sense his relief at that, and she elaborated. She should go back to Westport—to get a change of clothes, check the house, charge her cell phone in the car during the drive, and take care of mail and newspapers that might have accumulated. She did not tell him that she also expected a call from Francis. She'd been in touch with the girls by cell phone every day, but not Francis. She knew he'd expect to talk to her on Christmas. Eighteen Christmases they'd been together. This, their first apart.

"The roads will ice up again, sweetheart," Theo said, fluffing her hair around her face. "I won't be long at Yiayia's. Stay. Wait for me. You can even snoop around."

"Tempting, but I should go." She thought of the Renoir print. "I have something I'd like to give you," she said. "For the bedroom."

"Promise you'll be back."

"I promise."

He held her for a long time, and she broke away first.

The cold air felt wonderful when she left his overheated apartment. She drove to Westport with the windows open, singing Christmas carols. And she found she was in tears.

Before taking off her coat, she called Francis's California number. It was noon. Even with the three-hour time difference, they should be awake. No one answered. She couldn't reach their cells—maybe they'd turned their phones off at the movies. No, not at nine in the morning.

She forced herself not to worry, but tried all three numbers and the landline at half hour intervals. Finally, on the landline, Francis picked up. "Merry Christmas, poetry girl," and the sound of his voice brought tears again.

All three got on speakerphone. They'd been at church. Of course. The big Christmas Mass. Charlotte remembered what that was like, with everyone going to communion, everyone smiling and saying "Peace be with you" with hugs and handshakes.

Talking with them was like coming home from a long vacation. Familiar, but strange. The girls were excited, interrupting each other to tell her about the beach, about the shopping. Her mind was darting, only half listening to what they said. They assumed the snow had prevented her from flying. No one asked what she had been doing. She mentioned that she'd been asked to Christmas dinner at Natalie's. Equivocation, she knew, but so much easier to let them think it. Francis was the jovial, kind Francis he always was around the girls.

"You could still come," Francis said. "The girls miss you. I miss you."

"Wait till you see what he got you on Rodeo Drive," said Emily. "It's—"

"Shh," Abby said. "It's a surprise."

"I miss you too," Charlotte said truthfully.

"I love you, Mommy," Abby said, her voice high and young.

"Me too," said Emily.

"Me three," Francis chimed in.

"Merry Christmas," Charlotte said. "Love you too."

When Charlotte was upset, she organized small things, getting control of tiny areas where she could not control the large ones. She began weeding through her closet, color-coding everything. It was daunting to see how much gray she owned. She made a pile of it for the school's clothing drive and gathered lightweight cottons for Theo's apartment. Or California?

Her eye fell on the picture hanging awkwardly on Francis's robe hook. It would look wonderful in Theo's bedroom. What if Theo didn't want it? She decided to offer it. She took the white robe, wrapped it around the picture to protect the glass, put both in a green trash bag.

Her house was as quiet as a movie set after the actors had gone home. Her eye fell on some papers she had to correct. Their faces came flooding back. Valerie, China, Suzette. Even Caridad.

She recalled a study skills lesson she once taught. Take a container and a bag of stones, large and small. How to make the stones fit in the container? Put the biggest things in first.

What are the big things, Charlotte? What do you want? Without a doubt, the twins would be number one. But after the girls?

She remembered that Natalie was sure to observe her first thing after the vacation, her favorite tactic when someone was on the shit list. So Charlotte went on line trolling for essay topics. One, which she thought the kids might like, was: *What person, alive or dead, would you like to have dinner with?* For herself, she decided on Jane Austen. She wondered whom Theo would pick. Someone Greek. Socrates, probably. Soon she was typing away, making lessons, until she glanced out the window and saw it was dark.

☙☙☙

It was eerie, late Christmas night, pulling out of her still-snowy driveway and past the holiday lights of her neighbors. She drove to Riverdale, feeling more than a little broody, singing Christmas carols alone in the car. As she neared Theo's building, she forced herself to focus on the moment, to push away the nostalgia of Christmases past and the apprehension of future complications.

He opened the door, looked hard at her face. "You're early." He looked like Cro-Magnon man, his features distorted, and his eyes glaring.

She started babbling. "Merry Christmas, darling. I have a

question. What one person, alive or dead, would you like to have dinner with?"

"Alive or dead? I thought *you* were fucking dead. Jesus. Do you ever think? I was going to look for you myself but I was afraid I'd miss you. You could have called. I tried your cell over and over. And your land line's fucking unlisted."

"I left my cell in the car," she admitted. "I was charging it, and I just forgot to take it inside. But I'm fine."

"I'm not. You talked to him, didn't you? I can see it in your eyes."

"Francis? Of course I did."

"Joy to the world."

He turned around, did not offer to take the bulky packages from her arms.

She could not bear it, to think how he had worried. There could be no words. She put her things down in his foyer, took his hand. To her relief he followed her to the bedroom.

She lay on the bed, and opened her arms. He buried his face in her neck, inhaled her, sucking on the sensitive skin as though to assert ownership, perhaps even leave a mark. My God it felt wonderful. She was wildly excited. She strained against him, wanting his touch everywhere. He made her come with his mouth and then entered her and when she came again, she felt his shuddering and the spray of semen he sent deep inside her.

She could never, never give this up.

Then he rolled over. He wrapped himself in the blanket, and turned his back.

Next door's television blared something about the Pope's Christmas message. She touched Theo's shoulder blades. "Darling, I'm always going to talk to him. We have children together. A history."

He tugged the blanket to his chin and began snoring.

She lay there, edging near him for warmth, watching the headlights flash on the blinds. She began to pray, reciting the words she'd grown up with. *Forgive us our trespasses.*

I miss you. Me too. Me three. What would her daughters

think if they could see her now? Toward dawn, she fell asleep too, and woke to find him, like an oversized prairie dog, sitting up on the bed, watching her.

"I feel pretty bad," he said.

She sat up, reached a hand to touch his forehead.

"Not that kind of bad. Let's go into the kitchen," he said. "Could you make coffee?" He sounded about four years old.

"I need to get the robe I brought. It's cold in here."

"The heat isn't up yet."

He watched as she took her robe from around the framed Renoir print.

"It's beautiful. I saw the original once, in a museum. I bought a postcard."

"It's yours if you want it."

Mrs. O'Neill from next door had her TV on again, and Charlotte heard about a tragic accident. How terrible, a Christmas wedding. The bride and groom killed on the way to the reception. A little flower girl also.

He sat in boxers and tee shirt, looking gloomy.

"What's bothering you, Theo? Is this all just because I had a conversation on the phone with Francis?"

"A conversation? One look at your face, and I knew. You're thinking about going back to him."

She rinsed the coffee pot thoroughly, added fresh cold water, and measured the coffee with care.

"And I don't blame you," he added. "He's your kids' father."

They were silent while it percolated. She poured him a cup, almost added sugar and cream, as Francis liked it, but remembered in time. Theo took it black.

"You make great coffee, sweetheart. I'm going to miss this."

She did not want him to see her tears. She went to the cabinet and opened a package of English muffins, broke one apart and dropped each half in the toaster. Took a jar of honey from the cabinet. When the muffin was done, she spread honey on his half.

He frowned. "Don't fuss. I'm a big boy."

"I like doing things for you too, you know. Last night, Theo. My God."

He inclined his head, smiled very slightly. "Something to remember me by."

The heat was clicking, and the apartment began to grow warm. She heard water running in other apartments. The woman next door was listening to Morning Joe. Charlotte reached for his hand. "No, Theo. Something to look forward to."

He smiled with sad eyes. "We had a good time."

She hesitated. She was a fool to say it, a fool not to.

"Theo, darling, it's more than that. When I'm with you I feel so good, like the sun has just come out. With him, it's rain. Freezing November rain. All the time."

Light flickered in his eyes.

She continued. "It's so different with you. So peaceful. Fun. But not just fun. Joy. Halcyon Days. 'The teeming quietest happiest days of all. The brooding and blissful halcyon days.'"

He smiled that wide smile that made her think of a Steinway piano. "You and your poems. It helps me to hear that. But it makes what I have to say harder."

His neighbor turned the television off, as though trying to listen. The kitchen was silent. His eyes searched hers. Someone in the apartment above dropped something. "I'm sorry, Charlotte."

"Theo. You want to break it off?"

"I can't go through waiting for you to go back to your husband."

"But I'm not!"

"What? Do you see yourself living in this dump? You're already trying to fix it up. Pretty soon you'll be trying to fix me."

"But you're not broken."

"Yes, I am. I'm damaged goods. Look. I am going to hang up that picture, look at it every day, and remember our time here. And the person I'd go to dinner with? You. Just you. I'd like to take you to a fancy restaurant and hold your hand on top of the table. I'd like everyone to know I'm the guy with you. And I can't have that. All or nothing."

"We can do that." She walked to his chair, put her hand on his shoulder. "Are you leaving me?"

"I don't leave people. People leave me. I'm just helping you."

She traced his lips with her finger. "You'll have to put me out bodily. I refuse to go."

"Damn it to hell." He pulled her onto his lap. "Remind me to tell you never to listen to me."

"Oh God, Theo. You scared me."

"Just remember. I don't share."

❧

Valerie's Journal
DO NOT READ!
After Christmas vacation, the first day the school is so clean when you walk in, the floors shining, and even the desks with the gum scraped off the bottoms of them. It will take half a day to get back to normal.

Zamar broke up with Suzette and my friend Suzette she is cranky. She is also going to beat up any girl who goes anywhere near him. I try to tell her that you don't need a man. Look around. They just mess your life up. So Suzette gives me that look like who am I to talk. She's the only one who knows about the ring. I had to show somebody. Suzette isn't happy about it. Maybe she's hating on me a little.

I can't wear it of course except on a chain around my neck. It's real, an amethyst. I mean it's not a diamond or anything but it's serious jewelry. He said the ring meant, maybe after five years when he finished college he'd find me again. Five years! "Who makes

*plans five years ahead," I said, and he told me maybe
I should start.*

*So I think maybe I'm pre-engaged. Sort of. If Ro-
han knew, he would kill both of us. Or maybe just
Drew. I call him that now when I remember.*

*When I saw Murphy's class was dark, I thought
maybe she had a movie for us. It's so good to walk in
to class and there's a TV up and the lights are out but
that didn't happen. There was nobody in Murphy's
room but a note taped on the door. When I saw that
note, I figured Murphy was absent but no. They
changed her room.*

*Come to find out Murphy's new classroom is not
in such a good location, being the only room on this
long hallway and it used to be the band room when
we had a school band so the seats are kind of like a
stadium. It's also near the back stairs where business
transactions take place. You see Gareth there sometimes, just hanging. He never goes to class but he's
always in the halls. He is one crazy guy even for a
coconut which is what some ignorant people call him
because of where he's from. They say he wants to
take over Rohan's customers. Now Rohan, he's been
coming to school lately.*

*Lagakis is in the hall outside Murphy's room half
the day, walking around whistling. I mean, I wouldn't
care, but he has no idea of how to carry a tune. The
guy is seriously happy. He has this permanent smile
like all the time. They think they're keeping it on the
down low but her rings are bye-bye and everybody
can tell how they are with each other just looking at
them. You'd think he would dial back on the flowers,
if he wants to keep it quiet. Personally, I feel bad for
her daughters, but otherwise NOMB. None of my
business. Live and let live.*

*You know, I actually love writing those journals.
But writing in journals that's how I got in trouble*

again. I get this journal assignment from Murphy to write about these flowers she has, daffodils, and I put it not in Rohan's book that I keep at home but a second notebook I bought in the dollar store myself (I got the idea from the unreliable narrator thing) and let my grandmother check and whap! my grandmother hit first and asked questions later.

In my house, she said, you will not lie. No way that lady has daffodils blooming this time of year.

She thinks she knows everything my grandmother because she used to have a house down South with flowers and she said that I was making it up. But China says they even sell them in the AP she works in. Oh yeah, her stepfather made her get a job when he found out she cut class to be with Keith. He almost made her drop out of school.

I don't want to hear it, my grandmother says when I try to tell her. Anyway, she came to school to check on my attendance wearing that hat and I got to show her for myself.

A bunch of them in pots all over the windowsill and on this plant stand Murphy got special. My grandmother just shut up then. She didn't say anything but maybe she trusts me a little more now.

Oh, the journal deal is some corny thing about good memories being like daffodils, but I took off from there and wrote about one Christmas when I was little and my father got me a white fur coat. I can still see that coat in my mind's eye just like in that poem and it makes me cry.

Chapter 21

Cat and Mouse

Every day, Charlotte waited for the summons, but Natalie held back, a cat to her mouse. So far, Charlotte's teaching program was unaltered, although she had a different classroom, but she feared that would change in February, when the new semester began. She might have to quit. She didn't think she could manage the Renaissance kids, even with Theo standing guard.

The summons arrived during Regents week, the last week in January, when no classes were scheduled. Charlotte had thought that perhaps the students who had already "passed" would be required to take the English Regents again. But Suzette, Monroe, and other students whose grades were questionable, were not on the list.

Charlotte entered the principal's office to find Natalie seated at her desk, typing on her computer. The principal did not rise to great her, but motioned to a chair opposite her.

"You sent for me?"

Natalie continued to type. So Charlotte sat down at the long conference table and pulled out college essays long overdue for correction.

At that, Natalie looked up. "Ms. Murphy, I didn't call you down to give you space to correct papers." She rose and strode around the room dramatically, her high heels making clicking sounds. "Why, Charlotte? Why? I find what you did to be unspeakable."

Charlotte underlined a comma splice, wrote *run-on*, and shuffled the papers to select another essay.

"Is it possible to get your attention, Ms. Murphy?"

"You have it."

"All right. Obviously, our friendship, such as it was, is over. Any consideration that you might have come to expect from me will not be forthcoming."

"Very well." Charlotte stood.

"Sit down until I dismiss you." Natalie's tone softened. "As a professional, I can still value you as a teacher. I don't want this unfortunate misunderstanding—"

"You mean the Regents investigation?"

"I mean your disloyalty."

Charlotte sat. "By the way, what's been happening with that? With the Regents investigation?"

"Didn't anyone tell you? Oh, that's right. You live in your own world."

"What's that supposed to mean?"

Natalie smirked. "I think you know. Anyway, the superintendent is entirely on my side. We've agreed. There has been no real evidence."

"How can you say that? How can he believe it?"

Natalie banged her hand on the desk. "The investigation is over. That folder you produced was just a trumped up bit of flummery—trumped up by a miserable teacher who happens to be dead."

Flummery? "Who decided that?"

"Let's just say I am well connected."

"You mean protected?"

"Charlotte. My integrity was never impugned. I've been completely exonerated."

"You get to keep the bonus? It's all just swept under the rug?"

"I prefer to call it water under the bridge. And, to continue the metaphor, you're not helping anyone if you rock the boat."

"Rock the boat?"

"I've figured it out. And it's all down to Lagakis."

"What are you talking about?"

"You've been on your honeymoon."

"Excuse me?"

"You were seen. Oh, I would never have dreamed this. You of all people, Saint Charlotte, with him. But when I found out you were having an affair—how could you?—with *that*, I realized he's to blame."

Natalie let that sink in and then continued. "I am not prepared to forgive you. But I want you to know who you've been dealing with. He's a scoundrel, Charlotte. He's been playing with you like a toy. Did you hear me, Charlotte?"

Charlotte had been searching her memory, wondering who had seen her with Lagakis. But Natalie's voice brought her back to the present.

"Natalie," Charlotte stood up. "This is ludicrous. Excuse me."

"Listen to me, my fair weather friend. Your lover boy and Trombetta, between the two of them, cooked up a scheme to get to me. The only problem was that she died. She—she probably made the first call, but then she died and he didn't have the balls to report the so-called evidence. So he used you. He knew damn well you'd agree to help him clear out that locker in his office. *His* office, mind you. Isn't that what you said?"

Charlotte nodded, her heart pounding.

"Then it was a cinch for him to set you up. To get you to spill the beans to the guy from headquarters. About the so-called evidence."

"Natalie. I examined the papers. That is not so called evidence."

"But don't you see? You were meant to find them. He set you up."

So what? Theo had admitted this, that first night.

"Even if that were true, why should that matter? Suzette failed, Natalie. She deserved to fail. And I let it slide when I first heard that she passed. I figured it was another teacher, to tell the truth, rating the exams after me."

"That could be," Natalie said eagerly.

"No, Natalie. See? It wasn't the essays, where you have some leeway. They were already graded as high as they could be with the rubric we're given. No, it was the multiple choice. I had turned a blind eye, so to speak, to someone re-grading the essays. After all, essay grades can be subjective. But it was obvious that multiple choice answers had been erased and the right answers bubbled in."

The bell rang for the change of periods, and Charlotte started up and then realized that there were no classes during Regents week.

But Natalie had forgotten to turn off the bells. Lagakis was right. She knew nothing about running a school.

Now Natalie was on her feet, looming over Charlotte. "Think back, Charlotte. Remember how evil Trombetta was about the kids. Suzette, especially. She was a one-woman crusade against Suzette. And your boy—birds of a feather, dearie."

Natalie was talking again. "Ms. Murphy, Trombetta was against me from the start, and she was certainly against the kids. A lot of the kids, but especially Suzette. She probably had her heart attack from just thinking about her graduating. And she wouldn't want my numbers to go up either."

"I can see Trombetta doing it just to get back at the kids. But Theo—Mr. Lagakis—I don't think he'd do it."

"My dear, it's like the slaughter of the innocents, what that man did to you. That man looks down on the kids. Ask them. But that's not why he did what he did."

Charlotte remembered Theo mouthing off at the funeral about how the kids couldn't read.

Natalie continued. "I don't judge you, Charlotte. God knows you needed a little something after Francis. And I'm sure he's enjoying himself. Men do. But what your boy was after, what he's always been after, is my job."

Charlotte's head came up sharp. Theo?

Natalie was watching Charlotte's face closely. She reached over and patted Charlotte's hand, her nails red and sharply filed into pointed ovals.

"Sorry dear, but it's the harsh truth. He wants me out of here so he can be next in line. They'll close the school, turn it into a bunch of little learning communities and each of them needs a principal. It will take five people to do the job I'm doing alone. He went to some diploma mill and got all the credentials."

"He has it over the—" Charlotte almost told Natalie where he kept his diploma, but thought better of it.

Natalie went on. "He figures they'd make him the acting principal if I were out of here. And making *you* find the folder—that was actually intelligent."

"He is intelligent," Charlotte found herself defending him.

"I'm speaking as a friend, Charlotte. One who has known you for almost twenty years. And how long have you known him? How well have you known him? Believe me, dear. This guy was using you to get to me."

"*You're* using *him* to get *back* at me," Charlotte blurted out. And then regretted it instantly.

Natalie smiled. "That, dear Charlotte, is an excellent idea. I'm so glad you thought of it."

"I don't have to listen to this," Charlotte said and left the office without being dismissed.

She went to find Theo, but he was at yet another suspension hearing. Gang activity had been stepping up precipitously. When she saw him the next day, she told him about what Natalie had said. "So. She knows about us."

"I'm guessing she just suspects. You didn't say anything, did you? A bunch of kids have asked me about you already. Apparently, I'm smiling too much. And you really do look radiant."

"Thanks to you, if I do."

"Duh. But the thing is, Charlotte, do you believe what Natalie said about me wanting her job?"

"Of course not. Theo, is it true? Do you want to be principal?"

"Not on your life. It was bad enough on the force. I don't want to go over to the dark side."

"Natalie is going to try to use you to get to me. She's going after you, Theo."

"She's bluffing. I bet they close this school, and none of us will hear from her again. I'm not afraid of her. Don't worry about me. Let's just worry about you."

It was easy to believe him, to believe him and just enjoy being in love.

"Charlotte," he continued. "She must have been hearing rumors, at least. I want to apologize. I didn't mean to, but I took a chance with you, taking you to my place. I'm as bad as my father. You should stop coming over. Let's take a break. I want to take care of you, not hurt you. I thought we were being so careful. I'm so sorry."

Each day, after school, Charlotte had been going to Riverdale, parking her car in the underground garage of his apartment building. He had rented an additional space just for her. She told the twins she was involved in a study group.

When he suggested taking a break, she felt the smallest twinge of something she recognized, suspicion, but she pushed it down. "You're acting like we're the ones in the wrong," she said.

"Right and wrong isn't always black and white, Charlotte. You taught me that, with Valerie's referral."

"No break, Theo. I couldn't bear it.'

"You have to. Look, from now on we're going to have to be better than careful. I wouldn't put it past her to contact Francis."

❡❡❡

Valerie's Journal
PLEASE READ!

Well, my book Middlemarch *by George Eliot is extremely hard but getting good and has a lot of SAT words and since you're making me apply to college I go a little at a time and it's getting pretty good. What I do is if a new character gets introduced I write the name down and what he is in the book so I can look back if his name comes up again. Ms. Trombetta actually taught us that.*

In this book Middlemarch *by George Eliot, they have the main character Dorothea marrying this real old guy just because she thinks he can give her an education, which you couldn't get in those days if you were a girl.*

And a bunch of people are getting married to the wrong people, which is interesting to me being my parents did that too.

Except for this guy Fred who has a gambling problem but his girl Mary that he loves, and who loves him, won't marry him and he's waiting around for some old dude to die so he can inherit. I get that. Sometimes I wish my mother would just OD, meaning overdose, because seriously she might as well get it over with. I know that sounds cold but you don't know my mother.

My mother and father both went to college but it didn't do them good, which is why I started for my beautician license. I kind of like the idea that I can take care of myself but Drew says I can do whatever I want and maybe I should explore my options.

That's how he talks. He can't help it. In the book, (Middlemarch *by George Eliot) Dorothea is rich but she wants to help poor people kind of like you, miss. I guess. It must be nice to be rich and able to do exactly what you want.*

Things are not always what they seem, Valerie. It is good to explore your options. Ms. M.

CHAPTER 22

Chasing Rainbows

I don't *want* to take money from him," Charlotte said. "I can earn my own living."

"Look, the money is not just for you," Attorney Gordon said. "It's for your family—all of it. If you don't do this, I will write it in the record that you are going against my advice. You earned this," she said. "All the years you spent at home, helping him advance his career. And he's so much better off than you ever could be on a teacher's salary. Don't even think about it."

Ms. Gordon also made a case for speed. "I'd like things to move along as quickly as possible," she said, "to minimize the chances of Francis finding out about your…situation. With this man you've been seeing. He'll be more lenient if you are portrayed as innocent. Not that adultery is a crime," she added.

Adultery. A scarlet letter. But Francis—Charlotte realized that she was about to say something like "Francis started it," as if they were in kindergarten. But she nodded. "I'll try."

"Who else knows about this man?"

"Apparently, my boss, the principal of the school, suspects."

"Is she reliable? Will she keep your secret?"

"I doubt it."

"Then I advise you that you stop seeing him until the divorce is final."

"So long?"

"Charlotte—may I call you Charlotte? You may not realize that a divorce can be finalized three months after the return date, which in your case is next Tuesday. A lot of divorces kind of linger in the system, but I'd advise you to speed things up."

Just like that? Only three months? So short a time to dissolve a marriage, to sign away eighteen years of her life? But the marriage was irretrievable. No matter what happened, she could never be with Francis again. Why wait?

"Where do I sign?" Charlotte asked and, with a steady hand, wrote her name where Gordon indicated. The final divorce hearing could be held barely six months after she had first discovered Francis's infidelity.

When she brought this conversation back to Theo, she told him that, after all, he'd been right. She'd been advised to be discreet.

He was quiet, nodding assent. "Don't worry, sweetheart. You say April. In New York, it took me a year just to get started on divorce."

"I think it's different now. Besides, I live in Connecticut."

"April! Charlotte. We'll go out to dinner then and sit on a banquette side by side and hold hands right on the table. I can't wait for that. But meanwhile, we'll keep it on the low."

She had smiled to hear him use the students' slang.

ℰ✄ℰ✄

Valerie's Journal
DO NOT READ!
I was walking down the hall on my way to the li-

brary when I saw the principal and this guy in a suit. Of course, the principal had to stop me, as if she was my best friend in the world.

"Hello, Valerie dear," she says in that voice she has. It reminded me of when we rehearsed my handshake at Trombetta's funeral. I know how to act, of course, and so I said, "Good afternoon, Ms. Albert," like my home training says.

"This is the President of the Honor Society," she says to the suit. "Valerie Martin. One of the best and the brightest in the school. A graduating senior."

I know it's a big deal that I'm a senior that's graduating. My grandmother knows what's happening and she says our school got in trouble for a low graduation rate.

The suit sticks out his hand and says, "Congratulations, Valerie. And what are your plans for after graduation?" he says. Or something like that. I shake his hand but I thought that was a little rude. I mean, Ms. Albert didn't even bother to tell me his name or anything.

But my grandmother taught me to get even more polite when someone is rude, and I say "I'm sorry, sir. I didn't quite get your name."

And Albert gets a little red. Good.

"Calvin Margulis," he says, sticking out his hand again even though we already shook. But I just shake it again.

"Good morning, Mr. Margulis," I say. "In response to your question, I'm thinking about college."

Yes, I really said that. In response to your question. J. Crew, I mean Drew, loved to say that all the time when we went to the library thingy. Now of course we just go to his aunt's apartment.

"And what will you major in?" asks the suit.

"Biochemistry," I say, "but I need to talk to somebody about it. I'm thinking about medical school."

*I thought he would drop his teeth. And the princi-
pal is smiling like she's gonna break her face.*

*Now that thing I said about biochemistry and med-
ical school was purely J. Crew's idea. We don't even
have regular chemistry, let alone the bio kind, in this
school but we take cosmetological science as part of
the technical program and, even though the teacher
isn't much, I like reading the book. That is how I
learned about stuff like zinc for the fingernails. Oh
wait, I think I got that from notes which she writes on
the board, thank God, so I have something to copy to
show my grandmother every day.*

*"That is so exciting, Valerie," says the principal.
She like touches the guy on elbow. "This is what I've
been talking about. I gave up a guidance counselor
for him. I put up with his poor teaching because I
thought he could at least do crowd control. Meanwhile, I need more special safety officers here. He
costs the same as three security guards. He's worse
than useless and we're forced to neglect our best and
brightest. I'm building a case the usual way."*

*Then she kind of remembers that I'm standing
right there. It's funny how if you're quiet people forget that. Once she remembers of course, she tells me
to come in and talk to her any time. Her smile is so
bright you can tell she's had her teeth whitened. She
does her make-up okay, but she needs to get a little
work done on her forehead, and then she needs to
stop raising her eyebrows so much. My grandmother
always says black don't crack but lightskin women
start to show their age early.*

*"Good luck, Valerie Martinez," the suit says. "I
expect to hear good things about you later on."*

*Martinez? I must look Hispanic to him. I wonder
how much longer Mr. Lagakis is going to work here.*

CHAPTER 23

Valentine's Day

Natalie did not change Charlotte's program, and, for that, Charlotte was grateful. But Valentine's Day was difficult, even with the good kids.

Balloons arrived throughout the day—balloons and flowers. Roses—hard, tight little roses with no fragrance at all—were for sale in the school store. The volume of chatter in the class increased with each delivery, and then came to a halt when two boys, their eyes gleaming with the prospect of Valentine's sex, came to class with little gift bags topped with fluffy pink tissue. Joyful cries of *Bendito*! were heard, but some girls stared at those bags with slitted eyes. Then a girl named Daisy, pregnant and thrilled about it, entered, carrying a heart-shaped balloon.

"From my babyfather," she said.

Once again, coos of approbation and envious glances. The students were throbbing with hormones, excitement, and disappointment. How to harness the pounding anticipation, the swelling excitement, and the bitter pangs? Poetry. Only poetry.

But poetry was now forbidden. "All you English teachers love literature," the assistant principal, Mr. Eugene, had said at the most recent faculty conference. "That's all you ever want to teach. But our kids don't need literature. They need to pass the social studies Regents. That's what we need to meet our targets." He also insisted that students work in groups at all times.

One morning, Charlotte discovered that the closet in her classroom had been emptied of the anthologies she loved to use. Instead of her familiar books, she found new paperback workbooks that consisted of brief readings about social studies topics followed by multiple-choice questions. Even photocopying was under surveillance—all material had to go through Mr. Eugene.

But Charlotte found a way to be subversive. As dean, Theo had his own copier, albeit an ancient one, best suited for single copies. Charlotte made copies on Theo's machine, and then surreptitiously handed out thirty copies of a poem, instructing the students to keep the paperback social studies books open on their desks. They obeyed, instantly her co-conspirators. She wrote on the board: *Why are cities often founded near rivers?*

She called the students to order and asked them to open their notebooks to a fresh page, to date it February four-teenth. And then she asked them to answer the question: Can you love someone you don't trust?

"I like this topic," came a voice from the back of the room.

"That I can write about," someone else said. "Not like those rivers."

"Are you going to read this?" Valerie asked.

"Only if you want me to read it."

"Do we have to read it out loud?" said China.

"Only if you volunteer," Charlotte said patiently.

They knew the answers to these questions, but asked them anyway.

The students moved apart slightly in their groups as they wrote, and silence, blessed silence, filled the air. Charlotte began to write herself, supposedly modeling writing in a journal, but thought better of it and locked her book away, just in case. She saw Monroe look up at the sound of her key in the lock. He did not write at all, but simply sat, ob-serving. Charlotte smiled at him and mimicked the act of writing, pretending to scribble on her palm, and he shrugged.

She looked through the glass window of the door and saw Theo in the hall, speaking with the Teach for America rookie whom she had privately dubbed Miss Minnesota. The young teacher, Katy Knudsen, was tall, blonde, and astonishingly young. Knudsen pulled a heart-shaped lolli-pop out of her bag and offered it to Theo, who took it with a smile and placed it in the breast pocket of his jacket. His dimples were working full out.

Charlotte turned back to her class and gave a two-minute warning. She took out some brownies she'd baked and wrapped in cellophane and red ribbons. Then she walked around the room, quickly checking journals and placing a brownie on each desk. She invited her students to read aloud, but only China volunteered, waving her hand aloft to show off the heart design on her brightly painted nails. Charlotte walked over to China's desk and glanced at the girl's journal, and, after skimming it, gave her permission to read.

"Remember, we do not comment on one another's jour-nals," she reminded the class. "What we write is part of our-selves. Be respectful."

China was dressed in a tight red top, and a heart shaped cut-out showed her cleavage to advantage. She stood up to face the class, although Charlotte always allowed students to read from their seats.

"I didn't trust anyone," the girl read. "Until I met the love of my life, Keith. But I loved a lot of people you can't trust. Everybody in my family. And some people I thought were my friends back-stabbed me. You all know who I mean. Now the only one I trust is Keith."

Murmurs of assent filled the room, and then everyone looked over as the door opened again. Charlotte saw Rohan enter, carrying an oversize helium balloon. If he had not been so large himself, he might have been swept away by it, Mary Poppins style. Rohan was tall, with a fully developed chest and impressive musculature. He did not look like a teenager.

Behind Rohan came a student government messenger, delivering a single rose to Suzette from Zamar. Suzette's dark skin flushed, and then she flashed Zamar a smile. Apparently, they had reconciled. Suzette had simply beaten off the competition. Another rose came to China from Keith. Behind the messenger, Doris, the stooped-over school aide from the main office, walked in, delivering a bouquet of perfect red roses to Charlotte. She knew even before looking what the card would say. Sure enough. The card read, *To the wonderful mother of my beautiful girls.* Francis' secretary wrote the same thing every year.

These latter were not the tiny tight roses for sale for one dollar in the school store, but fully opened American Beauty roses. The messenger also delivered a tight red rose to Charlotte, which she hoped might be from Theo. The offerings from Lagakis Florist had stopped. But when she opened the card she saw it was from Rohan. A rose from the smartest boy, the handsomest boy, the most popular boy in the school, who happened to be highly placed in a gang.

"Thank you," she said, not mentioning his name but meeting his eyes. "But now, to our lesson." After the recent deliveries, she did not hold out much hope that the students would listen to her. But, amazingly, they brushed off the brownie crumbs and took up their photocopied sheets obediently. What good kids they really were, she thought. She did not deserve them, but they deserved, they needed, so much more than she could give them.

First, she wished them a Happy Valentine's Day. Then she briefly recounted the story of Cupid and Psyche, explaining how the God of Love had forbidden his beloved, Psyche, to see his face. How they made love in darkness, until curiosity and the envy of others prompted Psyche to light a candle and to look upon the face of Love. Psyche had loved, but had not trusted. As Charlotte spoke, she saw the students' faces looking up at her, full of interest in the old story.

"Where can I read that story?" China asked, and Charlotte automatically thought of Hamilton's *Mythology*. But no, they would not appreciate Hamilton's stilted prose. She hesitated.

"Just go on line," Valerie said. "They have everything there, right, miss?"

"Right. That's a much better idea," Charlotte agreed. "I should have said that."

"That's okay, miss," Rohan said. "We know you're old school."

"The Greek and Roman myths are well known to educated people," Charlotte said.

She was losing them. Talking too much. She saw them retreating into their own lives, into what mattered to them. How to make a connection? In a lightning stroke of inspiration, she asked Rohan to read the poem aloud. He shrugged and agreed.

He was easily the best reader in the class, perhaps in the school, and the students listened attentively to his clear neutral rendering of the poem. How much more readily students listened to each other than to their teachers. That, of course, was the basis of the principal's recent commandment to make the students work in groups at all times. But sometimes you had to bring the class together as a whole.

As Rohan's deep voice filled the room, the poem's words became Rohan's.

"Psyche with the Candle
by Archibald MacLeish

Love, which is the most difficult mystery
Asking from every young one answers
And from those most eager and most beautiful –
Love is a bird in a fist:

To hold it hides it, to look at it lets go.
It will twist loose, if you lift so much as a finger
It will stay if you cover it – stay but unknown and invisible
Either you keep it forever with fist closed
Or let it fling
Singing in fervor of sun and in song vanish.
There is no answer other to this mystery."

After thanking Rohan, Charlotte began with an easy question, one everyone could answer. "What do you see when you read this poem?"

Suzette held up a drawing of a bird, flying away from an outstretched hand. They had agreed that Suzette could draw her journal responses before writing them.

"Thank you, Suzette," Charlotte said, and she walked to her student's desk and asked gently," May I show everyone?"

Suzette shrugged. "I don't mind," she said.

"Suzette," Charlotte said, "has captured the central image and the central metaphor of the poem. She has captured in her drawing what the poet depicts in language to convey his theme, or meaning. Suzette has looked at an important question, how the poem means."

Suzette's dark skin reddened. "Stop trying to gas me up."

Charlotte ignored her. "Now, I'd like each of you to write down what you think that meaning is. Just in your own words."

As Charlotte spoke, she walked over to the window of her classroom door. There was Theo on patrol in the empty hallway. He winked at her as he walked by. She smiled and turned back to her class.

"What is fervor?" China asked.

"My bad," Charlotte said, and the class laughed at her outdated slang. "I should have mentioned that before. Does anyone know what fervor means?"

"Is it like fever?" China asked.

"Kind of. It means warmth, but emotional warmth."

"Like I have fervor for Keith," China said.

"It's more like you behave *with* fervor," Charlotte replied. "How do you feel about Keith?"

"He's the love of my life!" China answered.

"You said that *with* fervor," Charlotte said. "That's what I'm talking about."

"But the poem says *in* fervor," Rohan said. "Like this," and he quoted from the text.

"That's so good, Rohan," Charlotte said. "You're reading closely, and yes, in fervor is good too."

"Thanks, miss."

"Anyway," Charlotte said. "Look at the words in that penultimate, or next to last line. 'Singing in fervor of sun.' What kind of charge do you get from those words, positive or negative?"

"Positive," they chorused back.

Valerie's hand was up. "But the bird flies away," she said. "May I read, miss?"

This was unusual. Valerie rarely volunteered, although she always answered when called upon.

Charlotte walked over to Valerie's desk and let her eye quickly slip over the girl's purple script.

"Yes," Charlotte agreed. "Please do."

Valerie read from her journal, "In 'Cupid and Psyche,' by Archibald MacLeish, in my opinion, I think the poem means that you should keep love hidden. Otherwise the bird flies away."

How Charlotte hated that *in my opinion I think*. But the rules were: no corrections on journals. "Thanks, Valerie," Charlotte said.

"Anyone else? Look at the words of the poem," Charlotte said. "Look again at the penultimate line," and with that she wrote the word penultimate on the board. "That means next to last."

"I like those words you give us," Monroe said.

Rohan's hand was up. "I'd like to read what I wrote," he said.

"Of course," Charlotte replied.

Normally she would check the writing herself before allowing a student to read. She nodded, trusting him.

"The poem means," Rohan said, "that love is something you can't control. You can't hold it in. You can hide it— you can be, like, you don't care. But the poem means that you need to let it out, even if maybe you lose it."

"Yes!" Charlotte said, ignoring his bad grammar, and the class laughed.

"You say that with fervor, miss."

She should not have praised Rohan, Charlotte realized. She had broken her own rule.

"Can anyone comment," she asked, "About the title of the poem? How does the story of Psyche and Cupid enrich your understanding of the poem's meaning?"

Rohan's hand was up again, but Charlotte shook her head at him, trying to send him the thought—let someone else answer. He nodded, but no one else volunteered.

Suddenly, Monroe's hand waved wildly in the air. Now Valerie's hand was up too.

Valerie did not wait to be acknowledged. "Miss," she asked, unnecessarily loudly. "Are *all* cities founded near rivers?"

"Of course not," Charlotte said, genuinely mystified. Then she saw that the door had opened behind her and that Mr. Eugene was in the room. "Oh," she said, catching on. "But, as we have seen today, many cities are founded near rivers."

"Happy Valentine's, mister," said China to the assistant principal. "Did you get your wife a present?"

"Yeah, he gave her a package," Suzette said, and Charlotte saw several shoulders shake with laughter. Thank God, the laughter was suppressed.

"Good morning boys and girls," Mr. Eugene replied.

He had turned red at Suzette's remark, and Charlotte became very nervous. But China's diversionary tactic had worked. Eugene looked at the board, noted the question:

Why are cities often founded near rivers? The definition of penultimate stood next to it but he apparently did not bother to read farther than the focal question about rivers. He merely cast a cursory glance at the students, all of whom were sitting in their groups, looking at the new workbooks. Not a poem was in sight.

"Very good, boys and girls," Eugene said. And he quickly walked out.

Charlotte realized that she had been holding her breath and exhaled visibly. "Thank you," she said to Monroe and Valerie. "Thank you, class."

And with that, the bell rang. Rohan walked over to Valerie and attempted to tie the balloon around her wrist, Valerie shaking her head. They walked out together, not talking. Rohan was still holding the balloon.

Charlotte searched the room for copies of the poem, but there were none to be found. She erased the definition of penultimate and thought of another word for her vocabulary list: insubordination.

She had been insubordinate and technically could have been fired for what she did today. Natalie could have a field day with that. Charlotte thought it was a good lesson, but was that worth it?

She saw Theo in the hall and wanted to sob on his shoulder, but instead she handed him a brownie. "That's for the use of your copier," she said. "Thank you."

Theo apologized. "Look, I'm sorry, Charlotte. Eugene walked right past me. I couldn't warn you. How did it go?"

"Not a problem. I didn't even see him come in. But the kids saw him. The kids had my back."

"They usually do. But be careful."

Kids streamed around them, going to their next classes, exchanging hugs and high fives. Theo opened the brownie eagerly and swallowed it in two bites. "It's very good, sweetheart," he said. "I see you got flowers." His eyes were that dark shade they became when he was angry.

"Don't be jealous. That's just Francis's secretary."

"Yeah. Well—I have something for you, sweetheart, but not to give you here."

It was noisy in the hall, and impossible to be overheard. Still, Charlotte flashed him a look.

"I forgot," he said. "But they do know, the kids. They know everything."

Valerie passed and ignored Charlotte and Lagakis. Rohan walked behind her, still holding the balloon.

China ran up to Theo and Charlotte. "How come you didn't go to the dance on Friday?" she asked.

Charlotte had wanted to be a chaperone at the Valentine's Day dance. She had actually thought about it. It would be a way to see Theo under the cover of her job. But Theo had begged her to stay home. "I can't do my job and worry about you at the same time," he had said. "I need to know you're safe at home in Connecticut."

"Um, I had to stay home with my family," she said now to China.

"How come *you* went, mister?"

"I had to go," Theo said. "It's just part of my job."

"Miss Knudsen was there," China said, looking at Charlotte. "You should have come, miss."

eɔɐɔ

Valerie's Journal
DO NOT READ!
Well of course, you know I wasn't allowed to go to the Valentine's dance, even though it was at school. My grandmother made up some excuse, like she had to do something for the church, and I had to baby-sit the foster kids who, thank God, went to sleep. Well it might have been bad but guess what? I texted J. Crew and told him the coast was clear if he wanted to call me and he did.

Boy did we talk. Almost two hours on the phone.

First went back to that poem and kids dying and getting hurt and how come if there's a God he lets stuff like that happen. I started telling him about Suzette—I didn't use her name, just said a friend of mine—and how she loves to fight because it kind of takes her mind off other things, bad things that have happened to her. It's like fighting is her way to survive. And how she kind of explodes and I have to talk her down.

And he said how his parents always fought to, like, take their minds off other things too, and then he said "You know what, Valerie, you're really smart and maybe you should think about being a therapist or even a doctor not a hair stylist."

"But in the hair salon everybody goes there for therapy," I tell him and he laughed and said that proved his point that I understand people and just hearing him say it made me feel so good.

Now in school, teachers they always tell me I'm smart but I can't ever believe them. I figured it was just that my grandmother kept making me do the homework and have perfect attendance. And the other kids call me a brainiac if I answer too many questions in class, which is why I stay quiet.

Now Rohan, he really is smart. He doesn't even need to go to school to pass most of his tests. But he does read a lot. He started to do that when he was away. That's when he started pumping iron too.

But anyway Drew saying that stuff made me wonder if it isn't true. I guess I can kind of believe what he says since I figure he has like higher standards of excellence. Like his aunt Ms. Trombetta was always bragging about him for. She wasn't a bad teacher, just mean. But at least you could trust that when she taught you something, it was right. Not like some of the others who tell you stuff and the book says other stuff.

Anyway, it was ok that I didn't go to the dance and

anyway I heard all about it from Suzette and China and the big news was that there was a huge fight between Rohan and Gareth's crews outside the school. Ms. Knudsen almost got killed but Lagakis saved her and they left together. They were dancing together too. Murphy's gonna be mad, I bet.

CHAPTER 24

Green Eyes

S o how was the Valentine's Dance?" Charlotte asked
Theo. They allowed themselves a few conversations,
snatched during hall passing time.

"I got through it," Theo said "It's never easy to deal with
large groups of our scholars. You were better off at home."
He looked nervous about something. "Charlotte," he said. "I
need to talk to you. Can you come into the office later?
We'll leave the door open and all."

"Just to talk?"

"Unfortunately, yes," he said. "But we need—I want to
tell you something."

Just then Katy Knudsen ran up to Theo and flung her
arms around him. She was somewhere in her twenties, with
straight blonde hair halfway down her back, blue marbles
for eyes, and the deer-in-the-headlights look of new teachers. She could not control the Renaissance kids. No one
could. But she had persisted, unlike the other Teach for
America fellows.

"Oh, Theo!" Knudson said, kissing his cheek. "You are
so awesome. A lifesaver! And your car! It's so awesome!"

Students passing on their way to class stopped to look,
although they normally ignored teachers.

Theo? His school name was Ted but everyone just called

him Lagakis. And what was Knudsen doing in his car? Theo gave the girl a hug. His face was flushed bright red.

"Don't mention it. No need to thank me."

Charlotte stood and stared. They had her full attention.

"Theo," Knudson said to Lagakis. "You were *awesome*. Oh, hello, Mrs. Murphy."

"It's Ms."

Theo had that "I'm so proud of me" look his face wore when Charlotte had an orgasm. He was giving Miss Knudsen the full dimples.

"What a smooth ride we had."

Charlotte looked at Theo. If he had laughed, she would have kicked him. As it was, she wanted to throw up.

"Oops! That sounded a little off color, didn't it? But I'll never forget it. Gotta go," Katy said. "I'm late for a class I have to cover."

"See you later?" Lagakis called over to Charlotte.

"When it snows in hell," she answered sweetly, and turned on her heel. "Goodbye, *Theo*."

They hadn't been together since she'd had her talk with Gordon. Was he looking around already? Clearly, Knudsen was looking at *him*.

She stalked into her classroom and heard her students talking about some fight that had taken place after the dance. Charlotte marched to her desk, opened the drawer, and pulled out two rubber bands, one for each wrist. Memories of Francis played in her mind. She had not thought of the picture of him and Rosemary in a long time, but there it was again. Snap. Put it out of your mind, Charlotte, she told herself. Theo and Ms. Knudsen. Double snap.

But the rubber band trick wasn't working. She could imagine the conversation Theo wanted to have. A confession, probably. Some sort of dalliance that he realized she'd hear about.

As she taught, she saw him waiting outside the door, pretending to patrol and distracting her from teaching, and, when the bell finally rang to signal the end of the period, he came back into the classroom, put his hand on her back and practically pushed her into his office. Claustrophobia set in, and nausea came in waves. A volcano inside. Something to throw up in. There was a wastepaper basket. Better yet, just throw up all over the mess on his desk. The internal matching the external. Disorder in the universe, dissonance. Katy Knudsen's arms around him. Charlotte felt like she was going crazy.

He left the door carefully ajar and opened a folder, as if he were discussing a student's conduct with her.

"Could you open a window, at least?" she asked.

"Sure," he said, doing so. "You're not well?"

Cold air blew in, and she felt better. She saw a flock of small city sparrows settle on a telephone wire outside. Love is a bird in a fist. Her own journal prompt flung back at her: *Can you love someone you don't trust?*

"Never mind," she answered. "Why did you pull me in here?"

He started to crack his knuckles, a habit she detested. He cracked each finger, paused, and then cracked again. Each time he paused, she stiffened, waiting for the next one. She prayed, when he reached the last digit, that he would stop. Mercifully he did.

"Look, Charlotte. I didn't want to worry you, but last Friday night there was some trouble."

Was he going to start cracking his knuckles again? Her stomach was heaving.

"She walked right into it. The Knudsen kid. No common sense. I had to get her out of there. That's all it was."

"The kids mentioned that," she allowed cautiously.

"You see?" he said.

"Among other things. Like you left with her. Little Miss Minnesota."

"Oh, that."

"Yes, that."

"I didn't like to think of her riding the subway that late and I—"

He broke off mid-sentence and she tensed. Here it came. The confession. The excuses. But instead he stopped, staring at her with his head tilted sideways, for all the world the way her mother used to do.

She braced herself, trying not to feel it when it came. Not to feel it. Not to react.

Then he said, softly, "My God. You're jealous. It is so incredible to me. I'd actually feel flattered if—"

She snapped the rubber band.

"Not those damn rubber bands again." He reached over, seized one of her hands, and, before she could pull back again, carefully removed the band.

She retrieved and replaced it, giving another little snap. She folded her hands in her lap. She was far away, off in a place he could not reach.

"Jesus, Charlotte. Charlotte. Use your brain. You're too intelligent not to know how I feel about you. You're playing a game here."

The brown eyes now three shades darker. The brows a straight black line.

"Is that what all this has been to you?" she said. "A game?"

He looked as though she had hit him. "Are you out of your mind?"

She started to shiver. The breeze blowing in from the open window was blasting her. He pointed his chin toward the window, and when she nodded, he got up to close it. Be fair, she told herself. He's not Francis.

Trust him? She had seen the way Knudsen had smiled at him. And she had seen him smile back. But he did seem upset now. And he had come into her classroom to tell her, to explain. Perhaps it was really nothing. Probably it was nothing. Probably she was—conflating him with Francis. And there was the sex. The rainbow sex. She missed it.

"Oh," she said. "All right then. Let's just m—move on. Look. I—I don't feel very well."

Suddenly, he was all kindness and concern. "Oh, sweetheart. I'm an idiot. So I was right. I know how you ladies can get. That time of the month, right? I should have realized you're due." Perhaps the single most perfect thing he could say to make her angry again. But then he began talking very fast. "All right. Look—before you hear this from someone else—Natalie called me in before. She said I have to go into Kate's class this afternoon. Every afternoon, until she gets a handle on things. She can't manage her students and she needs my help."

Natalie. How perfect. She had set Knudsen in Theo's path. What sweet revenge.

But it was better not to react.

Now he continued. "Natalie gave me a direct order. Believe me, I don't need this—babysitting job."

It was even possible that he believed that. Charlotte summoned what she could of her dignity. "That I understand. Just part of your job."

"Thank God. You had me going there for a while," he said. "Then you're all right? We're all right?" Checking the door to be sure they were unobserved, he kissed her palm and closed her fist over the kiss. "God, I miss you." But he was already standing up. "I guess I better get over there now," he said, "To Kate's class. Natalie will check up on me. Close the door on your way out."

She had thought he would give her something for Valentine's Day.

Kate. He had called Miss Knudsen Kate. And she had called him Theo. Slowly Charlotte opened her fist and pressed her palm against her cheek.

ᘓᕽᘒ

Valerie's Journal
DO NOT READ!
Now one of the problems I have sometimes is when other people have really bad problems I just can't

feel them. I mean, there's only so much a person can feel.

So when China told me about how her stepfather does her, and how her mother doesn't say anything because they need the money he brings in, I felt bad, but after I told the guidance counselor Mr. King and saw China talking to him I kind of put it out of my mind. NOMB.

Now with Suzette it's different, because we really go back, and when she started getting all crazy about Zamar breaking up with her I really did feel bad, but see? It was a kind of normal thing—a guy breaking up with a girl. And even if Suzette is nowhere this side of normal, listening to her complain about it was a normal thing too. I felt bad for her I really did.

But this thing with Corny—when Corny OD'd right in history class I didn't feel anything at all. Except maybe guilty for being friends with Rohan.

Lucky Lagakis was the teacher for that class and he knows CPR maybe from when he was a cop or something but Corny fell over in class and Lagakis was on it in a flash. He was doing mouth to mouth and calling 911 practically simultaneously. And the class was just sitting there watching when the EMTs came and carried Corny away. Rohan just sat there with the rest of us, staring, like it was a TV show.

But what comes to mind is that it's really Rohan's fault. Now I have a good relationship with Rohan, ever since kindergarten, and I know he hasn't had it easy. But Rohan is the one who gets the drugs for Corny, and now when he comes around and starts talking to me I just have to think. I mean, he's like the same person who put glue in my hair in Miss Calcagni's class when we were both five, but sitting there watching them carry Corny out I had to wonder how I could even look in the mirror talking to Rohan. But see? I have to be polite.

And funny thing. Even though Lagakis must have figured out by now that Rohan is pushing most of the drugs in this school, if you don't count Gareth, it looks like Rohan and Lagakis are best buddies.

CHAPTER 25

Rainy Day

"Mom? Mom? *Mom*! Wake up! You're late!"
Charlotte struggled awake. All she wanted to do
lately was sleep. The sofa in the den where she
had been asleep felt so comfortable and she didn't want to
leave it.

"My God. Look at the time."

Ordinarily, she'd be showered and out of the house by
now. She could barely make it to school for her first class.
She tried to wake up quickly, but it felt like she was walking through sand. She felt so sad, so overwhelmingly sad.
Then it came back to her. Theo and Ms. Knudsen. *Katy.*

But here was Abigail, standing over her, still in her pajamas, or what passed for pajamas on a teenager—a long tee
shirt. Her red curls, like Charlotte's own, were out of control this morning. It must be raining out.

"Abigail. What's wrong? Why aren't you in the shower?"

"I—I don't feel well."

"Do you have a fever? Take your temperature." Charlotte pulled Abigail to her, felt her forehead. It was fine. She
kissed her daughter's cheek. "You feel pretty cool."

"I can be sick without a temperature."

"Take it."

"I knew you'd say that. It's ninety-nine. But I want to stay home today."

Abigail had never been fond of school, and since she was a small child she'd had bouts of illness that vanished as soon as she was ensconced in front of the television with cinnamon toast and tea. "Schoolitis" was the family name for Abby's maladies.

"Ninety-nine is not a real fever. Is your homework done? Do you have a test today?"

Shouldn't Charlotte know that? She had no idea, she realized, what was going on in the girls' school any more.

"Yes, my homework's done, and no I don't have a test today, but I just don't feel right."

It would be the perfect excuse to stay home herself—a sick child. But Abigail was seventeen now, old enough not just to stay alone but to babysit for younger children. And it was too late to call in sick.

"That's not a temperature. You have schoolitis."

"I couldn't stop coughing last night." Abby gave a little forced cough, to illustrate what she meant.

"It's probably a drip. Have some hot tea. You'll feel better after you have breakfast. Take some lozenges to school with you. Next week is President's Week. You can rest then. Go get dressed. I have to run."

Now Emily was in the room, fully dressed. "Are you letting her stay home again, Charlotte?" Emily said.

"Don't call me Charlotte. Call me Mom or Mother," Charlotte said a ritual response to her first name on Emily's lips.

Emily shrugged eloquently, conveying without words: *Start acting like a mother.* Deal with this later, Charlotte decided. God, she was tired.

Suddenly her foggy brain picked up on what Emily had said. "Again? What's this about again?"

"Oops." Emily said deliberately.

Charlotte saw Abigail shoot a twin-speak look at Emily. *Shut up,* the look said.

Once again, Emily shrugged, this time at her twin.

"I was tired," Abigail said. "I needed—I needed to sleep in."

The school always mailed notices to the parents if students were absent. Charlotte had not received anything. But since she had been leaving so early in the morning, either twin could easily have stayed home without her knowledge and screened the mail. She'd just assumed everything was all right. She needed to talk this over with them. With Abigail, really. But Emily too. Obviously, Emmy was concerned, or she would not have slipped and told on Abigail. And she'd need to talk with Francis too, Charlotte realized. She'd call him later.

She heard her own mother's voice calling to her through her sadness, coming through loud and clear. She felt her mother's fingers poking disapprovingly at her shoulder blades: Get up! Stand up straight. Head high. Best foot forward.

Charlotte took a quick shower, not washing her hair, and threw on yet another long skirt and sweater. Librarian style. She was late. She decided to call the principal.

Natalie answered her cell and was surprisingly pleasant. "Drive carefully," she'd said. "I'll arrange to cover your first class if you're late."

Because it was raining and later than usual, traffic was heavy. As she neared Stamford, she simply sat, as if in a parking lot, while an accident was cleared. As she sat, she thought about what was happening. She needed to reorganize her priorities. She was lost in a fever dream of missing Theo, neglecting her kids. And what had ever made her think that Theo was always going to be faithful? Perhaps just that she thought no one else wanted him. He was overweight and far from handsome and—wonderful in bed. And someone else did want him—someone who was young and unencumbered.

Her wipers were old—she needed to replace them—and they smeared the windshield in half circles. Once the acci-

dent was cleared, bullying trucks on Interstate 95, behind
schedule, tailgated and honked as she struggled to see
through the fogged-up windows, and as she passed Co-op
City, she was nearly in an accident with a car merging in
too quickly on the right. But she made it to school safely.
She arrived barely in time for her second class, and as she
hustled toward the room she saw Theo coming toward her
in the hallway. Miss Knudsen was with him, talking ear-
nestly. As Charlotte watched, the rookie teacher tripped and
fell into him and he automatically righted her, one hand on
her elbow, the other on her back. Oldest trick in the book,
Charlotte thought, as the girl's hand rested on his arm.
She'd done it herself, once.

He saw Charlotte before Knudsen did and raised his eyebrows. *Where were you?* But she hurried past them toward
the room. "Late," she said, unnecessarily.

"Everything all right, Mrs. Murphy?" Knudsen called
back at her. "They sent me to cover your class." It was interesting, how the young teacher never failed to work in that
Mrs. Charlotte had been calling herself Ms. for a few
months now, and had often invited the girl to call her Charlotte. Knudsen should have a talk with Emily.

"Yes, dear," Charlotte answered, turning around. "Just
overslept."

Dear. She hoped that achieved the right patronizing
touch. Theo stood apart from Knudsen, impassively watching Charlotte as she struggled, all thumbs, with her umbrella, briefcase, and papers, to open the door. She knew she
looked horrible in her old green raincoat that she'd thrown
on over her Marian Librarian clothes. Knudsen, of course,
was in brown cowboy boots and skinny jeans that left no
doubt as to the shape of her derriere.

"Oh good," Knudsen said. "Does that mean I don't have
to cover? Great. I was hoping to get some coffee when they
gave me the coverage." She pronounced it cah-fee.

Charlotte had skipped breakfast. She would kill for some
coffee. Would kill Knudsen for less.

"I have some cah-fee in the office," Theo said to Knudsen. "I usually do."

They already had a private joke, Charlotte noted. His voice, as always, was overly loud. Why did he assume that everyone wanted to listen to him?

""I love your caw-fee," Knudsen said, mimicking his New York accent.

"Come in to the office with me and I'll get you warmed up in a second. Get *it* warmed up, I mean. The cah-fee."

His face was red now. Was it possible that remark about warming her up had been a slip of the tongue? He seemed to be reverting to his old lecherous ways. How could she have forgotten that side of him?

The class, which had been talking joyously, immediately silenced when they saw her. She must look really bad. As she walked into the room where her class was waiting, she heard Knudsen's pealing Midwestern voice say to Theo, "You were so helpful yesterday. Bless your hear-r-r-r-r-t." Her rolling r's echoed through the hallway. She was not a rookie at everything, little Miss Minnesota.

Charlotte threw her coat and briefcase on the desk, started to pass out papers. Thank God she had a lesson prepared. But just then, Natalie appeared. What was this? A surprise observation? Perfect. It would be an appropriate terrorist tactic—pop in to observe when obviously it would take Charlotte a while to get her bearings.

But Natalie's face was concerned. "Charlotte," she said. "Your daughter's school called. The nurse said she couldn't reach you on your cell."

Charlotte's heart stopped beating.

"Now relax. I'm sure it's nothing terrible, but I think you'd better go," Natalie said. "Something about an asthma attack. I hate to think of you going back all that way in the rain, but the nurse was quite insistent."

"Asthma? Abigail never had asthma. Nobody in our family has asthma," Charlotte said defensively. Her heart was racing. Why had she come to work that morning? To see

Theo, of course. *Bad mother!* But thank God she hadn't let Abby stay home alone. At least she had the nurse with her.

"Look, the nurse said she's doing better, but she wants you there to take her to the doctor. Just go."

Natalie was acting really kind. In the old days Charlotte would have taken that for granted. But now, after she had betrayed Natalie to State Ed? Natalie was certainly being very generous.

"I'm a mother too," Natalie said, reading her mind. "Go."

"Thank you," Charlotte said. She snatched up her coat, started to struggle into it, and then decided not to bother.

"Believe me, I know what you're going through," Natalie said.

Knudsen and Theo were still standing nearby, and Natalie directed her next remark to the rookie teacher. "Those jeans are most unprofessional," she said. "We've spoken about this."

Theo was looking at Charlotte. "Can I do anything?" he asked.

"Yes, Mrs. Murphy," Knudsen chimed in. "We'd love to help you."

Charlotte shook her head. "Nothing."

"You can help by covering the class, after all," the principal said to Knudsen. "Get in there."

Knudsen looked panic stricken. "Theo?"

He shook his head. "You'll be fine. I'll stop by later."

"I hope your daughter's better, miss," a student said. This was followed by a chorus of good wishes from the other students in the class. "Take care of your daughter, miss. We'll be good."

As Charlotte started to walk away, Natalie caught up with her.

"Natalie, this is more than kind of you after what happened."

"Look, Charlotte. I'm not a monster. I know your girls—love them to death.' Natalie held out her arms to Charlotte, who entered them with relief. Natalie kissed her cheek.

When she emerged from Natalie's embrace, Charlotte saw Theo's eyes on her.

"I'll walk with you, Charlotte," he said.

"No. I'm in a terrible hurry."

He ignored her and followed her to the outside door, his long stride easily matching two of her quickest steps.

At the door, he stopped. "It's pouring. Put your coat on." He took her coat from her arm, held it for her. She set her briefcase on the floor and struggled into it, stepping away from him quickly.

Undeterred, he followed her outside, holding the umbrella over her. When they reached her car, he said, "Are you sure you can drive okay?"

"Positive."

He held the umbrella over her as she fumbled for her keys, tried to kiss her cheek as she opened the door. "Look," he said, "Don't be fooled by her Judas kiss. She must want something."

Why was he even talking about that? "That doesn't matter now," Charlotte said. "Will you get out of my way? Don't you see I can't talk now, Theo?"

From its usual place in the glove compartment her cell phone rang. She recognized the ring tone. Theo would too.

"Hello, Francis," she said into the phone. She climbed into the car, slamming the door in Theo's face.

She pressed the button for speaker phone and started driving.

"Charlotte," Francis said. "Thank goodness. They couldn't reach you so they called me in California. Where the hell are you?"

"I'm in the Bronx, Francis, on my way back to Connecticut. What's going on?"

"It's bad. The nurse wants to send her to the hospital. I gave permission for Sally Bailey to go with her."

Sally Bailey, their next door neighbor, was the emergency contact Charlotte had listed on the school form.

"Natalie said something about asthma?"

"Didn't you even call the nurse back?"

"I was about to," Charlotte said. "I'm trying the best I can to get back to Connecticut."

"Then don't bother to call. Abby is probably in the hospital by now. Just go."

"The hospital! But what's wrong with her?"

"The nurse thought it was asthma, but now she says it's probably pneumonia."

Somehow, Charlotte retraced her long drive, this time to Norwalk Hospital, a little nearer to the Bronx than Westport. When Charlotte arrived at the hospital, she found Abigail in a make-shift cubicle. Tubes were coming out of her nose and an IV drip was running to the back of her hand. Her cheeks were unusually pink. Charlotte rushed over and touched the girl's forehead. Unlike this morning, her daughter's face was very hot. Sally Bailey was still there, but she gave up her seat when she saw Charlotte. "I have to pick up my little guy at pre-school," she said. "I'm so glad you got here."

Charlotte thanked her, hugged her, and said, "I'll never forget this, Sally."

"I know," Sally said. "I'm a mother too."

"It probably started out as a cold," a twelve-year-old girl was saying. Where had she come from? "I'm Dr. Lee," the girl said. "Are you the mother?"

"Yes," Charlotte said. "I am her mother."

"Have you been feeling tired?" the doctor asked Abigail.

Abby nodded. "Exhausted. I could never get up in the morning." She looked over at Charlotte. "That's why I stayed home from school a couple of times. I figured I'd catch up on my sleep."

Charlotte started to say, "Why didn't you say something to me," but she stopped herself. Instead, she patted Abigail's knees under the thin hospital blanket and asked the doctor, "How do we get my daughter well?"

"I suspect she has a bacterial infection in her lungs, a

form of pneumonia which we've been seeing a bit of lately."

"But she had no fever this morning."

"Occasionally a patient is afebrile even with an infection, especially early in the morning. I need to wait until the labs come back, and I've ordered a chest X-ray. If it is bacterial, the infection usually responds quite well to an antibiotic, and we've started her on that intravenously. I'd prefer to keep her overnight, and then, all going well, send her home to your care. But no school. Dr. Wilson is your primary care doctor?"

Charlotte nodded.

"Let her rest for a few days, and then go to Dr. Wilson. He'll determine when she's ready to resume her full activities. And with a full course of antibiotics, of course."

"Am I contagious?" Abigail wanted to know. "I don't want my sister to get it."

"By the time you go home tomorrow you will no longer be contagious. But if your sister were going to get it, she would probably have it by now."

Emily! As the doctor disappeared Charlotte started to dial Emily's number. "Are you calling Emily?" Abby said. "You're better off texting her. It's eleven thirty. She's in class."

"I don't know how," Charlotte admitted.

"You are so lame," Abigail said, but fondly. "Give me your phone. They took mine and put it somewhere. What do you want to say?"

"You're too ill to do this."

"Not to text."

Charlotte handed over the phone.

"You have a message," Abby said after texting Emily.

"Never mind that," Charlotte answered, taking her phone back. "It's just someone from school. Try to rest. I'm going to take good care of you."

ↄ∕ↄↄ∕ↄ

Valerie's Journal
DO NOT READ!
I AM STRESSED OUT!
I feel like screaming.

Can you believe it I might not graduate? After so many years of playing by all the stupid rules, somebody goes ahead and changes the Regents scores, that's what they're saying, and maybe we all have to take the tests again and what if I don't pass? If I don't pass, I swear I'll get Rohan to kill someone. It only costs twenty-five dollars. He'd probably give me a discount and I think I'm gonna make a list. And put the damn principal on top.

Yeah, yeah, I know I'll pass, but still, it's a lot to ask. My grandmother says in the Parents Association they're talking about maybe getting rid of her, the principal not my grandmother, but it's too late for the school. They're gonna close it. And so even if I do graduate it will be like what high school did you go to? Oh yeah? I never heard of it. Can you believe it? All the trouble we took to pick this high school and now it might now even exist anymore. And I know I passed that test. But what I have to do now is concentrate on passing my state boards so I can get my license and work. That has to be priority one.

And it's plenty of stress just getting into the school building now. There were two cop cars in front of the school this morning before the doors even opened but I don't know if they're real cops or just safety and security ones. They call them peace officers, which is like what Murphy calls an oxymoron I think. Like jumbo shrimp.

There's not a fight every day there's like five fights and Lagakis is starting to look as old as dirt. His hair is very dry and brittle. He better be careful or he'll be bald soon.

And with Murphy absent, I couldn't even write in

this journal, which Murphy locked up because I actually asked her to, which is so ironic. So I got Monroe to open the locker where Murphy keeps it. Somehow, I never thought about her being absent because she never was before. But you can't really count on anything.

Problems? Let me count the ways, as Murphy would say. My mother who is in recovery mostly but still has her moments, which is why I'm with my grandmother. My grandmother. Not just a trip but a whole journey. She has me on lockdown 24/7 because she thinks I'm going to turn out like my mother so I have to lie to her to see you know who. My father I never see because my grandmother doesn't think I should see him in jail. Rohan. He hangs around me like white on rice, always looking like he'll kill any guy who comes near me. Which of course nobody does, except of course Drew that Rohan doesn't know about.

And Drew is another headache because he totally doesn't get anything. He's all about college next year and that he wants me to go to his prom and he even says he wants me to take him to ours.

I have to admit that I think about the prom a lot. But even if we get to have a graduation and a prom Drew is NOT going. We are not on the same page there. What I want to do is dress up and dance at my own prom with my own friends, ride in a limo with Suzette, China, Keith, Monroe, and go to the school after party, on the Circle Line and then go home solo too. Rohan won't be allowed at our prom because of his poor attendance or they'll make up something else.

In my opinion, J. Crew totally would ruin my night. And I don't want to be his black girlfriend at his prom either but he doesn't see it that way. Plus, my grandmother would take me out if she knew. Su-

*zette says look at Lagakis and how he's playing Mur-
phy with Knudsen. Well Suzette says after a while
that's what I can expect from J. Crew. Plus a ton of
other problems. She thinks I should dump him. But I
can't explain to her what I feel. Even though he
doesn't have a clue about my life right now, I think
I'm in love with him. We talk a lot, but about different
stuff. Interesting stuff,, which takes me away, and then
when I get back to my own life I feel clear in my head.*

*I wish Murphy would come back. I want to talk to
her about all of this. But I guess she has her own
problems, with her daughter sick and all. I think how
lucky those girls are to have her to talk to. I wish she
were my mother but you don't get to pick your relatives.*

*Yesterday in class Knudsen gave us a get well card
to sign for Murphy's daughter, the one who's sick.
Knudsen says she'll mail it to the hospital. So we all
signed it, at least the ones in class.*

*Knudsen can't teach. She just stands at the board
and says stuff like "I'm waiting" for people to get
quiet and lots of luck with that. Then when she turns
around to write on the board...well...well, you know
Suzette started a little nickname Miss Knutie with no
Booty and when she turns around somebody is sure to
yell it out. So she has Lagakis on speed dial and he
shows up if there isn't a fight going on and gives us
that riot act thing he does, so everybody shuts up and
she writes the assignment on the board. I copy it—you
know that—but nobody else does it. Suzette drew a
picture on the board of Knudsen and Lagakis doing
the nasty and everybody started laughing. I wish I
could give somebody custody of his brain.*

CHAPTER 26

Francis Tries Again

Abby lay in the hospital bed, listless, mostly sleeping. Francis flew in from California. At first, it seemed as though Charlotte would not lose many days from school, because of the President's Week break, but when the week was over, Abby was no better.

Natalie was actually kind about it. "Take as long as you need," she told Charlotte. "Just arrange for the doctor to write some kind of note for you—say that you were seen on those dates—and we'll count it as medically excused."

But Francis cautioned Charlotte against accepting Natalie's favor. As they sat in the hospital together, Charlotte had told him about the scandal at school and her conflict with Natalie.

It was strange, but since they'd been separated, he'd begun listening to her as he had not during the years they were together.

"Don't make Wilson lie about some trumped up illness. It just gives Natalie something to hold over you."

"I'll lose my pay for these days."

"That's nothing—what they pay you. Best to tell the truth. It usually is."

"Funny, to hear you talking about telling the truth," she couldn't resist saying.

That old constipated look was on his face. "I'm trying to help you out here."

"I know, Francis. Truce?"

"Truce. By the way, have you been gaining weight? You're looking very well."

"I think I've lost five pounds this week alone, Francis."

"Oh. Well, then, perhaps you've redistributed," he said. "Very becoming."

"All right. Francis. Truce."

He told her a little about Rosemary. She was, he said, very strict. "Not like you. If I have a late meeting or a business trip, she calls to check up on me, and then she checks with the hotel to see if I'm really staying there. She's turning into a nag." His voice was complaining, but he smiled rather proudly.

Maybe he thought of this surveillance as a sign of caring. I should have been more suspicious, Charlotte thought. More aware of his activities, his life away from us.

It had been years since she'd spent so much time with Francis. They fell into their old habit of working the daily crossword together. Emily came to the hospital every day, after school of course, and she beamed when she saw Francis and Charlotte bent over the puzzle.

Abigail's temperature fluctuated, sometimes hovering near normal and other times spiking. Despite the antibiotics, the fever stubbornly refused to go away. Francis wanted Dr. Wilson to call in a specialist in lung diseases, but the physician said that he just needed to find the right antibiotic—that when he did, their daughter would get better. He insisted that Abby remain in the hospital until she was afebrile.

"That alone worries me," Francis said to Charlotte when Abby was sleeping. "They kick people out in twenty-four hours, even if they've had brain surgery." He'd been surfing the web, looking up mononucleosis, Lyme disease, and even leukemia. "Doctors don't know everything," he said. "But they have to act like they do."

Because Abigail was still a teenager, she was given a

room in the children's section, which was empty. Charlotte was glad her daughter did not have to share a room with an adult, but instead had a private room with brightly painted walls and cheerful pictures of animals. The only drawback was that there was a lovely private bath in the room, and there was no pretext to leave the room to call Theo. Charlotte made an effort to call him when she could break away, but it was difficult. She managed to leave a voice message on his phone. "Abigail is still in the hospital, and Francis is here," she had said. "Please don't call. I'll try to reach you."

In another message she had said, "It's bad. The doctor doesn't seem to know what to do for her. She has pneumonia but it isn't responding to treatment. We're at the hospital all the time, and I can't talk to you."

Theo belonged to another world, another time, not this enclave of a pretend intact family.

"You are such good parents, here all the time," a pink-clad nurse said, watching them play cards with Abby. The nurses were lovely, especially this one, who bustled around and teased Abby about being a teenager who probably took long showers. But cheerful surroundings and upbeat nurses were not enough to get their daughter better. Mornings, when Abby's temperature was typically at its lowest point, they would be hopeful, but each afternoon it would rise, despite the IV cocktail that poured antibiotics into her slender body.

The twins had inherited Charlotte's curly red hair, but, unless they were very late indeed, both girls made sure to blow it dry and straight every morning. However, now Abigail's hair curled around her face, much as it had when she was seven, and she looked young and fragile lying in the bed, hooked up to a monitor that beeped regularly.

Like a much younger child, Abigail personified the monitor, smiled when it beeped, even, in her fever, beeping back at it. "My other twin," she said.

Charlotte grew more and more worried.

Emily joined them in the hospital every day after school.

During the late afternoon and early evenings, the four played cards and board games rather than looking at the tiny TV affixed to the wall, Abigail joining in but drifting back to sleep after her turn. Each day they filled out menu cards and ate hospital food on trays.

At first Charlotte thought of Theo a great deal, fantasized conversations with him, imagined what he'd say if he were able to watch her going through the day. But more and more, her mind drifted from him. He was, she thought, like the alto parts of a choral piece, always present, but not the melody. Sometimes she noticed, in surprise, that she had not thought about Theo for hours. As work had been a way of obliterating the breakup of her marriage from her thoughts, worry about Abigail pushed Theo to another part of her brain.

She called him at times when she knew he could not answer. She left a message, said not to call, and he didn't. Perversely, that annoyed her. She spent so much time with Francis that her messages to Theo were squeezed in during random moments of privacy. They became more and more terse and formulaic. *No change. Don't call. Can't talk. Gotta go.*

Theo had no place in this foursome. For they appeared to be a real family, except that, when they went home, Francis slept in the guest room. As Abby's condition worsened, Charlotte stopped even trying to call Theo.

The fever was erratic, occasionally spiking to a worrisome high and then retreating back to near normal. Dr. Wilson kept introducing them to a parade of new doctors—doctors, Francis said cynically, who would each shake their hands, and say hello to Abby, and then send an enormous bill.

On Friday, Wilson brought a dark-haired woman, Dr. Cynthia Solaris, to examine Abigail. "We're lucky to get her," Wilson said in an aside to Francis. "A friend of a friend introduced us, and she asked if I had any interesting cases. Does she have your permission to examine Abigail?"

Francis agreed immediately, and Charlotte acquiesced in silence. Solaris did not bother to shake their hands or even acknowledge them, but she examined Abby thoroughly and then suggested a combination of antibiotics, speaking only to Wilson as though Abby were a science experiment they were working on together. Charlotte disliked the idea of Abby being an "interesting case." The woman had no bed-side manner at all, but handled the child brusquely and left without bothering even to say goodbye.

But Francis was not bothered. "Art Wilson has a great bedside manner, but he doesn't have a clue what to do with our daughter. This Solaris is probably a busy person, and that means she's successful."

"I don't think he has a great bedside manner. Have you noticed that he only speaks to you, not to me? And while I'm on the subject, you never even asked me before you agreed to let Solaris examine Abigail. I'm her mother, and you should speak with me before going ahead. As it happens, I agree. We need another perspective. But in the future, ask."

Francis was taken aback and actually apologized. "I guess poetry girl has gotten used to running the show," he said.

"I'm not a girl, poetry or otherwise," she replied.

"Yes, *ma'am.*"

Francis told Charlotte that he'd lost confidence in Wilson, and he suspected that, with Solaris, kickbacks were the order of the day. "They're all thieves. And they're all in it together."

However, Solaris *did* have a clue. Soon after being treated by Solaris, Abby ate her breakfast of cereal and milk with relish. "I'm starved," she said. "This cereal is great."

Her temperature had been normal for nearly twelve hours. If she remained afebrile for twenty-four more hours she would be able to go home the next day. Emily had been part of the vigil at her sister's bedside but, on this particular Saturday, she had taken some time off to be with Ryan.

When Charlotte heard footsteps echoing down the corridor, she turned toward the doorway, expecting to see Emily, but instead saw a pink-coated volunteer enter the room with a large bouquet of yellow spring flowers. Charlotte immediately recognized the logo on the cellophane wrapped around the flowers. *Lagakis Florist.*

Daffodils. After that first night, he'd read the poem to please her. Then he'd brought pots of the yellow flowers to her classroom—out of season then. Daffodils. We'll always have daffodils.

The flowers were already arranged in a dark blue vase, with a little wet sponge beneath them to keep them fresh. The lady in pink set them on Abby's tray, but Francis moved them to the window ledge. "They're probably full of pollen," he said. "She doesn't need that now."

Theo would never think of that. He was not Abigail's father.

That night, Charlotte dreamed of Theo. Somehow he had come into her bed in Westport. She turned to put her arms around him. His hands were squeezing her breasts, flicking at her nipples. It did not feel like Theo, gentle, wonderful Theo. It felt like—

"Hello, poetry girl."

"Francis? What are you doing?"

"We're still married."

CHAPTER 27

On the Horns of a Dilemma

When Abby had been afebrile for twenty-four hours, she was discharged. A follow-up visit was scheduled for Tuesday, and, with Dr. Wilson's approval, she was pronounced ready to resume normal activity on Thursday. Francis stayed for the follow-up and then booked a return flight to California. Charlotte cooked him a farewell breakfast.

His eyes bored into her as he rattled his newspaper. "I forgot what a good cook you are."

"Oh," Emily said, "She's gotten even better. She cooks new stuff now. What's that eggplanty thing you make?'

"Moussaka."

"No carbs. You should try it."

"I don't think you'd like it, Francis."

"I can be more adventurous now. Apparently, you can too."

Charlotte let that pass. Now she was overcome by nausea and somehow at the same time by hunger. She took a piece of bacon, savoring its salty flavor.

Francis kept staring at her. She looked away and let her eyes fall on the daffodils, now fully open on the dining room table.

As she drove him to the airport he said, "Charlotte. I ran

into Jack Bailey this morning when I went out to get the newspaper. He said there was some guy here at Christmas?"

God help me, she thought.

"Oh. I thought I told you—the car broke down and this man from school with relatives here drove me home—then the tree fell down in the storm." That was the truth, or at least part of it.

"Jack said his car was parked here all night."

"It was too icy for him to leave. I had to let him stay."

Francis let it hang there, but Charlotte was on the phone with Renata Gordon within seconds of his departure.

⁂

Francis returned to California, and Charlotte returned to work. As she walked through the familiar doorway, she was greeted by so many dear and well-known faces: George, Mr. King, even the assistant principal Mr. Eugene, who had been extremely friendly since observing her on Valentine's Day.

One and all welcomed her back. She quickened her steps, anxious to see Theo, to ask to speak with him later on, during her free period. She longed to go immediately to Theo's office, but protocol dictated that she stop first at the principal's office. Natalie greeted her warmly, considering.

"How is Abigail?" she asked.

"Much better. She's back on full activity."

"Great. Sit down, Charlotte. We have some catching up to do."

"Oh, I certainly do. I haven't seen my students in forever."

"No. I mean we—as in you and I—have to talk."

"Can't it wait? I have to check my mail and prepare for my first class."

"Very well. But see me third period. When you're free."

Natalie walked her to the door. To her surprise Theo was

in the outer office. He looked up, and away. It seemed as though he were growing a beard.

"I'm so glad you're back on board," Natalie said to Charlotte.

"You've been really generous," Charlotte said. Natalie held out her arms, and Charlotte automatically went into them, feeling Theo's eyes on her all the while.

"Come in, Mr. Lagakis," Natalie said.

"I'm waiting for the chapter leader," Theo replied.

The union chapter leader? That meant Theo was in some kind of trouble. Big trouble.

"Hello, Theo," Charlotte said.

"Mrs. Murphy," he replied. Even in that small office there was a great space between them. His eyes were on the floor.

"See you later?" Charlotte knew Natalie was listening but she didn't care.

He shrugged. "I doubt it."

At this, the union chapter leader appeared and clapped Lagakis on the shoulder. "Sorry I'm late, Ted," he said. "Let's get this done." And the three disappeared into Natalie's office.

Charlotte went upstairs woodenly. As she passed Theo's office, she was surprised to see a light on. There was Miss Knudsen, drinking coffee out of the cup Charlotte had come to think of as her own.

Charlotte would have hurried by, but Knudsen rose and beckoned to her.

"How's your daughter?"

"Better. Thanks for the card."

A faint scent of strawberries came from the young girl. Strawberry bubble gum. Charlotte wondered if Theo liked it. "What's going on with Theo? I saw him in Natalie's office with the chapter leader."

Knudsen patted Charlotte on the head. "You're such a sweet lady. I guess it's not easy, coming back to this. Have you checked your messages lately?"

Valerie's Journal
DO NOT READ!

Sweet are the uses of adversity
Which, like the toad, ugly and venomous,
Wears yet a precious jewel in his head;
And this our life, exempt from public haunt,
Finds tongues in trees, books in running brooks,
Sermons in stones, and good in everything.

This was our new poem we had today and you can see that Murphy's back, finally. I think it kind of surprised a couple of kids that the principal was visiting. I guess Murphy knew—she had her little lesson ready and even had candy for us. But this time I didn't actually like the candy—Sour Patch Kids. Then she passed out something else, and it was mad good. Little white nougat things with fruit flavor dots. So good, after the other stuff.

She gave some out to the principal sitting in the back too, but she didn't want any.

All this stuff took a long time and then she thanked us for our nice card and Suzette has to ask if Abigail liked the picture she drew.

So she said her daughter getting sick was a bad time, but like, there was good there too—that her other daughter and her were having problems and they got closer. So the adversity sort of brought the family together. Not like in my family.

Then she gives us the poem and we talk about the stuff in it, you know, the images and similes but the bell rang before Murphy could finish—she's off her game, I guess, but it was good to have her back.

So after class I asked if I could talk to her and she said maybe I could help her, actually, and she takes out this ancient cell phone and starts asking me about texting. She should get another phone. She doesn't know anything about how to use hers. I think she's worse than my grandmother.

I started to tell her about Drew and how I want to keep him separate from my friends at school and she listened to me, and didn't say anything. But when I finished she said she totally got it about trying to keep two things separate. She even had a name for it—compartmentalize—but sometimes you can't. You got to figure out a way to make stuff fit together she told me. Decide what's important and what's not so much. Prioritize, she called it.

Anyway I thought it was funny she didn't know how to even get a text off her phone. That thing is mad old. I started to show her. But then Murphy got up and threw up into the waste-basket—really hurled. It was disgusting. I guess it was the Sour Patch Kids.

Murphy was in no shape to listen. But those texts she got were pretty interesting. NOMB, of course.

CHAPTER 28

Observation

When Charlotte visited Natalie a few days later for a post observation conference, she was given an observation report to read:

Dear Mrs. Murphy:

When I visited your period six English class today, you were in the process of distributing candy to the class, which is against school rules. The bell rang before you were able to complete a poetry "lesson." You detained a student, Valerie Martin, assuring her that you would write a pass to her next teacher, which is educationally unsound and may lead to missed instruction.

As we have discussed, poetry is not a good choice for this group. More accessible writings—such as those in the workbook I specifically told you to use—would be more appropriate to academically challenged youngsters. Furthermore, going against my direct order is tantamount to insubordination and may result in termination of your teaching license.

I expect that your next observation will resume the formerly high standard of teaching you exhibited before your extended unexcused absence.

This was an unsatisfactory lesson.

Sincerely,

Natalie Albert, Principal

I have received a copy of this report and understand that it is being placed in my file.

_____
Teacher's Signature

Charlotte could not believe what she was reading. "Wow, Natalie. It was really that bad?"

"Not necessarily. It all depends on your attitude. If you are willing to cooperate with me, there might be other ways to look at your lesson."

"Cooperate? What does that mean?"

"It means I just got a rather tiresome phone call. There will be another visit from the state. May I count on your support this time?"

"About the Regents again? I thought you were exonerated."

"I was, of course. This is a pure formality. But it would be helpful this time if you back me up. And then this observation wouldn't have to go in your teacher's file." Natalie picked up the observation report and dangled it over the wastebasket. "It could go in the circular file."

"Just do what you think is fair," Charlotte said.

"Oh, I will, believe me. And there is one more thing. It's about your Romeo."

Charlotte felt her mouth go dry.

"Lagakis—he's on his last legs. Gave him three unsatisfactory ratings and I've got someone from headquarters at Tweed coming to observe him. I'll have his license, believe you me, and maybe yours, too."

"Take our licenses? How? Why?"

"You know why. Now, dear friend, in the not so distant past I've given you a lot of professional development. You've attended workshops at headquarters, gotten a lot of training from the educational specialists there."

Charlotte shrugged. "Those specialists? To them, teaching is all about a check-list some genius developed. Teach to the test. Drill and kill. Nothing about reaching out to kids on a personal level, no mention of tailoring the lesson to meet the kids where they are."

Natalie pinned her eyes on Charlotte. "The check list is an important tool for evaluation. And, my dear, if Lagakis *somehow* becomes aware of that checklist, I'll know whom to blame. And you can guess what will happen to your license too. Insubordination is a serious offense. You can and will be fired. Do you understand?"

"Oh, I understand. Very well." Charlotte signed where indicated. She put the cap on her pen and shoved the report back at the principal. "Natalie," she said. "Fuck you."

CHAPTER 29

Boundaries

That same day, as Charlotte was going down the back stairs, she saw Theo on a landing, looking out the window at a side street. He didn't turn around, but she saw by the set of his shoulders that he knew she was there.

She didn't know whether to ignore him and walk behind him, saying nothing, or stop and try to talk, but her feet kept moving down the stairs of their own accord. She paused on the bottom step, holding tight to the handrail.

On the floor below, a math teacher with a loud voice was reviewing definitions. "Parabola. Boundary points," wafted out.

She decided to try. "Theo," she said. "I want to talk to you."

He kept his eyes trained out the window. "There's going to be a fight," he said "Get yourself into a classroom and lock the door."

"I want to say thanks for the flowers. My daughter loved them."

His brows knit together and he continued looking out the window. "You didn't answer even one of my texts."

She almost throttled him. Was that the trouble? "Texts? Don't you realize? How self-absorbed can you be? My daughter was in the hospital. And texts? Theo, I don't ever even look for texts."

"I see. I'm the one who is self-absorbed. And when were you planning to join the current century?"

"You know I'm not good at that stuff."

He did not take his eyes from the window. "If you wanted to hear from me, you'd have found a way. But your daughter—she's all right now, isn't she? Has been for a while. And still no word from you. And Francis with you all week. It all adds up."

She shook her head, *no*, and then realized he couldn't see her, as he was still looking out the window.

His tone was grim. "I guess that's what I expected. Right from the beginning."

"Theo, I can explain."

"It's not important now. I don't get a vote, frankly, about what you do with your husband. But Charlotte, *this* is important. Listen to me. Have you seen Rohan today?"

"I don't have Rohan in class until later."

"Well, if he shows up, I want you to call me. Don't let him see you do it. And keep him in the room."

"What are you going to do?"

"Just talk to him. He's been violating patrol. There's a big fight coming down, and he's in the middle of it. Not like this. A really big one A turf war, I guess you'd call it."

"Be careful, Theo."

He spoke into the phone again. "Yeah, George. I see them. Looks like Gareth's got a big crew there." He turned back to her. "I have to concentrate on this."

She touched his arm. "But, Theo, I didn't. We didn't," she said softly.

He shrugged her arm off and kept his eyes on the window. "Who gives a shit?"

"One question."

"Yeah, make it quick."

"Theo. Look. I know what Natalie's been up to."

"Oh, she can't do much. Just take away my license."

"I want to help you."

His voice got very soft, and his face was pale. "Jesus. I don't want your *help*, Mrs. Murphy. I honestly don't feel like seeing you at *all*. Just clear out of here. The fight is about to start."

☙☙☙

Valerie's Journal
DO NOT READ!

You know, once I saw a calendar with a picture of Yellowstone Park and there was this geyser there went off every day. They call it Old Faithful but they should have named it Suzette. She goes off at least once a day even if nobody crosses her. Sometimes I can talk her down. Suzette, I mean. We sit on the staircase between the fourth and fifth floor and I let her braid my hair. We're friends because her mother has the same little problem mine has only worse and they took Suzette away from her mother and put her with her pops. My mom has a job and everything, way downtown in Manhattan in the work program they have instead of welfare and mostly her little problem doesn't show so much. But back to Suzette. Her pops isn't bad, but he can't do anything being he works like two jobs. And the both of them are crammed up together at night like rats in this one room apartment and that's partly why I guess Suzette goes off all the time. Once Suzette told me how when she was little and lived with her mom there was this curtain that her mother went behind with the men. That's why they put her with her father. My grandmother says my mother does that too but I don't know if that's true. Yeah, they were right to take me away from her. My mother. But she almost talked her way out of that. Made something up and the stupid social worker be-

lieved her, of course. Straight or high, she is really smart, my mother, and can make you believe anything. She has a job in an office and everything. Not a regular office, but a WEP place where you work instead of getting welfare, but still it's an office. She has a tenant off the books and when she gets high who do you think the tenant calls? Not my grandmother. My grandmother won't do anything for her but she lets me go. I gave the tenant my cell number and so I get the call. Me. At least it's better than calling the police. Lots of times when you report something it just gets worse.

So anyway, me and Suzette were sitting on the back staircase. I was trying to talk her down like I have to when she goes into her volcano stage and all of a sudden we hear them.

"Charlotte," he says. "Go to your classroom and lock the door."

That's how I knew they thought they were by themselves. Him calling her Charlotte.

It figures. Everybody else in the whole school knows Gareth is outside waiting for Rohan. Everybody except Murphy. But hey, she's been absent for a while and she's maybe sick. I mean, she threw up. So I cut her some slack.

So instead of paying attention to what's going on outside, she starts thanking him for some flowers he sent her daughter. Suzette starts to laugh but I shushed her up. I admit it, I'm nosy and I want to listen.

And he's not too smooth either. Instead of asking how her daughter is doing, which would be the right thing, he acts like he knows everything about how she is and starts in about Francis—that's her husband—and going on about her not texting him back.

It's funny in a way because you can tell from what he's saying and the walkie talkie that he's still trying to figure out if the crews are lining up on the side street and she's not getting the picture, keeps going on about trying to help him with some lesson or other he's got to teach.

Then he gets all quiet. Tells her he doesn't want her help. I had read some of those texts he sent before she took the phone from me. She's such a klutz. She is so smart but so stupid.

So then his walkie-talkie starts going and he says to her get into a classroom and stay away from windows. He runs down the stairs and she comes back upstairs and I poke Suzette to stand up and make believe we just got there.

Murphy's got this wild look in her eyes and I don't think it's about a poem.

"Have you seen Ms. Knudsen?" is all she says.

CHAPTER 30

Proxy

"Here's a check list. Use this."

"Can we go over it?"

"Sure. He's got to teach to the test. Figure out what the kids need to pass the social studies Regents and just drill them on that."

"I think he's already doing that."

"Then we'll concentrate on the bells and whistles."

"Tell me again what to do."

"Practice with him, Katy. Get a timer, or use your cell phone. Whatever. Make sure his mini-lesson is exactly six minutes long. Make sure he writes something on the kids' papers—something about state standards. With a rubric and put that on the board too."

"Got it." Knudsen was actually taking notes.

"His lesson has to have group work. Six minutes of a mini-lesson and then they break into groups. Talk to Rohan about giving a presentation."

"I can't do that."

"Then I will. You check Theo's bulletin boards. Make sure there's current work every single day."

"That I can do. I had a whole course in bulletin boards."

"Great. There should be a hand-out. Typed. His hand-writing is awful. There has to be an instructional objective on the handout and he has to refer to it at the end of his lesson. Maybe we can type them up together. I'll help you."

"What about homework, Charlotte?"

"He'll know about that—he'll assign it. And let him have a sponge activity."

"What's that?"

"In case he finishes early, there has to be something for the kids to do so instruction is bell-to-bell."

"Anything else?"

"Use the timer again for a summary. Set it so that the kids finish their group work ten minutes before the bell. Have the kids report out of their groups."

"How do I do this? I mean, how do I get him to listen to me?"

"He loves to help people. Make believe that you need to see him do this—that he's helping you do something for graduate school."

"He'll say it's a big waste of time. A dog and pony show."

"That's how you survive in this system. Just don't tell him I spoke with you. He can be a little stubborn, and he might not listen if he knew."

CHAPTER 31

Out of Bounds

After Charlotte's encounter with Theo on the landing, the skirmish he'd been monitoring had been squashed by the appearance of the cops. Nothing actually happened, but tension filled the school, much like the atmosphere in summer when a hurricane is about to start. As the days passed, Charlotte began to understand how distracted Theo must have been as she'd attempted to have a conversation about their relationship and about the way Natalie was harassing him. He avoided her for the rest of the week, nodding politely if they passed in the hall, but not saying so much as a hello. She continued to coach him by proxy, showing Katy exactly what he had to do when the Tweed Twerp, as the evaluators were called, came to observe him.

Charlotte had always had what her mother referred to as a delicate stomach. When things upset her, she became nauseated. Now, it seemed, her stomach was always upset. Her nausea grew worse and worse until she finally called Dr. Wilson, who squeezed her in for an appointment after school. She'd been feeling run-down, with stomach upset, she said, and Dr. Wilson had said it was probably just the loss of estrogen in a woman of her age. And perhaps a reaction to the reduction in stress after Abby's recovery.

"Adrenalin is a great thing," he said. "But when you don't need it, and the levels go down, you feel the way you're describing. It probably is hormonal. You're what—thirty eight? A little young, but probably menopausal. Go get a facial and go shopping. Retail therapy. Works for my wife."

Charlotte bristled at his patronizing tone. A facial? What a nerve. But shopping sounded like a good idea. She would go shopping for another doctor, she decided.

To her surprise, Wilson's office called the next day, insisting that she come in immediately for a follow-up visit. Charlotte went right after work, more than a little worried.

As soon as she arrived she found herself seated across from him in his office. Wilson didn't want to examine her again. Only to talk.

"The lab results came back, and I was right. It's hormonal. I thought it might be perimenopause, but we're talking entirely different hormones. You do realize you're pregnant, dear?"

Even before he said the word, Charlotte guessed. She was late. Very late. She'd known for some time. But she hadn't faced it.

Her throat felt dry and tight when she tried to swallow. "Do you think I might have a glass of water?"

Wilson went to the adjoining bathroom, filled a cup of water from the sink, and handed it to her.

The water tasted terrible and smelled worse. She set the cup down on his desk and managed a faint thank you.

"You seem surprised," Wilson said carefully. "These surprises are often the best possible things that can happen."

"I've been surprised before."

He shuffled a few papers on his desk, not looking at her. "But if you wish, we can make it un-happen."

Charlotte's hand went to her stomach. She understood that he was offering to terminate the pregnancy. She wondered if he knew about her separation from Francis. The two sometimes played golf together. Was that why Wilson had summoned her into the office instead of merely calling?

"When is the due date?" she asked.

"I'd imagine you'd know better than I. When was your last period?"

"I was never regular. Or very good at arithmetic." The understatement of the year.

"You'd better see your ob-gyn. He'll be better at figuring that out than I would."

"I'm sure *she* will," Charlotte replied.

Had Theo lied about his bad swimmers? He would want the child, would offer to stay with her if she told him. But she did not want another partnership of obligation. And if she didn't tell him, everyone would think the child was Francis's. Except Francis. Unless, of course, she hurried to California. And then what?

Wilson continued. "There are tests we can run, you know. And you ought to start on folic acid and prenatal vitamins, just in case."

A baby. Just when she was almost finished with raising the twins. Could she go through it all again?

Charlotte sat quietly while Wilson wrote out the name of the prenatal vitamins he preferred.

"Doctor," she said. "If you happen to speak to Francis, would you mind not mentioning this?"

"Of course. You'll want to tell him yourself."

"I'm not sure what I want to do. I need to speak to my ob-gyn."

"Yes, call him right away."

"He's a she."

"Ah. Speaking of lady doctors," Wilson said. "How is little Abigail doing? Dr. Solaris called asking about her."

The surly specialist? "She's doing really well."

"Solaris will be pleased. She called especially to find out how our little girl is doing."

"I'm kind of surprised at that," Charlotte said. "I mean, we're eternally grateful that she helped you cure Abby, but she didn't seem too interested. She was such a cold fish. We thought it was just a science experiment to her."

"She mentioned some relative that put her on to the case," Wilson said. "You know that fur store on Main Street?"

"Main Street in Westport?"

"Yes. Lukakis...or something like that. Solaris—Lukakis—they all know each other, those Greeks."

Charlotte closed her eyes, her heart in her stomach. "Yes. I've heard that."

"I guess somebody asked Solaris to look into your daughter's case at Norwalk Hospital and they said I was her doctor."

"Who asked?" Charlotte's voice was barely a whisper. Her throat was still so dry. She stared at the cup of water. No. She couldn't possibly keep it down.

"I figured you knew, or I wouldn't have said anything. Solaris didn't want a fuss made. I understand it was a colleague of yours who knows her."

Charlotte blinked away tears. *Theo.*

"Dr. Solaris is a big shot from Manhattan. You'd never see her in a suburban hospital as a rule. She doesn't see many patients. Mostly does research. Cutting edge. It was a privilege, working with her."

No wonder Theo never asked how Abigail was doing. He'd found out through the Greek grapevine. No matter what he thought about her now, when he'd used his relations and their wide network of contacts to help her daughter, he'd acted with generosity. With love. He had loved her then, even though she'd ignored his calls and texts. Even though she'd sat with Francis in the hospital every day, pretending to be part of a perfect family. Why had she been so careless of Theo's feelings? So wrapped up in her own worry that she'd left him out of her life?

Charlotte left Wilson's office filled with remorse and shame. But soon another feeling surged up from her very core. Her eyes fell upon a patch of early daffodils someone had planted in a sunny corner outside the office. She nodded back at their golden heads and formed a desperate resolve.

She had to thank Theo for helping Abby, for saving her child. And then perhaps she would tell him about his.

ϾͻϾͻ

Valerie's Journal
DO NOT READ!
Today spring is in the air. I get a little sad now, thinking that I won't be riding the bus anymore to school. And I won't be seeing my friends anymore. Or my teachers. At least they didn't close the school before I could graduate. They'll close it next year though, which basically means they'll give it another name. I hope they pick a better one.

Maybe the best thing about spring is that my birthday is in May and I'm gonna be eighteen. My grandmother has been easing up on me a little more every day, which is so strange—all my life she's been suspicious, almost like she'd enjoy finding out that I was cutting school or messing up but now I'm definitely graduating. So I told her what I really want to do on my birthday, which is to go upstate with her when she visits my father.

She was not happy about that, believe me, and kept saying stuff like "But who is going to watch the foster kids?" But I told her that, after all, I'll be eighteen and old enough to vote even and I need to see him. It's been more than ten years she's kept me away. And I never even talked to him on the phone. And I know she has.

And that's when the really bad thing happened. She sat me down and told me that my father doesn't want to see me. Or what she actually said was that he doesn't want me to see him. "He's ashamed," she said. He just wants to remember me like a little seven year old kid, and he wants me to think of him like he was then. And his face is all disfigured from when he got shot.

"I don't care about that," I say.

"Yeah, but he does," she tells me.

And that got me so mad. Mad at him, but mostly mad at my grandmother. All she ever does is talk about how terrible my mother is, and how she dragged my father down.

But bad as my mother is, and she's bad, at least she always wanted to see me, even if it was just to try to bum some cigarette money off me when she'd spent all her salary on junk.

I got so mad at my grandmother that I started throwing things in the house, took down this vase she keeps on the high shelf and never even uses since she doesn't have a garden up here like she did down South. She came here to help raise me and she brought that vase but anyway I took it and threw it out the window. There were a couple people on the street and they hardly even looked up when it fell but it didn't hit anyone. Anyway, my grandmother just looked at me real mild and said, "Does that make you feel better?"

It made me feel guilty and bad, but I looked around for something else to throw out the window.

"All these years," I said to her. "Making pretend my father loved me."

"He loves you Valerie. Best he can." She said this real quiet.

You know what I thought of? I thought of the funeral for Trombetta and how Murphy told me most people did the best they can. And how Trombetta would have said well sometimes your best just isn't good enough.

My grandmother's hair was covered in this red scarf I had given her for Christmas and I remembered how I was surprised that she ever actually wore that, since most of the time with a gift she just puts it away for a special occasion and that's the end of it. But she'd taken it out the box and put it right on, and she wears it all the time now. It's like she had decided the special occasion was here.

"I knew this day would come," she said to me after I threw the vase. "That wasn't my idea, to tell you today."

"When were you going to tell me?" I said. She had chicken on the stove for dinner and it was starting to spatter but she just left it there making a mess. I got up, moved it off the heat, and threw it in the garbage.

"Do you feel better yet?" she said. "Would it have been better, you knowing it all along? Would that have made it easier for you growing up? I don't even know if what I did was right. But it felt right. But maybe it was just easier."

My grandmother has these big eyes and there were big tears in them. She didn't even wipe them, just let them fall.

I made my voice mean, like she would when she thought I cut school or something. "I can't trust you now," I said to her. "Can't trust anybody, I guess."

"Well, that's what happens," she said. "My child is the one who did the wrong and I get the blame."

Little Nadar came in to ask for something and he saw Grandma crying and went back out into the living room real quick. I almost felt glad to see how scared he looked, to see somebody else feel like I felt, but then I felt bad for him. At least I had my own grandmother to raise me. He has nobody, except us.

"How can I trust you?" I said again.

She had stopped crying. She took a dish towel and wiped her eyes. She would never do that, use a dish towel on herself. She is crazy clean. She has to be when the social worker comes to check on the foster kids.

*"How can you trust me? The one that raised you
up and put hot cereal in you every morning before
school and made sure you went to school clean and
neat? Checked your homework every single night."*

Now she was sounding more like Grandma.

*"How can you trust me? Valerie Martin, you can
trust me just as much as I trust you."*

"What do you mean, Grandma?"

"You been lying to me, girl."

*"Grandma, I'm sick of this. I been doing good all
my life. Going to school. Getting high marks. Graduating."*

I got mad all over again, just thinking about all
those years of keeping her rules. She has a least a
thousand rules and I keep all of them, or at least I
used to. From washing my hands before I touch food
to dusting every day to turning off the lights before
leaving the room to checking and re-checking my
homework before I show it to her to never leaving the
house until I look perfect.

She had been yelling at me, but now her voice got
real quiet again. *"Same as I can trust you, now you
wear that chain around your neck and never even tell
me about that boy that give it to you."*

She said every word just a little quieter, like she
was in the choir at church doing a special effect before the big finale.

Inside the foster kids were getting loud and you
could tell pretty soon they'd be fighting. I could hear
the television channel change to one with commercials, which is against my grandmother's rules.

"How did you know?" I asked.

*"And what was I, born yesterday? You going off
the library all the time? And that chain around your
neck—that wasn't gonna be missed by these old eyes
that's been watching you like a hawk since you were
born. When that chain showed up right around*

Christmas and you with your lips all swoll up I knew something was up."

"You didn't say anything. You never say anything."

"What's the use of that? Anybody could see there was no use saying anything. You're almost grown. You've come into your womanhood. It troubled me though."

I started to cry again. "Daddy won't see me?"

She got up from her chair now. It takes her a longer time to do that than it used to. But she got up and put her arms around me and pulled me into her chest. My grandmother has a really big chest, like a pillow. She's not normally a hugger. More of a hitter. The hug felt good. I wanted to relax into it, but I was still mad at her. I knew I should be mad at my father, properly. Or somebody else. But she was the one in front of me and I was mad.

It would stay with me forever, like watching my father get arrested and get shot in the face by the cop when I was seven had stayed forever. He'd been in the street trying to kill my mother for getting high again.

He had his hands around her throat and someone called the cops and I saw the whole thing from the stoop where I was sitting. No one knew about that but Suzette for a really long time. And now Drew, after we talked about little kids getting hurt in that poem at the library, it just kind of poured out of me.

When I told him, he said he realized that he had thought he had problems but he never did. And later he said that's when he started to love me. And I said I didn't want him to feel sorry for me and he said he never would, that I could probably do anything at all with my life if I could get through something like that.

"Why won't my daddy see me? Doesn't he know I've been doing good?"

Grandma just nodded then. "Valerie, you're a good girl," she said to me.

I almost couldn't believe it, that she actually said that. She never says anything like that. Just told me she was watching me, that kind of thing. I got to like hearing that she was watching me.

"You're almost grown, and I can't keep you on lockdown forever. You should bring that boy here to meet me. You're being careful, aren't you?"

"Yes, Grandma," I say, because there's no way denying that I know what she means. And still in her arms, I pull the chain out and show her the ring. She looked at it hard.

"It's real, isn't it?" she says.

Chapter 32

Celebrating Herself

She had known it would be a Monday. The idea was to infuse as much surprise and confusion as possible into the experience—and everyone was disoriented on Mondays.

That particular morning, Charlotte arrived early, walking extra carefully in new high heels, which, irrationally, she'd bought to celebrate the life growing within her. She'd bought a new sweater too, Aegean blue, as her new best friend, the saleswoman in Bloomingdales told her, low necked and clingy. The principal's door was shut.

Up the staircase in her high heels, holding cautiously to the metal railing. In her classroom, Katy was waiting. The girl wore a blue scarf, glittering with a golden border in the Greek key pattern.

"Beautiful scarf," Charlotte said.

"Theo's present," the young teacher replied. "He realized I was trying to help him. But really it should go to you."

Charlotte felt her stomach twist, although the nausea had gone away. She was blooming, her face pink, her breasts high and round.

Katy must have seen Theo if she had received the scarf.

"You saw him?" she asked Katy.

The girl was fiddling with a fat novel. *Middlemarch.* "I

got in early to get some reading done," she said. "It's happening. Just the way you said. There's a guy in a suit sitting in the principal's office. Somebody important. There are pastries."

"She always observes on a Monday."

"Or after a teacher has been absent? Like with you?"

"Yes, you're catching on. Is he ready?"

"I have no idea."

Charlotte went about her usual routine, locking her purse in the locker, just keeping a few dollars in her pocket for lunch later. This was a safety issue Theo had drilled into her, and she continued it.

"Yo, miss, nice threads!"

Monroe poked his head in the doorway and then walked in, followed by Valerie and Suzette.

"Hi, kids," Charlotte said. "How was your weekend?"

"Bad," they said in unison.

Suzette walked over and fingered Charlotte's new sweater. "Cashmere," she reported. "Best quality."

"How do you know that?" Katy asked.

"You think I don't know good stuff? Miss Knutie?"

"Knudsen," Charlotte corrected.

The kids called Kate "the Knutie with no Bootie." She was glad nothing rhymed with Murphy, and they had never figured out what rhymed with Charlotte.

She changed the subject to diffuse the tension. "I was just about to book an appointment with you," Charlotte said to Suzette, who flushed with pleasure.

"Ms. Murphy, you really need a haircut." That was Valerie. "Miss, your hair is a disaster. An emergency." She pulled a plastic wrapped brush from her handbag. "It's clean, miss. I just bought it in CVS." She threw the brush to Suzette, who caught it easily. "Do something," Valerie said.

Charlotte submitted to Suzette's vigorous ministrations while Katy looked on in silence.

"You have Mr. Lagakis later?" Charlotte said to the kids.

"Yeah, for social studies."

"Do me this one favor," Charlotte said. "Go easy."

Valerie nodded. "Yeah, we saw the principal's door was closed. And Ms. Corbo is all pissed off because some guy in a suit took her space in the parking lot. All right, miss. We'll be good. We know how to take care of our teachers."

During her next two classes, Charlotte's students couldn't stop talking about her hair—whipped into shape by Suzette—her cashmere sweater, her high heels. "I'm celebrating myself," she told them. "You should too."

"Then let us use your credit card," someone said.

"Shhhh," others in the class said. "Let the lady teach."

For that day's lesson, she had chosen Walt Whitman's "Song of Myself." For homework, she assigned them to write a poem.

"Can it be rap?" a boy asked.

"Absolutely."

"Does it have to be rap?" another asked.

"It just has to celebrate yourself," she said. "Write about the joy in your life."

"I got nothing to celebrate," one girl said.

"Then fake it," Charlotte replied. "'Assume a virtue if you have it not.' That's from Shakespeare. Or write about not having joy. About hard things in your life."

"Adversity?" The same girl nodded toward the word wall. "I can do that."

"Exactly." Charlotte looked at the young faces around her. "I love you kids," she said. Where had that come from? Out of nowhere. Out of her own joy in new life.

"You love us?" a boy named Armando said incredulously.

He was tall as an adult, but looked six, with a round face and clear brown skin. Charlotte doubted that he had to shave, although he was a senior. He always dressed in gray or beige knit shirts.

"Write what is inside you, and it will be good," was all she said at first. Then, "Yes, Armando, I do. I love you. Every one."

CHAPTER 33

A la Bodega

Charlotte posted herself in the hallway, watching the door, but she took a few minutes to use the rest room, and when she emerged the principal's door was open. Natalie and the Twerp were eating, but Theo was not there. A very bad sign, if they had not included him in their lunch.

When George saw her standing there, she asked where Dean Lagakis might be. "He's probably in the bodega," the security guard told her.

"I'm going for coffee," Charlotte told him.

"Good luck, girly," he said.

He was on to her. Apparently everyone was. Except Theo.

He was not in the bodega, but she saw his big black car drive down the street, toward the school parking lot. She walked behind two boys into the bodega. Two boys with hoods drawn up around their faces. One carried a package.

The tiny woman behind the counter froze, holding the coffee pot poised as though to throw it at the boys. The short order cook came and stood behind her.

"It's a Tek 9," Charlotte heard one boy say.

There was something familiar about the way that the boys walked. "Rohan? Monroe?" Charlotte said.

"Hi, miss," they turned and answered in unison.

"You're not about to cut my class, are you?"

"No, miss. We wouldn't do that," Rohan said.

She wondered if he had gone to Theo's today.

"So what's this about a Tek 9?" she asked.

It was Rohan who answered. "It's a new app for my phone."

"Oh. You know me. I'm old school," she replied. "Come to class. I miss you, Rohan."

"I'll be there later, miss."

The boys left, apparently not interested in sharing their lunch period with their English teacher. The woman at the counter put the coffee pot down, and the short order cook returned to frying his peppers and onions. The boys did not bother to close the door behind them.

Charlotte sat on the tall stool beside the tiny counter and ordered a sandwich to stay, just as Theo walked in. He hesitated at the threshold. Much to her relief, he did not turn around, but walked toward her.

"Charlotte." He stood next to her, put his elbow on the counter. Their faces were at equal levels.

She smiled. "I was hoping to see you. How did it go? Your lesson?"

"I think it went really well."

"Want to talk about it?"

"No." He cracked his knuckles. His ring was gone, she noticed.

Her sandwich was ready. The short order cook put it before her and looked at Theo.

"Just coffee." He saw that she had not ordered a drink and said, "Make it two."

The little woman, Providencia, came over with coffee for them both. Charlotte waved hers away. "No café, gracias. *Tiene leche? Leche caliente?*"

The woman nodded. "*Si.*"

Theo did not seem to hear or follow the conversation, but he looked for the sugar container and started playing with it.

He added sugar to his coffee, much too much sugar, seeming not to notice as the white grains fell into his cup. He would not look at her, although he was close enough to touch her.

It was painful, being ignored by this man who'd never missed an opportunity to stroke her hair, to squeeze her hand. But when Abigail was in the hospital, she'd marooned herself onto a little island of the past, when the four of them were a family. She'd been afraid, superstitious even, that not doing so would mean her daughter would die. That she could be happy or be a good mother but not both. And yet he had saved her daughter's life, or at least hastened the recovery. Tears in her eyes, she said, "Theo? I'm sorry I didn't contact you when Abby was sick. I was so afraid we would lose her, I—I shut down."

"I'm glad she's okay."

Before she could lose her nerve, she continued, "I know this was supposed to be a secret, but I'm too selfish not to say something. I have to thank you. I know. What you did for Abigail. Getting Solaris to see her."

He made his Cro-Magnon face, his forehead becoming a ridge over his eyes, which he kept trained on his coffee cup. "I told her not to say anything."

"It was my doctor who let it slip. On behalf of my whole family I thank you from the bottom of my heart."

"Bullshit. You know I did it for you." He added still more sugar to his coffee. Soon the spoon would be able to stand by itself.

"Don't you take your coffee black?"

"Only when you make it. Let's stop playing games, Charlotte. That message. What were you trying to say?"

She was mystified. "What message?"

"Come on, Charlotte! 'No other man exists for me.'"

Those words. They sounded very familiar. "*Middlemarch!*" she said.

"I'm sure that makes sense to you," he said. "But so what if it's March?"

"No, silly. It's a nineteenth century novel. A really good read." Charlotte could visualize the cover as it sat on Knudsen's desk. Dorothea in her funny widow's bonnet. Ladislaw in his tall top hat. "That's where it's from. It's when Dorothea realizes that Will Ladislaw loves her. Rosamond Vincy says that for him, no woman exists besides Dorothea."

"Oh, yeah. Katy is always dragging that around. And you're always quoting some book." His face was weary, as though jet lagged, shadowed with his heavy beard. He ran his hand over it. "I had almost forgotten how pretty you are. And today. You look *really* spectacular in that sweater." He looked at her breasts, not at her face. "It's been killing me to see you every day."

"You were upset with me. You still are."

He pretended to hold a phone to his ear. "'Don't call. Francis is back.' And I'm thinking of you and him and every day looking at that damn picture you gave me and finally I took it down. And yeah, you could say I was *upset*. And of course then Natalie started observing me every day."

"Are you still angry?"

"You kind of softened me up with the Katy thing—getting her to give me all those tips."

"You knew? All along?"

"Of course. Hey, Katy's a nice kid, but she's no Charlotte. So that taught me to hope. And then to get a text from you, to think you'd go to the trouble of figuring out how to text. God, Charlotte, that's what I needed to hear, when I most needed to hear it. All, or nothing at all. That's it for me. So—my lesson—I rocked. I felt like I could fly. They're probably gonna make me the next chancellor. Thanks to you."

"But—" Charlotte changed her mind mid-sentence. "*Middlemarch.* You should read it. It's by George Elliot."

"A *guy* wrote that?"

"No, that was the name she wrote under."

"Shit!"

A beautiful Latina girl entered the store, and he looked at her with ostentatious approval as she walked, hips swaying gently, past their table.

"Theo!"

"Why the fuck not? This happens every time I think I'm gonna get what I want. You didn't send it, did you?"

She was happy not to lie, sad to tell the truth. "I locked my phone up this morning. I haven't touched it," she admitted. "But it's true. No other man exists for me, Theo."

"Except Francis. I guess you slept with him?"

"He tried," she hedged.

Theo's brows almost hid his eyes.

"The truth, Charlotte."

Their audience of two watched. The short order cook stopped chopping peppers. Outside, she saw Monroe and Rohan. She watched through the open doorway as they walked to the awning of the Fix a Flat shop. Rohan handed Monroe a package, and the two split up. Monroe headed to the school.

Rohan disappeared behind a parked car. He seemed to fade away.

"I'm a big boy, Charlotte. Give it to me straight. What did you do when he tried?"

"Verbatim?"

"Just fucking tell me what you did."

"I said, 'I know what I want now, Francis, and it's not you.'"

He stirred the coffee until it spilled over.

"Stop that, Theo. It's annoying."

He looked up. His eyes ranged over her. "That sweater. Never wear it again. It's making me insane."

"I bought it for you. I'll wear it just for you. I didn't send the text," she said. "But I mean it. It's true."

"I want to hear you say it." He sounded embarrassed.

"Theodore Lagakis, no other man exists for me."

That wide wonderful smile. Those dimples. Not handsome. Not at all handsome. But such dimples. She held out her hand. He took it, kissed her palm, and closed her fingers over the kiss.

China's boyfriend Keith came into the bodega just then and yelled, "Busted."

"This will be all over the school in two minutes," Charlotte said.

"Like I give a shit."

"Are we okay? Are you happy?" she asked.

"Sure. Especially since now I don't have to read the book." Then he reached into his coat pocket. "I got you something."

"I hope it's a scarf. I love Kate's."

"I'll get you a dozen of those, two dozen, if you want. But this—I've been holding on to it since Valentine's Day. When I got that text…well, after my observation, I went home and got it. Here."

He handed her a small box, wrapped in Valentine's Day paper. A very small box. A jewelry box.

She closed her eyes. She hoped it wasn't a diamond. She had enough of diamonds. Hers were in the vault, waiting for a day the twins needed something. She hoped it wasn't a ring. No more rings.

She opened the box—Lagakis Jewelers—and saw a small pendant on a delicate silvery chain. The stone was blue, the same color as the one in his ring.

"Wear it inside your sweater for now," he said. "If you're happy with it. With me."

She whispered. "So happy. I'm almost afraid to be this happy, Theo. It is exactly right. It looks like it was designed for me."

"It was. By me. My uncle took the stone out. The family jewels, that's what you've got here."

She placed it around her neck and turned so that he could fasten it. He lightly kissed the back of her neck as he fastened the clasp. Providencia and the cook burst into applause. She turned around to show him and he watched as she tucked it inside her sweater. "Till April."

Providencia came with the warm milk, beaming. *"Felicidades, Señora."*

"So what's with the warm milk?"

Should she tell him? Not yet. One thing at a time. "Lately, I have an upset stomach."

"I hope it goes away."

"Oh, I'm sure it will." *In about eighteen years.* "By the way, Theo, how do you know Dr. Solaris?"

"Oh. I thought—so nobody told you?"

"Told me what?"

"She owes me big time. I paid for her whole medical school. With the insurance money."

"From when your parents died?"

Theo nodded.

"Why did you do that? Is she one of your cousins?"

"No, sweethcart. She's my ex."

∽∾∽

They couldn't wait until April. That very afternoon, in his apartment, an Aegean blue sweater lay in a heap on the floor, under the picture of a red-haired bather, restored to its old place.

Rainbows formed through the cracks in his broken blinds.

She poked his dimple—newly shaven—and said, "Theo, I want to learn more about technology. So what's a Tek 9?"

He sat up. "Where did you hear about that?"

"Rohan came into the bodega talking about it with Monroe. He said it was a new thing for the phone."

"Jesus, Charlotte. Why didn't you say something before?" He reached for the phone.

"Where are you going? What's wrong?"

"Charlotte, a Tek 9 is a gun."

∽∾∽

Valerie's Journal
DO NOT READ!
China is seriously annoying. First, she takes my chocolate milk, then she gives me shit.

She says, "I'm actually doing you a favor. We know you like vanilla now. What the hell is that fat book?"

I tell her Middlemarch *and it's camouflage for my grandmother. So she gives me shit about using big words, like camouflage is a big word.*

A food fight starts. A container of milk, half empty, spattered nearby. "George can't handle this. He's older than dirt. Where's Lagakis?" I say.

"They gave him time off I guess. Hey—Lagakis passed. They're gonna let him stay."

"How do you know?"

"My boy Keith was in the principal's office running off some notes for Mr. Eugene. He saw some stuff in the wastebasket. They're giving Lagakis a satisfactory."

"You know that's all down to Rohan."

"Yeah, well, Rohan owes for the parole office thing. Anyway, Keith spies Lagakis come out of the office with this big Kool-Aid smile, and he lights out for the bodega like a bat out of hell."

"I bet Murphy's in the bodega."

"Yeah, she is. Guess what? Keith and Hector cut out and guess what? Lagakis and Murphy were in there holding hands."

I couldn't help it. I let out a big whoop. "Intervention!"

"There you go with another big word. I mean, I like you, Valerie, but you've changed. You never used to be like this."

"Yes I was, China. I was always like this. I just never let it show."

See? I had talked the whole thing over with Mon-

roe. You know he opens anything anywhere and it wasn't hard to get a hold of Murphy's phone. She keeps it in that locker. So we got Lagakis's number from Knudsen—I told her I needed to tell Lagakis something about Rohan and the gangs. Maybe she bought it, but anyway she gave me the number and I figured Murphy would probably say something like the lady in Middlemarch, *and so I texted "No other man exists for me." Just short and sweet and didn't sign it or anything since he'd figure it came from her phone.*

We stuffed her phone back in her locker and she never even knew.

Lagakis and Rohan have gotten real tight lately and when the important suit guy came in, you know what? Lagakis had Rohan teaching the class. Rohan was talking about the organization of gangs. How it was kind of like in the middle ages, with the lord, the vassals, the serfs, and even the wannabees, who were kind of like pages or maybe apprentices in the guilds. He talked about how back then there were the jousts and how everyone wore colors of their people, kind of like it is right now.

Well, everyone knows Rohan is mad smart but I think the guy in the suit won't be bothering Lagakis anymore. Not if Rohan has anything to do with it. Like I said, he and Lagakis have gotten real tight. Lagakis is trying to make sure Rohan doesn't break parole but it isn't easy for Rohan with Gareth and the other crew always dogging him.

❧❧❧

Valerie's Journal Special Edition
DO NOT READ!
I never liked March, even before the Memorial

*Service for Ms. Trombetta, RIP. No holidays except
for the Catholic schools like JC goes to, and it's too
cold to stand outside, but the trees by the zoo are
starting to get that yellow color they get before they
turn green and you're about to get trapped inside
school. I remember riding on the bus past the Botani-
cal Gardens that morning and seeing all the daffodils,
like in the poem. I was thinking that March is like
spring fever without the spring. We were reading
"Julius Caesar by William Shakespeare. They said
"Beware the Ides of March" in it. Rohan had gotten
all into that play. He was coming to school every day
again.*

*You would think somebody would have tipped off
the cops. Maybe somebody did but they just took their
time to come. I hate to tell you but at the last big
fight, after the Valentine's Dance, I heard one of them
told Lagakis "Next time let a few of them kill each
other before you call us."*

*Now at first, this memorial thing was just ordinary
and boring like any assembly. First old Dr. Haas with
the bad comb-over was playing parade music on the
piano. Then these skinny boys from South America or
someplace—I don't know them because they never go
to any classes except the ones all in Spanish—go
marching up the aisle of the auditorium in their little
white shirts holding up the flags and keeping time to
the music like they were in the army. They got to the
front of the auditorium and they started doing this
routine where they all turn around and click their
heels looking so serious and proud. Not one of them
could protect you from a flea.*

*Being I was MC, I had to be up on stage with the
principal and all the English teachers. Lagakis was
on stage too, probably because he was Trombetta's
friend. He had on a white shirt and that blue suit he
wore to Trombetta's funeral. He was standing right*

behind Murphy probably staring at her, since Murphy had also dressed up and looked great. I can remember thinking how perfect her hair came out for a change since she wore it up and had these little tendrils coming down around her face. She had on a knit dress in cobalt. I think she's finally putting on weight.

It's funny what you remember. I had been all worried over what to wear. You know my grandmother was in the audience along with three or four other parents from the Parent's Association. She brought the foster kids with her. Anyway, I remember I was so glad the Christmas dress my grandmother picked out was not an option because the school came through with a rule that we—all of us on stage—had to wear some kind of black pants or skirt and white top. J. Crew gave me the thumbs up when he saw me. I just winked back very serious and didn't crack a smile. Supposedly, we don't know each other. But he looked really cute in what he was wearing—jacket but no tie like something out of the catalog. He has a great build. I swear that guy could model. It's weird to think that he was actually related to Trombetta, RIP.

Anyway, the whole place was full of kids that some of them never even met Trombetta or had her for English but everybody hated her just for the hell of it. So kids were restless pretty soon. When Trombetta's sister gave a speech, they started clapping right in the middle of it, to give her the hint it was time to sit down. I hate it when they are so rude.

And then we heard it right outside the school. I mean if you live around here you get to know what the start of a fight sounds like, a big roar of people screaming, glass breaking, and maybe some shots. But it's funny how people will think that their school or their neighborhood is safe and everybody else's is dangerous. When a fight happens afterward, probably you hear people say, "Well, the fight was not on my

*block, or maybe there was a shooting on my block,
but not on my side of the street, or even it was on my
side of the street but not near my building. Or not on
the side of the building where my window is."*

*My grandmother always tells me that when you
hear a fight get started, get the hell away from there
or at least stay away from the window or hit the floor
in case somebody starts shooting. But what do you
think everybody does? Everybody starts running out
of the auditorium, running to the fight. Practically the
whole school ran out there. Yeah, I know. It's just
human nature. And Lagakis leaves the stage running
and he's talking on his cell phone I guess calling 911.
He should have quit right there. He should not have
got involved because it was outside the school and
none of his business. That's what everyone said, anyway. So it was his own fault in a way. But you know
he used to be a cop and so he probably just automatically went. Plus, I guess he thought he had to try to
get the kids who ran outside back in the building. I
give him that. He put himself out there for us. I remember how he said once he was like his grandfa-
ther, a shepherd, rounding up the sheep.*

*The whole thing didn't take that long, but it seems
like a long time when you're sitting there and everything is happening outside. Even if I had wanted to
run out, with my grandmother there I wouldn't risk it.
She would have no chance out there and I knew if I
ran out she'd run after me. So I went into the audience and sat with my grandmother. It was weird to
have her sitting there, in her hat with the navy polka
dot bow on it that matched her blouse. Weird but in a
good way. It's like if she's there I'm safe, even though
I know it isn't true.*

*I can still hear the shots. If I close my eyes, I can
hear the whole thing. I can see Lagakis standing in
the back of the auditorium trying to keep people from*

leaving, along with the security guards. Kids were giving him a hard time but he kept a lot of people inside. Some of them I bet just needed somebody to blame staying inside on. They didn't really want to go out. He kept going outside and coming back in with more kids. But then after the last time when he left the building, we started hearing shots. It was terrible, sitting in there, not knowing what was happening, scared somebody was coming in and we were like sitting ducks going to get shot.

And then finally we heard the sirens, and there's cops all over the room, and we see China coming in running down the aisle, and I stand up and make her come over to where we're sitting. By this time Murphy is standing near us, she's sitting talking to the foster kids real calm but you can see her eyes wandering to the back of the auditorium.

China is all excited to be telling us what happened. She loves to be the one to tell you things.

"The cops shot Rohan," she yells out.

All around the people started repeating what she said. "They got Rohan. The cops got Rohan."

You could hear voices from outside still shouting, but no more shots.

She was looking at me to kind of get my reaction. And to tell you the truth I didn't have one because I didn't believe it. But my grandmother reacted right away.

"Oh, sweet Jesus. Why they have to shoot him?" Now my grandmother is rocking back and forth. My grandmother knew Rohan from when he was a little boy.

I told you we were in kindergarten together and she goes to the same church as one of his aunts. So she was crying about Rohan and I guess she's thinking about my father and how he almost got killed by the cops. They shot my father when he was arrested,

*but he got better in a prison hospital. One of the fos-
ter kids started crying, and Murphy picked him up
and put him in her lap and kissed him on the head
and he put his thumb in his mouth and closed his
eyes. I saw China look at Murphy holding the foster
kid and I knew she was thinking how she didn't have
that as a kid, somebody to hold her when she cried.
See? I was thinking all different things not really
about Rohan.*

*"Is he going to—is he all right?" Murphy was ask-
ing about Rohan. She was really asking was he alive
or dead.*

*China is jumping from one foot to the other, and
she says something but it's so noisy in there I could
barely hear her. To tell the truth I really didn't take in
what she was saying.*

*So China grabs my arm and screams in my ear.
"Valerie! Listen! It was Gareth. Gareth, he was
shooting into the crowd where Rohan was at."*

*Gareth? I remember how Rohan's boys gave
Gareth a beat down after Valentines. I guess it was
just a matter of time before Gareth came back at him.*

*Now China is screaming. "Valerie! Rohan shot
Gareth."*

"Bullshit," I said.

"For real," she tells me. "He was packing."

*China is not making sense. "What?" I say. "What
are you talking about? What gun?"*

*I knew he had a gun of course. A Tek 9. Once he
kind of bragged on it to me, but you know that didn't
impress me.*

*"You know Rohan had a gun," China said. Now
Murphy is looking over at China, her mouth hanging
open.*

*"Lagakis was standing out in front, trying to get
Rohan to come inside. Somebody, I think one of
Gareth's boys but I don't know, his hood was up and*

then he ran away, hit Lagakis on the back of the head with a pipe. Cracked his skull wide open. You never want to see that much blood."

"Oh my God! What happened? Is he all right?" This was Murphy talking now.

"He fell down, miss, on his face right on the sidewalk. When Lagakis fell Rohan took his gun and went after Gareth."

"Is he alive?" Murphy asks. You knew she was talking about Lagakis, not Gareth.

"I don't know, miss. Maybe."

I swear it was like China was almost happy, she was so excited to know what happened and to be the one to tell everyone.

Murphy, she has this terrible look on her face. She takes the foster kid and puts him in my grandmother's lap and she is all white around the lips. I think she's going to faint but she just stands up real straight and starts for the back of the auditorium.

Murphy starts to go running out. Me and China held her back and then J. Crew kind of tackled her and just held her down. By this time, there were cops in the auditorium and they were walking up and down the aisle with their big stomachs out, telling everyone to just sit there. Some kid wouldn't stay in his seat and they put cuffs on him and everybody settled down then. By this time, Murphy is rocking back and forth in the seat just like my grandmother did.

"I never even told him," I hear her say. "He never even knew."

"He knew you loved him, miss," China said. "Everybody knew."

But Murphy kept rocking back and forth and crying.

You know stuff doesn't really hit you right away and very random stuff goes through your brain. I remember thinking that the cops were looking for a rea-

son to shoot Rohan. Rohan would never have resisted arrest or anything like that. Rohan isn't violent unless he can't help it. He probably had to shoot Gareth for respect. Or maybe he was trying to save Lagakis's life. Like I said, those two got pretty tight.

One sound I hate it's the sound of the ambulance. A whole bunch of ambulances came. They put you in an ambulance even if you're dead or alive, but by being in the auditorium we didn't know who was going to the hospital and who was going to the morgue.

CHAPTER 34

Meeting Yiayia

Charlotte sat in the hospital lobby, watching the elevator doors. She sat perched on an ice-cold vinyl sofa, surrounded by unnaturally green plastic plants. No right to sit in the family lounge upstairs. She had seen Gus walk in with a woman who could only be Yiayia. She put her hand up to wave and he nodded slightly, recognizing her but not stopping.

She should call the twins. Tell them what had happened, in case they heard it on the news. Tell them she was safe.

They had finally spoken about her separation from Francis. Abigail was the one who opened the subject. She'd come running in with her letter of acceptance to the University of Connecticut, which had rolling admissions.

"That's great," Charlotte had said. "In the honor program?"

"Don't push it," Abby replied. "I'm just glad I got in to the Storrs campus. You're not moving to California, are you? I hope you're staying here? If I go to UConn will I be able to drive back to see you guys on weekends?"

"I'm staying," Charlotte said. "You can come home anytime you want. Bring anyone you want. But not Dad."

"Is Dad ever coming back?" Abigail asked.

Charlotte had been careful not to badmouth Francis. She

had read enough advice books to know not to do that. But she'd been truthful. "To visit. Whenever he wants, of course. But not to live here with me."

Emily came into the kitchen, where they'd been talking, to take an apple from the fridge.

"Wash it first," Charlotte had said automatically.

"God, Mom. I *know* that." Emily said. "What's this about Dad?"

"He's not coming back," Abby said. "Mom just told me."

"Obviously," Emily said. "Rosemary would have a fit, since she keeps him on such a short leash. Maybe you should have done that, Mom."

Charlotte bit her tongue.

Emily continued. "I happen to like Rosemary, Mom, but frankly it's really awful the way she's always tracking Dad down—like she doesn't trust him."

Because she can't, Charlotte thought. "So. You met her?"

"She made us Christmas dinner. He just said she was a friend. But I knew instantly. Because she's like a bloodhound with Dad."

"Dad doesn't seem to mind," Charlotte said. "And that seems to be what matters."

"I love Dad, but he's kind of a dog," Emily said. "I heard you chuck him out of bed that night when Abby was still in the hospital. Good for you."

Charlotte said nothing.

Emily continued. "Yeah, yeah, I know. United front. But I don't blame you, Mom. If Ryan did me the way Dad did you—"

Then Abigail said, "Why didn't you guys tell us earlier, Mom? You let us think you were still together—even when I was sick."

"I told you, dummy, when we were in California and Rosemary was always around," Emily said. "I knew a long time ago. I mean, Mom, I used to get so mad at you. Always doing your school stuff and him coming in late every night. You never had a clue. All I could think was, no matter what, I don't want to be like you. I mean, he basically had to throw it in your face." Emily paused. "Sorry. But that's the truth."

Charlotte answered Abigail's question first. "Dad—and I—" She amended what she'd been going to say. "—didn't want you girls to worry. He—we—thought it might—"

"Let me guess," Emily said. "Affect our SAT scores?"

"Well, yes," Charlotte admitted.

"Typical. So typical of you, Mom. You're such a—teacher."

"I love hearing you say that," Charlotte had said.

"Say what? That you're a teacher?"

"No. *Mom*." Now, for Emily's question. "Emily, I guess I did know, deep down. But I didn't want it to be that way. I wanted you girls to have your father. He loves you."

"Mom. I mean, what century is this? Half the kids in my class, their parents are divorced. They still hang out, the cool ones, anyway."

Mom. No sweeter sound. But could she go through raising another child? Alone, quite possibly. One thing at a time. Think about Theo first.

Now as she sat waiting in the hospital, she saw Gus walking out, holding Yiayia's hand and she ran up to them. "Gus," she said, "Wait. How is he?"

He walked over. "Hello, lady," he said. "How's your car?"

He must be alive. He must be doing well, for Gus to ask such an inane question.

"How is Theo?" she asked, breathlessly.

"He's in the ICU," Gus said.

The ICU. She knew that already. She'd been pestering the information desk for information about him, and that was all she'd been able to obtain. She'd even called on her cell phone and asked, embarrassed to go up to the desk again.

"I know where he is. But *how* is he?"

"Bad. He has God knows how many staples in the back of his head. They won't let him eat and they have somebody watching him, in case his brain is gonna get damaged. Lucky to be alive. Cynthia is in there with him."

"Cynthia?"

"His wife. You know. Cynthia Solaris."

His wife?

Yiayia said something in Greek and Gus said, "Oh, sorry. I mean his ex-wife."

"Is he going to be all right?"

"Cynthia said she's not sure."

Charlotte shuddered. She knew head injuries were dangerous. She gave Gus a card with her phone number on it. "Please, call me," she said. "Keep me in the loop. I need to know how he is, what the doctor says."

Yiayia had been standing off to the side, a tiny figure all in black. She said something else to Gus in Greek, and he nodded. "She wants to know how your daughter is."

"My daughter?"

"The one that was sick. The Greek grapevine. Yiayia knows everything."

"She's fine," Charlotte said. "Thanks to Theo. And—and Cynthia."

To Charlotte's surprise, Yiayia opened her arms, and Charlotte went into them. Something of her smelled of Theo, perhaps soap they both used, or perhaps she had just kissed her grandson. Charlotte gathered Yiayia's tiny frame into her arms and together they cried.

❦

Valerie's Journal
PLEASE DO NOT READ
I have to get ready for my Easter but I almost don't feel like it. Visiting Rohan in the hospital is just

going through the motions. He's got all this stuff attached to him. He doesn't know you're there and maybe that's why nobody even comes, not even his people any more. Just me and, once in a while, Murphy or one of his aunts. They let me in because his aunt told them I was family and sometimes I do the thing they show you in the movie, like squeeze his hand and say Rohan if you feel this squeeze back or wiggle your toes but nothing happens. There's just this bleep thing that monitors him—nothing else to talk to.

Rohan's aunt says the doctor wants her to give permission to harvest his organs but she won't give permission because she figures they'll never bother to save him then. I have to tell my grandmother that if that ever happens to me I want them to let me be a donor. Might as well help out somebody else.

It's so weird to be holding Rohan's hand. He always took care of his nails but they've been growing out and he doesn't even know it, so I asked if I could give him a manicure and they said I could.

I talked to him a little while I was working on his nails just like they taught us to in cosmetology class and sometimes I looked up and hoped maybe I could catch a little flutter but he just lay there asleep. I told him about how Gareth got picked up by the cops in about a minute and that he's gonna be away for a really long time, probably building his power base. I told Rohan to hurry up and get well so Gareth's crew wouldn't be the new thing.

I went down memory lane about kindergarten and how he put gum in my hair back then, and reminisced a little bit about how just last month he had taught Lagakis's class about how the gangs are organized. I mentioned all his boys that I knew about by name but nothing. Not a blink or a squeeze.

I know the emergency room of this hospital like my

own house since my mother is usually brought there whenever she has a relapse. But I've never been in this part of the hospital before. It's pretty noisy most of the time, with nurses and doctors walking really quickly with their shoes making noise on the linoleum floor and the phone ringing non-stop but Rohan just sleeps on so peaceful like one of his own customers nodding out. It's kind of weird knowing that Rohan is one of the ones who sells drugs to people like my mother, and worse to young kids, yet he's so nice to me. It's always been that way, that he was nice to me, and he even gave me this special book at Christmas. My grandmother would make me give it back if she knew. Tainted, she would say. I don't know if that's actually true. Lagakis told us in social studies that some people believe when you do good for people it makes good karma for you in the next life. Maybe Rohan giving me that book was good karma for him. And he did save Lagakis's life. Gareth was gonna beat Lagakis to death, partly as revenge for that time Lagakis nearly took him out, and partly because he was tight with Rohan. It also didn't hurt that Lagakis was the big hero a while back with Corny. See? It gave Gareth more prestige that way—to take down somebody whose picture was in the paper. That was so Gareth could get his own picture in the paper. Some of those guys, all they worry about is to go out big and get written up. Some of them would kill you just because you walked in front of them and didn't say excuse me. But Rohan wasn't like that.

So I just told Rohan that everybody in my grandmother's church is praying for him, and then I finished the manicure and just walked out by myself walking behind a doctor to the elevator and trying to match my steps to hers.

CHAPTER 35

Two Documents

Renata was with Charlotte when the divorce became final. "You're one damn good lawyer," Francis had said, shaking Renata's hand. "Got me to sign over half my life."

"I wish you well," Charlotte said to him. "You and Rosemary."

"Goodbye, poetry girl," he'd said. "I'll pay for their college. And you can keep the house. Your mother helped us buy it, giving us the down payment. Of course, I made the payments all these years. But that's it. It's all yours. Your Greek god can do the rest."

"I'll do the rest, as you put it, myself, Francis. And you're welcome to visit the girls any time."

"Yeah, in the guest room," he said.

"Maybe you'd be more comfortable at the inn in town," she'd said. "You and your—you and Rosemary."

Charlotte had not even known that her mother had helped him buy the house. However, Mother had been clever. She'd insisted that the house be in Charlotte's name. And Charlotte did not feel in the least guilty that she got to keep the house in Westport.

She remembered what Renata had said about how she'd helped Francis advance his career. It was true. All through

the many years of her stay-at-home motherhood, she'd put
his comfort above her own.

"Get a paternity test right away," Renata had insisted
when Charlotte came to her with the news of her pregnancy.
"You're lucky. They can do it now pretty easily. You won't
even need amnio."

"I know it's Theo's," Charlotte had said.

"Do it, Charlotte. This way, Francis has no claim. The
baby was conceived while he was your husband," Renata
said. "He has a legal claim, and he's annoyed with you.
He'll be even more annoyed when he finds out you're pregnant. Don't give him ammunition."

It was easy to get DNA evidence from Theo's apartment,
and, of course, the child was his. If it had not been Theo's,
it would have been an immaculate conception, for she had
not been with anyone else. Her due date was in late September. Charlotte was pretty sure conception had happened
Christmas night, after she returned from Westport. She was
aware of the irony of getting pregnant by accident, not once
but twice. People made the same mistakes over and over.
But this did not feel like a mistake.

If the baby were a girl she would have been called Joy.
But Charlotte was having a boy. He would have to be
named after Theo's own father, Angelis. That was the
Greek tradition, she'd been told. And told. Yiayia knew
more English than she let on. She'd read the paternity test
results with a magnifying glass, and then embraced Charlotte for a long time. Theo's belief that he was infertile was
down to Solaris, Charlotte imagined. She must have tricked
Theo with a phony lab report, and then taken birth control
pills.

Charlotte did consider the possibility that Theo had misled her, just as he'd misled her about the Regents folders.
That he'd been trying all along to get her pregnant. And if
he had? She'd have let him. Full speed ahead. If she'd been
rational, thoughtful, she'd have insisted on protection from
pregnancy, or proof of his infertility, from the beginning.

But each time they'd been together, rational thought vanished. She, a grown woman, a mother of teenagers, had been as powerless, irresponsible, and heedless as a sixteen year old swept away by raging hormones. She thought of Sara Teasdale's poem, "Barter." *Give all you have for loveliness. Give and never count the cost.*

She had done so, and it had been worth it. She had known passion, had made over her complacent life for loveliness.

Life has loveliness to sell,
All beautiful and splendid things,
Blue waves whitened on a cliff,
Soaring fire that sways and sings,
And children's faces looking up
Holding wonder like a cup.

Life has loveliness to sell,
Music like a curve of gold,
Scent of pine trees in the rain,
Eyes that love you, arms that hold,
And for your spirit's still delight,
Holy thoughts that star the night.

Spend all you have for loveliness,
Buy it and never count the cost;
For one white singing hour of peace
Count many a year of strife well lost,
And for a breath of ecstasy
Give all you have been, or could be.

Life has loveliness to sell,
All beautiful and splendid things,
Blue waves whitened on a cliff,
Soaring fire that sways and sings,
And children's faces looking up
Holding wonder like a cup.

Life has loveliness to sell,
Music like a curve of gold,
Scent of pine trees in the rain,
Eyes that love you, arms that hold,
And for your spirit's still delight,
Holy thoughts that star the night.

Spend all you have for loveliness,
Buy it and never count the cost;
For one white singing hour of peace
Count many a year of strife well lost,
And for a breath of ecstasy
Give all you have been, or could be.

Life has loveliness to sell,
All beautiful and splendid things,
Blue waves whitened on a cliff,
Soaring fire that sways and sings,
And children's faces looking up
Holding wonder like a cup.

Life has loveliness to sell,
Music like a curve of gold,
Scent of pine trees in the rain,
Eyes that love you, arms that hold,
And for your spirit's still delight,
Holy thoughts that star the night.

Spend all you have for loveliness,
Buy it and never count the cost;
For one white singing hour of peace
Count many a year of strife well lost,
And for a breath of ecstasy
Give all you have been, or could be.

Would Theo have tricked her this way? Taken a chance?
Natalie would think so, of course. Charlotte didn't much

care. She wanted this child, his child. She wished over and over that she had told him that day in the bodega, the day he had been so wildly happy. She could have made him even happier. But when she visited him in the hospital, he didn't even register her presence. The doctors had deliberately put him into a coma to preserve his brain, and he lay there, a large unconscious presence. However, she held his hand, still so warm to her touch, and, when they were alone, whispered her news in his ear. He never moved.

෴

Last Journal of Valerie Martin
READ IF YOU WANT
I remember there were sirens. A traffic jam. A hearse. Another car loaded with flowers. Limousines carrying men and women in dark clothing. A cop on a motorcycle dressed in a leather jacket just in case. A couple of regular police in cars. It was an important funeral. He would have been proud.
Murphy was driving Lagakis's car real slow with the lights on all the way to the church from the funeral parlor. First, we had to drive around the block of the school. It's like a tradition. It was weird to see everyone on the sidewalk watching to see the hearse go by. Suzette and Monroe and I were sitting in the back, feeling really solemn. At the church, they wanted ed me to talk, and give a eulogy, but I just couldn't. Murphy said she couldn't talk either. She was crying so hard I don't know how she could see to drive. I saw him in the coffin and he was looking so big, still, with those wide shoulders. They got the colors right, but his face still looked like a ball of wax. He'd been on a regulator or respirator or a something for a long time. Everyone agreed it was better this way than living like a vegetable. He was only the second dead

*person I ever saw, but I have to tell you it was easier
to see Trombetta.*

*I had on the same outfit. I wore it to Trombetta's
and to the Memorial Service and now to this funeral.
After today, I plan to throw it away. Speaking of
Trombetta—one person who is not going to the funeral is Drew. In fact, going to the memorial convinced
him he didn't want to go to my prom. I'm still wearing the ring he gave me on a chain around my neck,
though, and after my birthday, I actually introduced
him to my grandmother and she just said pleased to
meet you the way she would to anybody. So that went
ok. We officially know each other now and every now
and then I throw his name into the conversation very
casually and she doesn't say anything. We text, and I
know we're gonna see each other all summer until we
both go to college. Maybe after. He's going to some
college in New York, Columbia. At the dinner, I'm going to take the ring and wear it outside the dress. And
maybe leave it that way. Like Murphy. She has something she wears around her neck too. It looks like the
ring I always noticed on Lagakis's pinky finger.*

*After we graduate Murphy is taking us out to din-
ner, me and a few friends. I'm gonna take a chance
and bring Drew along with Suzette and Zamar and
China and Keith and of course Monroe. Baby steps.
We're going to a restaurant that one of Lagakis's uncles or cousins or something owns where they have
tablecloths. We have to dress up. I'm going to wear
the dress I wore to the prom. It's strapless knee
length. Purple. Drew says he's going to get me or-
chids to put in my hair, which of course I will wear up
to show off the dress. I went to the actual prom with
Monroe, who came out to me that night. He still is
keeping it on the down low for everyone else, which is
smart. About Monroe: Come to find out he can hardly
see but they just put him in special ed. I'm trying to*

convince him to save for contacts because, you know of course, a guy can't wear glasses around here, especially if he's gay.

You could see it was killing Lagakis that Murphy was driving but they aren't letting him drive yet, Murphy said. He had double vision for a while. He has a doctor's appointment next week and she figures probably they'll let him then. He keeps saying that he's fine and he wants to take over the wheel and she won't let him. So she's driving his car, and he keeps telling her to watch this and slow down and speed up like he was gonna grab the wheel any minute. You'd think they were married.

Murphy is starting to show. She got her divorce from Mr. Murphy and I guess that's good because the kid is from Lagakis. He's mad happy, was passing out candy cigars at the prom. She is having a boy. Just one, not twins. She hopes.

We got to the church and, even though he looks like Frankenstein with those staple things in the back of his head, he still helped her out of the car like she was some delicate flower. He's gonna be ok, she said. The hair will grow on the back of his head, and he'll be as handsome as before. That, of course, is her opinion. But I guess that's what matters.

Oh, and I'm going to college—LaGuardia here in New York. Trombetta, RIP, actually left me money for the tuition, and remember Murphy made me apply to all these colleges? Well, I got in there. But I'm not going to sleep there or anything. And I'm still going to do hair on the side. And I haven't ruled out medical school.

The prom was dedicated to Rohan, which was kind of funny since if he'd been able to go, they wouldn't have let him. He was still alive then, sort of. Murphy went to the prom with Lagakis, but they only danced a couple of slow dances. I think he wanted to do more but she was very strict and made him sit down. I heard her yelling at him and he just laughed but he sat and pulled her down on his lap. In front of everybody. She got right up, though. When they danced slow, he held her real nice and respectful and they both laughed about something. One time Monroe asked her to dance fast, and she got up, and she wasn't bad even with her stomach sticking out just a little. She looked nice in this blue dress but the flat shoes kind of spoiled it. Lagakis sat on the side and watched her with that proud look he gets. I think it's a big deal that he made her pregnant, which is funny, because most people have to struggle and work just to not get pregnant. I think she looks better than she ever did but she always had pretty good potential with just a little effort, which we tell her and she doesn't listen.

I helped Suzette do Murphy's hair for the prom. I offered to do it when she gets married but she didn't say yes or no. I don't even know if they're getting married. She said something about how a piece of paper shouldn't matter. She also said she's gonna come back to work when the kid is born but you know what? I bet Lagakis will talk her into getting married. I bet she stays home with her kid too, once she sees it. I hope it looks like her not him. Her daughters probably will help her with the baby since they're going to college in Connecticut where she lives. But different schools.

Ms. Knudsen came to the prom with her old boyfriend. They are the worst dancers I've ever seen. She's gonna go back to Minnesota with him and open some kind of store. Something to do with fish. Bait and tackle, I think she said. It's good she won't be teaching. She was bad. She and Murphy are real tight now. It's funny how we used to think she was after Lagakis. Her boyfriend is much younger and better looking with blond hair and glasses. Kind of a taller J. Crew. I still call him that sometimes and he doesn't mind any more.

At graduation, Ms. Albert the principal told us that next year she's gonna take a better principal's job in someplace. Arizona, I think. Or maybe Arkansas. My grandmother is in the PTA and she told me that really Albert got the boot for faking the Regents but they let her finish out the year and she was just using a cover story.

You know we all had to re-take the Regents. But it's all good. Even though when we took the test again, it was the hottest possible day in June and, of course, no air conditioning but all my friends still passed, even Monroe. Murphy thinks Suzette passed because of the drawing she did but the truth is I always kind of figured Suzette cheated off me. Monroe I know couldn't have being he can't see far enough to copy. But then again he might have stolen the answer key from the vault where they keep the state tests and stuff when they get delivered. He told me, Monroe, in strictest confidence, that he broke in there once to hide Rohan's gun in there for him and then to take it out on the day of the Memorial. Not that it would be so tough getting anything past old George. He needs to retire.

Monroe is worried about that karma thing, but I told him no, that Rohan made him do it and the bad karma is all Rohan's. Anyway, he's getting out of school and working for this locksmith someone in Lagakis's family knows and he will be strictly cool about it, believe me. When he saves enough money for contact lenses, he'll try to get his license to give massages. We all know how to be professionals, see? But we need the paperwork. I used to think that was the only reason to go to school, but my mind is opened up now. Thanks to Drew, and I guess Murphy and the

*poems and the journals. She was the one who thought
we were good enough for those poems and got me
started at the library workshop.*

*Suzette has a job lined up in a beauty shop but just
kind of entry level since she didn't pass the state li-
censing boards. She's planning to work for herself off
the books at home once she builds up some clients
and also gets enough money to get her own apartment. That's if she can just keep the volcano from
erupting.*

*The kind of bad thing is that China is HIV positive
which you know isn't a death sentence exactly now
since they have medication. They call it living with
HIV. The really bad thing is that she isn't telling
Keith. I talked to Mr. King about it, my guidance
counselor, not saying her name of course but just asking if I should tell the boyfriend. I didn't give her
name, but he guessed and he said right away that
he'd talk to China and give her a chance to tell Keith
herself. She's scared to tell him because she's sure
he'll quit her. He probably will. And it's not her fault.
It's not like she could say to her stepfather no glove
no love when she was only ten.*

*Maybe Mr. Eugene the assistant principal will be
the new principal. If that goes down I know it will be
the same old, same old, with Lagakis getting grief.
They don't get along too well. My grandmother said
Lagakis and Murphy were the ones who told on Ms.
Albert. Anyway, Eugene is always going on about
tests scores. It's bad enough we had to pass all these
stupid tests but some of the people who run the school
act so ignorant about it. It's like they don't see that
they're affecting our actual lives because they want
the money when the scores go up. Why can't people
see what that does to people? I'm glad I'm getting
out.*

I supposed you can tell that I'm talking about all

these other people trying not to talk about Rohan because it's really hard. I mean, I knew him since we went to kindergarten and when we got to the funeral parlor, his aunt had all his school pictures up from PS 89 where we both went. I guess you could say he went out big, which of course he would have liked—a hero saving Lagakis's life. Gareth is in jail, and you know he'll just start building up his body until he gets as big as Rohan.

Those shoulders. I can still see them lying there, useless in the coffin. He probably could have played football or something if we had a team, which of course we don't. Rohan didn't get into DeWitt Clinton where he really wanted to go. I could never see him doing hair. Our school was his twelfth choice out of twelve, but it's where they put him. His aunt didn't know how to work the system like my grandmother does.

Anyway, when we got to the funeral, nobody wanted to speak a eulogy, but of course old Lagakis had to get up and run his mouth. He starts out saying that he's Greek (surprise) and that he knows all about tragedy and then he says the greatest tragedy is that somebody like Rohan, so smart and so talented, didn't get the chance to live up to his potential. Then he reads this story about a Passed Around Child that Rohan liked and, even though he can't read it with that expression Murphy has, he reads loud with a voice that grabs everyone's attention and we all got the point and it was definitely time to take out the Kleenex. I had skipped mascara knowing in advance what was going to happen. Rohan's aunt asked me again did I want to say something because he always liked me, but you know me. I stayed quiet.

CHAPTER 36

Visitors

The aunts, uncles, and cousins finally went home. Theo's family had camped out throughout the birth, talking loudly in Greek, drinking endless cups of coffee, passing around baklava provided by Yiayia. The room was filled with flowers and balloons in bright blue. Charlotte was animated, relaxed, chatty even. She was on drugs.

A caesarean, naturally. Charlotte was small and the baby was huge. Now she lay, unable to fall asleep, her swollen legs attached to a machine that compressed them at intervals. Theo stretched out on the too-short chaise-lounge provided for rooming-in dads. His eyes, creased with tiredness, never left the bed where Charlotte nursed. The drugs would not affect the baby, she'd been assured.

A lactation consultant came in to explain how to achieve a good latch, but Angel needed no coaching. "At the head of the class," the woman said. "The best I've ever seen. Your son is a natural, Charlotte," she said.

"*Our* son." Theo rose, stood over the bed, ran his hand over the little dark head. "He knows a good thing when he sees it."

The woman nodded and left, placing her card on the bedside table. "Just in case. But I doubt you'll need me."

The baby had dimples. A broad back and shoulders threatening to burst from his swaddling blanket. His newborn footprint measured four inches. He weighed ten pounds and was twenty-four inches long. A strong neck that turned toward his father's voice.

Theo scrubbed the baby's cheek with the gentlest of knuckles. "I think he smiled at me just now."

"He's not supposed to do that," Charlotte said.

"Guess he didn't read the book."

When the baby went to sleep, Charlotte placed her pinky in the rosebud mouth, separating him from her nipple. He opened one eye but closed it again. His skin was red and dark against her white breast. Abigail kissed his hand and marveled. "Such a big hand, for a baby."

"I can't wait to play softball with him. He won't need a mitt," Emily said.

"He'll be great at the piano," said Abigail.

"Let him be a baby first," Charlotte protested.

"His eyes are blue, like ours," Emily said.

Theo frowned.

Charlotte smiled at him. "They may change."

Footsteps sounded in the hall. Angel's eyes opened, fixed on his mother's face, his lips moving, rooting.

"Cover yourself, sweetheart." Theo got up and stood in front of Charlotte and Angel. Abigail stood ready with a receiving blanket and Charlotte kissed the downy dark head. But he kept rooting, looking for her swollen breast. "He won't stop."

Valerie walked in first, dressed in jeans and hoody, embellished with purple sequins around the collar. She was followed by J. Crew, in a Columbia sweatshirt, and Monroe, whose dreadlocks flowed over something with a designer logo.

Suzette entered last, dressed in bright orange pants and matching halter top.

"What's with the orange? Were you working construction this summer?" Theo asked.

Charlotte gave Theo a warning headshake. "Come see the baby."

Angel began to cry, a loud wail. "He's hungry," Charlotte said, uncovering her breast. Theo quickly stepped in front of her again, facing the kids.

"Let's wait in the hall," said J. Crew. His ears were bright red. He'd given the other kids a lift from the Bronx.

"Deal with it," Valerie said, punching him on the arm. "We brought him something, miss. Me and Suzette." She offered a small box. Through the plastic top Charlotte could see a baby's comb and brush. Theo had to stop Suzette from going to work on the baby's hair right there.

"I wasn't gonna hurt him. Poor kid. He looks just like you, mister," Suzette said, giving Theo the finger.

"'The child is father of the man,'" Charlotte said.

"Wordsworth?" asked J. Crew.

"Obviously," Valerie replied.

End

About the Author

Jacqueline Grandsire Goldstein, born and raised in the Bronx, taught high school English there for 25 years. She enjoyed giving pizza parties for her students to celebrate the life of her favorite author, Jane Austen. Goldstein attends the Writing Institute at Sarah Lawrence College and is a member of the Romance Writers of America. Her work has appeared in *The New York Times*, *The Westchester Review*, and *The Examiner News*. The mother of two adult daughters, she now lives with her husband in Westchester, New York.

She blogs at tomorrowbeckons.wordpress.com. You can also find her on Facebook as Jacqueline Goldstein Author and follow her on Twitter @jacquigoldstein. Visit her website, jacquelinegoldstein.com, and say hello!